All That Remains

By

Michele G. Miller

All That Remains (From The Wreckage, book 3)
Michele G Miller
Copyright © 2014 by Michele G Miller

License Notes

This book is a work of fiction. Any names, places, characters, and incidents are either products of the author's imagination or, if real, are used fictitiously. Any resemblances to any persons, living or dead, are completely coincidental.

For more information:
http://michelegmillerbooks.com
Cover design by Starla Huchton of Designed by Starla
Edited by Samantha Eaton-Roberts

Other Titles by Author

The Prophecy of Tyalbrook Trilogy - YA Fantasy Romance

Never Let You Fall
Never Let You Go
Never Without You - Avail Late 2014

The Last Call Series - NA Contemporary Romance

Last Call (Suspense)

From The Wreckage Series - Coming of Age Drama

From The Wreckage
Out of Ruins
All That Remains

Table of Contents

⚓

Contents Continued

To my readers. You are *MY* anchor.

"When he kisses her, storms rise beneath her skin;
For she is the ocean, and he is her moon."

~ Unknown

Prologue

West

Gilded Copper.

It's the color he searches for every time he steps onto the sprawling A&M campus. A fiery red, laced with golden highlights that curl around a slim porcelain neck as it arches back inviting his lips in for a taste.

Nine months ago, he twisted that copper hair around his fingers as his lips skimmed the slim column of *her* throat reveling in the taste he could never get enough of. Nine months ago, he climbed behind the wheel of his Jeep to take *her* back to his place to enjoy more of *her* taste when an angry addict decided to play chicken with them. Nine months ago, he'd slammed his vehicle into a silver sports car, breaking *her* body and his heart.

Seven months of counseling have brought him back to the place where he was his happiest once upon a time. He stands under the heavy branches of The Century Tree at A&M watching couples come and go, holding hands on their way to someplace or another, and it reminds him of *her*.

He doesn't do it often, stand under the tree and allow himself to think of *her*. He usually reminisces in his room, in private, where he's able to beat himself up for all the ridiculous choices he has made. In the almost two months since he walked out of the rehab, he's maintained his distance, choosing to stay at the house he shares with his brothers and Mindy, or on campus at Freemont. Freemont, the junior feeder college across town from A&M where he'd made the conscious decision to start school instead of attending A&M.

It was a decision not entirely of his own making, but it was a good decision in the end. He's rekindled one of the many loves he'd given up when his mother passed away six years ago. He is now playing quarterback for Freemont Junior College as a walk on. His first game is a little over a week away. Nine days and he's not sure how much anonymity he will have anymore. At some point, he has to find her and tell her where he is and what he's doing. He owes her that much.

His body is too weary to think of such things. He'd come to the campus to hang out with Austin and take it easy, and yet, here he is, under the tree again, wondering when he will see her. He has no idea if she'll be here for fall semester or if, perhaps, she's already there. He can't imagine her giving up the dream she had to attend A&M, regardless of all that happened. He stands there, wondering what she will say when he reappears in her life. He's tempted to call Danica back at Crestdale Victory Center, the rehab, and get another one of her pep talks; instead, he decides to skip hanging with Austin and go home. He should leave before he gets the notion to knock on every dorm door on campus calling her name.

As he prepares to leave, laughter rings out nearby and he pauses as the familiar music reaches him. His pulse speeds up as he peers across the campus to a couple.

Gilded Copper.

Every muscle in his body tenses at the sight of her. Darkness is encroaching, long shadows growing everywhere he looks, but there - across the grass walking away from where he stands - God is shining the last bit of his August sun on Jules Blacklin's silky red hair. The strands are sending off imaginary sparks as her hair swings along her back in vivid contrast to the white top she is wearing.

A million words come to, and leave, his parted lips before he is able to utter them. The second he comprehends how perfect this moment is, how it must be fate for her to be here at this exact time; he's also reminded that two inches over is a person walking next to her. Her arm is threaded through his, and as she throws her head back while laughing merrily at something he's said, her partner turns his head and West is punched in the gut by a betrayal of epic proportions.

Standing by the girl he once pledged to marry is one of only three people he has always trusted with every ounce of his being. Smiling at Jules, his hand lifting and tugging playfully on her long ponytail, is Austin. West's brother.

One

Seven Weeks Earlier

<u>West</u>

"It's crazy how little you can actually know about yourself."

"How do you mean?" Dr. Steel's ever moving pen stops working over her notepad as she tilts her head up, her small eyes narrowing as she looks at West.

The first time she'd looked at him that way, he'd felt as if he were a bug under a microscope. Her features always remain smooth, unchanged by anything he says; but those eyes? Those eyes are comparable to the tractor beam from the Death Star; they latch on, and West feels as if she's pulling every bit of his soul from him.

"I'm amused, that's all."

She pushes her tongue forward making a clucking sound, once. It's a tell. One of the many he's picked up on from her in his seven months at Crestdale. It means they'll sit there all day until he spills the proverbial beans. He starts to wonder if he should have kept his mouth shut.

"All right, all right," West mutters, sinking farther into the leather chair in her office. He props his feet on a stool in front of him, the picture of a relaxed man. If only. "I was thinking about it all last night. Football, my mom, the tornado… Jules." He stops there, because saying her name always cuts him just enough to make him pause, the need to take a breath is overwhelming.

The pause, the breathing, it's one of *his* tells. She's picked up on the way he pauses every time he speaks Jules name during his time at Crestdale. Dr. Steel sits there quietly and she waits, as she does every time, knowing he will continue on in a moment.

"I'm glad I decided to stay here this past month," West admits for the first time out loud.

"Do you think it's helped?"

"Yeah."

When Dani had suggested he wasn't ready to go home and fight for Jules, he'd been angry at first. As if she knew anything about him, about their relationship, anyway. She was right, though. West wasn't ready to face Jules yet because he hadn't faced himself.

"West, do you think you can tell me about the night of the tornado?" The way she speaks with very little inflection amazes him. The soothing monotone words never feel threatening the way everyone else's always does. Somehow, it made her easier to talk to. The family grief counselor he'd seen right after his mom passed away always put emphasis on his name, drawing it out with her southern Texas drawl. Obviously a transplant to the south, Dr. Steel's sentences are quick and to the point.

"Again? Haven't you heard it enough?"

"I'd like to hear more about your time spent with Jules. We need to talk about her before you leave, don't you agree?"

He shrugs, well aware of his issues with talking about Jules. For the past seven months, six required by the deal his dad made to get him out of any trouble over the wreck and the one extra one he decided he needed to admit to his issues, they'd covered all of his issues with his family. They'd yet to discuss his trouble with Jules. That one scares him still. Talking about her means he's closer to trying to see her, and seeing her means she can say no to hearing him out.

Reluctantly, he looks up from the leather bracelets on his arm and answers her. "Yeah, we can."

She lets out a small sigh, and West can just make out the slow sinking of her shoulders as she releases the air. It makes him smile for some unknown reason.

"You can begin wherever you want, West. It's your story to tell."

"It's thinking of Jules and our story that made me think about how little I knew about myself." She nods; a silent urging, telling him it's okay to continue. He appreciates the way she listens to him without putting words in his mouth. "Before her, I thought I was maybe a little screwed up, a little depressed still over my mom, angry at the world... you know all that angst-ridden, teen cliché stuff. After her, I knew what I really was."

Her brow raises, and her pen once again moves over the pad of paper on her lap.

"I was wrecked."

Two

<u>West</u>

"I hated going to the Shack on Friday nights, it was always packed full of football players, cheerleaders, and all of the students who wanted to be around them. The ones who were hoping for instant popularity because they were seen with the cool crowd. Do you know how many girls give it up to jocks in the back of their pick-ups for a chance to hang on their arms for a few weeks?" West asks, his face twisting in disgust. "I hated that scene."

"Then why were you there?"

"I was there before the crowd rolled in. Ironically, I was flirting with a girl who worked there. She was a friend of Lauren's, and she seemed willing to hang out, so I was waiting for her shift to end. I can't even remember her name anymore. It would have meant nothing to either one of us."

"It?" Dr. Steel cocks her head.

"Sex."

"So you were hanging around hoping to score with some girl you didn't know."

Those words coming from Dr. Steel's lips sound crass. West nods, stifling a laugh with a shrug. "Um, yeah. Basically."

"Basically? Did you do that often? Sleep with girls for no reason?" His brows raise as she adds, "Well, for no reason beyond the obvious ones?"

He feels the heat in his face at her obtrusive questions, but she looks cool as a cucumber. Her right leg crosses over her left, the tip of her shoe tapping the air to the beat of some unknown song as she takes notes on the little pad in her lap. She is not easily shaken. Her face – similar to her monotone voice - is always a clean slate of thoughtfulness.

He chuckles at her inclusion of "the obvious reasons" for sex. "I wasn't a monk, if that's what you're asking."

She clears her throat.

"West, you just finished telling me how much you hated being around the crowd at The Ice Shack and put down the players who used their status to get sex, but you did the same thing?"

"No. No, I didn't do the same thing." She raises a brow in silent challenge and West squirms in his seat. "I mean, yeah… I did sleep with my fair share of girls, but most of them were friends I partied with. There were no strings attached, no using my assumed popularity to get into some chick's pants. I could list the girls I've been with, and they would all tell you we're still friends."

"Friends with benefits, then?"

He shudders with a smile, "Seriously? How are those words coming from your mouth? You're a doctor."

"A doctor, West. Not a monk." She laughs, throwing his phrase back at him.

He laughs with her. Her humor is why he finds it so easy to talk with her. She gets it in a way no other psychologist has in the years he's been in and out of offices at his dad's request. She doesn't look down on him, and she doesn't tell him he's too young; she just gets it.

"So what does my sex life have to do with anything?" he asks after a moment.

"I'm curious how you felt about these girls. In this month since you've opened up to me, you have not mentioned anyone you cared about. With the exception of Jules, of course." West watches as she flips through a few sheets on her notepad. "Did you not care for any of the girls you slept with?"

The question makes him feel like a scumbag. As if maybe he is as bad as the guys who use their status as a campus jock to rack up as many notches on their headboards as they can. It doesn't sit well with him to think anyone would assume he is another prick looking for easy sex. It was never that way and yet, maybe it was.

"Honestly, I slept with the chicks I was friends with. The ones who knew there would be nothing between us when it was over. I didn't do relationships. I tried once with Carley, and that was good enough. When we broke up, I decided attachments weren't for me."

Dr. Steel's tongue clucks again. "Until Jules."

"Yep."

"All right. Tell me the story. Why Jules Blacklin?"

Why, indeed! he ponders, sinking down into the chair and stretching his legs out. "I saw her standing there that night and I fell for her. It was instant. I was gone before I opened my mouth. I'd known her most of my life; I'd watched her, knew she was with another guy even... but that night when she sat at that table and I looked up... it was over for me."

"You fell for her before the tornado hit?"

"Yeah. In all honesty, I fell for her in the seventh grade. Maybe even before that. But when I kissed her that first time, I turned into a dumb pre-teen boy with a major hard-on and I had no idea what to do. Then my mom took a turn for the worse, and I dropped everything. Like we discussed."

"And five years later, you're finally sitting across from the girl you fell for once and what?" she prods lightly.

Reminiscing the last year has been a favorite, and most hated, pastime of his. So many things with Jules were perfect and worth the memories, and then there are the things he'd rather forget; the sights, sounds, and smells of the wreck that could have killed her. The very wreck that tore them apart.

"And I gave her crap and fell in love." He smiles.

"You saved her life." Dr. Steel points out unnecessarily.

"And she saved mine."

She taps her pen cap to her lips once and nods. "Why do you think that? Who knows what would have happened that night?"

West shifts in his chair, looking towards the window as he gathers his thoughts. "I'm not talking about the tornado. I'm talking about life. I mean... yea, there's a chance that if I hadn't bumped into her that night I might have run and been fine. Or I could have run and been like some of the others who weren't lucky enough to make it. But, I'm talking about how she saved me from myself. She pulled me out of my shell."

"That's a lot of responsibility to place on another's shoulders. From what I understand, you did the same for her."

West jerks back at that. "What do you mean? Did you talk to her?"

She shakes her head, pursing her lips. "No."

"Then, how do you... why, why would you bring her up? Who told you that?"

"West, it is my job to know all the ins and outs of what has happened in your life so I can help you. You know I've spoken to your brothers and father about that time. Now tell me, do you think that's a fair assessment? You both used the other to lean on?"

He runs his palm over his face, scrubbing at his tired eyes as the memories come back to him.

I'll be your strength, he'd offered her at the vigil when she didn't know how she'd get through everything. *You were my anchor,* he'd told her at the cornfield as he explained how he was able to stay so calm when they were trapped in the Grier house.

"Yeah," he admits on a shaky breath. "We did lean on each other. We were both so scared and broken separately, but it was as if we were whole when we were together."

"That is a lot to weight to put on a brand new love. Do you think

• • •
10

perhaps the stress of going through the tornado propelled you two into your relationship? Your father says you jumped into things with her pretty quickly."

"My dad worries about everything I do. Our relationship was quick, yes. We were pushed together by something crazy and scary and life changing, but that's not all there was between us. We were real. One hundred and twenty percent real, Dr. Steel. If you can't accept that, then I'm done now." West's hands go up defensively before he shrugs and crosses them over his chest. There were naysayers from day one when it came to their relationship. Everyone wanted to say it was a fling, a passing phase. Jules' parents worried she was rebounding from Stuart Daniels, and West's friends thought he was after a hot piece of action.

Dr. Steel looks up from her notes and taps the tip of the pen lightly on the paper. "I believe you, West. If it hadn't meant anything to you, you wouldn't be here. You walked away from her the same way you you walked away from football after your mother died. As I explained to you before, you get scared, you blame yourself, and you punish yourself. You love deeply and you don't forgive yourself for the things that aren't your fault. You hurt yourself thinking you're doing the right thing, but in the end you lose out on all the good. You lose out on having the life you deserve. And then, bitterness and anger are all that remains."

Three

West

Anger and bitterness are all that remain.

West is lying across the small dorm-like bed in his room, thinking about Dr. Steel's comments, when a knock sounds at the door.

"Yeah?" he calls out.

A black head of hair peeks in as Dani's long fingers wrap around the frame and push the door open. "You done with your exit interview?" she asks, slipping her willowy frame through the small crack and falling onto the bed next to him.

If it weren't for her advice four weeks ago, he would have left Crestdale already. He would have gone back to Tyler, found Jules, and begged her for her understanding. Then, he would have probably run away and lost her again at the first sign of trouble.

"Yeah. I'm a free man."

Dani laughs lightly and West rolls to his side to stare at his new friend. He recalls the first day he met her, walking into his first group meeting a month ago. She'd challenged everything he said about why he was at Crestdale, even before he knew her name. She'd boldly shared her external scars with him that day, and as the weeks passed, she'd shared her internal ones, as well. Her story made his look like a fairy tale, yet she never criticized him for his weakness. He would

● ● ●
12

miss her more than he thought possible.

"You're going to go straight to her, aren't you?" Dani asks.

"Am I that obvious?"

"You're that in love. You're that full of regret," she points out, kicking his leg with the toe of her sneaker.

"Dr. Steel says I should stay away from her." West shakes his head and sits up, sliding back to lean up against the wall. "Like this is some twelve step program and seeing her will make me relapse."

"What do you think?"

"I think -" He stops. "I'm scared as hell of what she thinks of me. What if she hates me? What if she sees me and walks away? What if she believes what everyone else does?"

Dani sits up with a deep sigh and rests her back against the wall next to West.

"So, I ask again, what do you think?"

From the moment he walked away from Jules, after an argument with her family following the wreck and the proceeding legal issues, people had been trying to insinuate that what Jules and he had was nothing more than a fling. They made it seem as if their relationship was brought on by their shared grief and the traumatic events that occurred the night of the tornado. His family attributed the fact that he never dealt with the death of his mother properly to his feelings for Jules. Psychiatrists insinuated post-traumatic stress.

"I don't know anymore."

"B. S."

"Excuse me?"

"Don't give me your lame wishy-washy answers, West Rutledge. I've been there. Done that. Remember?"

Dani would know. She's been in and out of treatment facilities all over for years, dealing with her own demons. She never fails to call him out on it, using the easy answer to get out of a tough question. Resigning himself to telling Dani the truth, he typically holds back, even from Dr. Steel, West edges off the bed and opens the lid of a nearby box. His room is half packed; his dad will arrive in the morning to bring him home for a few days before moving him to the house he will be sharing with Carson and Mindy closer to his new school. He pulls out a thick manila envelope and hands it to Dani. The name 'Jules' is scratched across it in black.

"I wrote to her," he explains when her wide eyes register the weight of the envelope. "Every night. Sometimes twice a day. I wrote her songs, letters, and rambling explanations of what I was doing here. I told her about you, about the trees in the courtyard, the posters in the counseling room. So much crap, I'm almost embarrassed by it. Almost… but not."

"Because you love her."

He nods. "Because I love her."

Dani bites her top lip and her eyes shine as she turns the envelope in her hands.

"I have a favor to ask of you?" West picks up a book at the foot of the bed and drops it into the box as he speaks. "Will you hold onto those for me?"

"The letters! Why? You should give them to her. Mail them. This would show her where your heart lies, West. You could prove to her you did it all for her."

"I want to win her back. I don't want to show her all of that pain if I don't have too. I want to get myself together, get started at school, and then go after her. Start fresh."

"Do you doubt her feelings for you?"

He doesn't waver. "Surprisingly, no."

"I envy you," Dani admits as she sets the letters next to her on the bed.

"Ha! You envy me? How many times have you called me out on my crap in the past few weeks? What is it you envy, exactly?"

"All of it. You've never faltered when it comes to how you feel about Jules. Not really. You've tried to throw a bunch of 'I don't know' and 'what if it wasn't real' crap at me, but we both know that's exactly what it was. Crap. You're in love with her, and you've made it clear that you believe she was in love you. Most days I'm still struggling to believe I deserve to live, I envy you for knowing it."

"Dani." West tries not to speak too harshly as he pushes her legs over and sits on the edge of the bed. He doesn't fully understand her struggle, but he doesn't need to.

"Sorry." She shrugs.

"You know what? If it weren't for you, I wouldn't be here. You're going to figure it out, too." He stops when her knee bumps into his back. Her turns around and sees the frown that has formed upon her face.

"Why don't I help you finish packing before we go down to dinner?" she asks, changing the subject.

They make quick work on the few things he keeps in his room and walk to dinner in silence. They sit at a round table in the cafeteria for the last time and complain about the lack of seasoning on the chicken, as usual. Dani picks at her roll, tearing small bites off and chewing them slowly as West studies her. She's too thin. Too fragile. He wonders how she's going to handle things after he leaves. He worries about her in the same way he would Mindy, or the sister he's never had.

They walk around the courtyard, under the shade of the large trees, and she grills him on football and his new school. She asks him what classes he might take first in the fall and about the new car he wants to buy.

They finally return to his room before lights out so she can grab his envelope of letters and Dani cracks, pulling West close.

"Win her back and live happily ever after for me. Okay?" she murmurs, her forehead pressing against his chest. It's the closest physical contact they've ever shared. Her head leans on him and her hands grasp the sides of his shirt desperately. He rubs her thin upper arms slowly.

"You can come to our wedding," he teases, frowning to himself when she shakes her head. "Dani, I'll call you with my new number the moment I have it. I promise. We can talk every day if you want. My leaving doesn't mean we can't stay in touch."

"You don't have to-"

West moves her a step back. "I want to. I'm probably gonna need your help, too. You know I'm a screw up when it comes to love."

"You're not anymore. You know what you want now. Only now you need to go and get it," she insists with a winsome smile.

She leaves a few minutes later with his letters in her hand, and he falls onto his bed for his last night at Crestdale. Dani's right. As he falls asleep, he can't help but smile at the realization that he's no longer scared to find Jules and win her back. Two months. He'll take July and August to train and prepare for football, get his feet back under him, and then he'll contact Jules.

The following morning, as he drives away with his dad for the first time in seven months, he catches sight of Dani's baggy clothes and black hair standing by a tree at the gate in the courtyard. He turns, keeping his eyes on her for as long as he can until she disappears as their car takes a corner. He left her a letter, too. It's at the front desk scheduled to be delivered to her later this afternoon. He hopes she'll read it and accept his words the way he accepted hers four weeks ago. He hopes that someday he will be able to introduce Jules to Dani. Introduce the two girls who've changed his life in such important ways. He vows he will see Dani again, outside of Crestdale, living the life she deserves to live, too.

"You're smiling," his dad remarks, his eyes flicking briefly from the road to West's face. "Glad to be out of there, huh?"

"Yeah."

"I'm glad to have you back, too. So are your brothers, and

Mindy. West…"

His father's voice is full of trepidation. They've had minimal meetings over the last few months. They've had family counseling sessions, but they'd all been when West was still in denial about his feelings. Once he decided he truly did need help, he'd asked that his father not be involved. It wasn't personal; it was something he wanted to handle on his own as an adult. Grieving his mother, leaving Jules… those were things he needed to cope with on his own.

"Dad, don't," he interrupts before his father can apologize for things he doesn't need to apologize for. "You working out the deal to get me to Crestdale saved me. I needed to stop pushing everything and everyone away. I needed to deal with Mom and what happened to Jules. I needed to know it wasn't my fault."

"Son, I never once thought it was your fault. None of it."

"I know that, but I thought it was. I blamed myself, and part of me will probably always come back to those moments and feed the little doubts in my head. If I hadn't stayed at CVC, I don't know when I would have dealt with it. I wasn't trying to lock you out of my life when I asked to stay for this last month. I was trying to be the man you've always taught me to be."

His father nods, quietly accepting West's explanation. His face is drawn tight and his fingers grip the steering wheel as they drive towards Tyler and the life he'd left behind.

Four

Jules

Alone in her dorm room, Jules throws on the shortest and tightest spandex mini she can find, along with a slashed up neon tee, and teases her ponytail as high and messy as she can. In the background, eighties music blares from her computer as she touches up the heavy eye make-up that completes her look. She grabs an armload of bangle bracelets and heads out, making her way to the first floor where her new friends are waiting.

While most of her friends from high school are taking trips and enjoying their last summer of freedom, she's been in school taking two of her core biology classes and wallowing in self-pity all summer. Leaving Tyler had seemed like such a great idea back in April when Dr. Morgan had suggested it. She'd thought maybe if Jules was to get away from all of the memories it would help her feel more confident in facing her future. So, she decided to enroll in the summer semester at A&M, and it's been working… to a degree.

She's spent most of the past eight weeks in seclusion in her empty dorm room or studying in the library. Her goal had been to be left alone. Goal accomplished, until tonight.

Two of the girls in her Biology II class had been begging her to hang out ever since they started their first track of bio in June. Now, after several weeks of backing out and making up excuses, she's finally relented and agreed to go to a party in exchange for an all-night cram session before final exam. It seemed a good deal at the time, but as she rides the elevator down to the first floor of her building, she's starting to question her decision.

"Jules!" Debbie, a short athletic girl with large brown eyes and a short pixie haircut, shouts as Jules steps off the elevator and into the common area. "We were wondering if we were going to have to come after you."

Jules glances at her phone. Eight-thirty. Right on time. She rolls her eyes and waves, making her way to the small group of costumed co-eds standing around outside of her classmates' dorm. A few of the girls are already sipping from cups and Jules can't help but glance around to be sure the R.A. isn't lurking around to catch their underage drinking.

Always the good girl, Jules, she sighs, as her brain mocks her.

When she'd agreed to go to 'a party' with Debbie and Lisa, she had no idea exactly who was throwing the party. As they drive off campus and into a nearby neighborhood filled with nearly identical houses all decorated with school colors and Greek letters, she starts to get the hint. They're still three weeks from the official move-in day for fall semester, so she's surprised there's much going on on campus right now. But A&M isn't Tyler, Texas. This isn't backwoods bonfires and high school. Jules is about to get her first real taste of college life.

It was an interesting sight, all of the tacky eighties gear and crazy drunk co-eds wandering around the small box house with the neatly trimmed yard. Entering the house, she reminds herself of the plan:

Follow all the rules about college parties you've learned from countless on-line articles, your friends back home, and even Mom and Dad.

Number One: Don't drink anything you didn't pour or watch being poured.
Number Two: Don't put your cup down.
Number Three: Don't leave said party with a boy drunk.
Number Four: Don't leave said party with any boy. (That one was her parents'.)

Debbie, Lisa, and the other girls don't seem to subscribe to her strict list and she soon finds herself deserted, nursing a warm beer from the keg, and standing amongst a group of be-wigged, glam-rock wannabes when someone calls her name over the din.

"Jules?"

She lifts her head as she searches for the owner of the vaguely familiar voice. Turning to her left, she spots someone heading her way. He is shirtless, wearing dog tags and faded jeans, and he is carrying a volleyball. Her jaw drops as she takes in Austin Rutledge.

"Jules! There you are!" he bellows, practically diving to her side. His arm knocks her beer cup, causing it to spill, as he pulls her into his bare chest. His mouth presses snuggly against her ear and his breath is ridiculously hot as he speaks.

"Save me, please," he implores as he takes her cup from her while his arm wraps around her lower back. She pulls back instinctively and his hand tugs her closer. "Jules, please work with me here."

She's startled by his request. The last time she'd spoken to Austin he'd just delivered her heart a death blow by way of the 'Dear John' letter West left her. She's tempted to pull back and slap him, but when a thick southern accent whines 'Austin,' in three long distinct syllables, she has to cover a laugh at his predicament.

Austin loosens his grip on her back and Jules laughs as she takes in the Madonna look-alike standing before her. The bleached blonde appears to be reenacting the 'Like A Virgin' video with her white lace bustier and mini. Her eyebrows are painted on thick and dark, and her eyelids are hidden by blue shimmering shadow. Jules imagines there must be a pretty girl underneath the layers of make-up, though it's hard to tell.

Austin nods at Madonna, tossing his volleyball prop into the air and catching it. "Sorry, hun. I'm taken tonight." Jules tries to keep a blank face as Madonna pouts and sends her a look before she turns and starts flirting with Bruce Springsteen.

Once Madonna is occupied elsewhere, Austin looks down at Jules for a few moments as she stands rooted to the floor with her teeth eating her bottom lip in agitation. Finally, he smiles, tugging her into his side and leading her away from the hair band groupies she'd been talking to. Without thinking, Jules follows him, shouldering out from under his arm the moment they reach the relative peace and quiet of the outside.

"What the -" she starts, taking several steps into the backyard before rounding on him. He keeps pace, and she practically runs into his chest when she turns. "- hell?" she finishes.

"Sorry." His hand runs through his hair as he tucks the ball under his arm. "I saw you and I acted. I didn't think... I needed to get away from that girl."

"Seriously? No 'Hi, Jules?' No 'How you been? What's up?' How about 'Sorry I tore the rug out from underneath you and didn't return your calls after the last time I saw you?'" she fumes, holding her hand up to his chest to stop him from coming closer as she steps back. "Instead, you see me at a party and automatically assume I'll help keep you safe from your harem of hoes?"

It's Austin's turn to look stunned as Jules shakes her head, drops her cup to the ground, and bumps into his shoulder as she walks past him back into the house without another word.

"I don't have a harem of hoes." Austin's low whisper carries a note of humor to it as he sneaks up on her.

She'd stayed clear of him for thirty minutes by talking to the hair band boys and dancing with her classmates. When she snuck into the dark corner to people watch and take a breath, she realizes she should have looked for him first. She didn't, and now here he is beside her, his demeanor so similar to West's that she has to close her eyes and swallow hard before she can look at him again.

"It was one girl, who seemed cool until she opened her mouth. I couldn't get her to take no for an answer. So yes, I used you." He leans against the wall, spinning the ball in his hand in front of his waist.

Taking a long sip of her new drink, she props her shoulder against the wall, too. She lets her eyes look at him then, honestly look at him, and she can see the remorse in his somber face.

His head dips down, his shoulders hunching forward, as he offers a simple and sincere, "I'm sorry."

Her own head bobs of its own volition, in understanding, and her lips curl up in a small smile as she speaks.

"So you're saying you've lost that loving feeling?"

She tries not to laugh at her own joke. She bites her tongue, purses her lips, and even rolls her head the other way, but the look on Austin's face is priceless and when he starts to laugh, the sound makes her heart leap. It's deep and strong, like West's, but happier and a little bubblier somehow. She sags against the wall laughing, her hand pressing to her stomach when it starts to ache. It's been a long, long time since she's had something truly funny to laugh at.

"Jules?" His serious voice freezes a giggle right on her lips. She wipes a tear of hilarity from her eye.

"Yeah?"

"I'm really sorry. I didn't want to give you that letter. He's my brother, and I did it for him."

She touches his forearm and he stops.

"Can we not talk about him?"

"But, I want -."

She huffs, pushing off the wall. "No. Like you said, you did it for him. I'm sorry. My attitude was uncalled for. You don't owe me an explanation Austin. Let's just agree to not discuss him, okay?"

"Deal."

Jules leans back against the wall next to Austin, her arm bumping into his as they watch the party around them in silence. She wants to ask about West. She wants to know how he is, where he's been and if he's even home yet. But she can't. Asking would mean she is interested, and she's spent the past seven months since he left trying to get over him.

"Can I ask you to dance?"

Jules allows herself to nod and puts her hand in his as they weave their way through the crowd and find a space large enough for their bodies to fit. They smile timidly at each other as they move to the synthesizer beat of an old Duran Duran song, and Jules is grateful for all of the eighties songs she's listened to with her parents on road trips. She hums along to the catchy tune as they dance around in circles. No one in the room is dancing in a fashion that makes any sense. Instead, they are mimicking moves seen in old movies and television episodes. The dancing breaks the ice as Austin scrutinizes her face.

"What?" she finally asks when she catches him staring at her for the third time in one song.

"Nothing."

She lifts her brow, and he shrugs. The tempo of their dancing begins to slow as the current song morphs into a slow rock beat and Jules finds herself standing there unsure of what to do next. Austin isn't bothered one bit. Holding his volleyball between his hands, he lifts his arms and lassos her in the middle, pulling her closer to his chest.

She stiffens as his volleyball pushes at her back pressing her closer to him before she relents and carefully wraps her hands around his neck. His bare skin is hot, and she feels somewhat awkward touching him this way.

"I've never slow danced with a volleyball before."

His lips twitch. "Yeah, I guess I don't need it." He looks around and nods at something, releasing one arm from around her and tosses the ball behind her back.

"You didn't have to get rid of it."

"Nah, I'd rather hold onto you than my ball."

Austin's eyes widen at his own comment, and the silent pause that follows is rife with tension. Jules' chest rises as she takes a deep breath, biting her tongue at the dirty joke she wants to blurt out while processing the meaning of his words.

"Let's not make a joke about balls, okay?" He sighs with a shake of his head, and the dam is broken.

Throwing her head back, Jules falls into another fit of laughter at Austin Rutledge's expense. When he offers her a ride home several hours later, she agrees. Debbie had left early with a guy Jules didn't know and Lisa is sitting in a corner chatting and doesn't look ready to leave anytime soon.

When they walk out to his car, he pulls a tee shirt out and slips it on, much to Jules relief, and maybe a small amount of disappointment. Hot abs and strong muscles are nice to look at. Why does it matter if they belong to your ex's brother?

"You know, Maverick, this scene really calls for a motorcycle." Jules quips, thinking of his Top Gun inspired costume and the motorcycle Tom Cruise rides around on in the movie. "What happened to yours?" she asks, taking in his little blue sports car.

"Oh, I still have it. It's at home. I don't typically ride it to parties."

"No? I guess it's not the best vehicle to have when you're trying to bring home girls, huh?"

His eyes narrow at the way she says 'girls,' but he doesn't rise to her bait. She wants to kick herself for insinuating that he is used to picking up girls and bringing them home. She'd meant it, and she wouldn't deny it, but he's been nice to her and she has no reason to be snarky with him.

She pulls her door handle to get in the car and mumbles, "Sorry, I-."

"Jules, don't." Austin interrupts her action. Leaning against the car with his elbows propped on the top, he stares at her across the vehicle. "I'm sure West told you enough about me to know that what you said was accurate. You're right, a motorcycle isn't the best way to get half drunk girls home from a party, but truth is I don't bring it to parties because it's been stolen more than once and I usually find it in some crazy spot on campus due to some idiots drunken prank."

She hears his explanation, but all of her focus is on the one word he said that she wishes he hadn't: West. It is too much for her at the moment, and she finds herself sinking against the car, pressing her body against the door and asking him the question she's wanted to ask from the moment she first saw him.

"How is he?"

Silence looms between them as he looks at her. Austin's features became sad as he counters her question with one of his own.

"How are you?"

She doesn't answer. He doesn't ask again. They both slide into the vehicle and, with the exception of him asking where she lives and her telling him the name of her building, they don't speak again. Austin drives onto campus, walks her to her building, and makes sure she gets inside safely. Then, he turns around and leaves. Jules returns to the solitude of her empty dorm.

Five

Jules

Three days later, Jules is leaving her building on the way to grab a late lunch when she spots Austin's head in a crowd of co-eds from her building. She wavers, not sure if he's shown up to see her or if perhaps he's there for someone else. *Maybe he was walking by and ended up being mobbed by groupies,* she thinks. Deciding to walk on by, she hurries onto the grass to cut around the group when his voice calls after her.

"Wait up, Jules." She stops as he disentangles himself from the posse around him and takes a few quick strides to her side. "I stopped by yesterday, but you weren't around."

"Yeah, I have class first thing, followed by lab until 1:35 each day. Why were you looking for me?"

"I thought we could hang. Maybe talk some."

She shakes her head, "You know what, Austin? I don't think that's a great idea."

"Oh, c'mon. I'm sorry for the other night. You asked about West and I should have answered you instead of playing games. He's good. He's been-."

"No! No. La la la…" She mumbles incoherently to get him to stop speaking. "Don't tell me. I don't want to know. Not from you. I mean, it's not your place. I shouldn't have asked."

His light laughter brings a smile to her face. "Okay then, back to our original deal? No mention of 'you know who.'"

He shudders playfully, and she rolls her eyes with a grin as she looks up at him, blinking into the sunlight shining behind his head. In the daylight, she can see all of the similarities he has with West; they're hard to look at, but she can also see the things that are uniquely Austin. Separating the two is essential to her as she studies him. Austin's hair is the same color as West's, but it's cropped shorter, spiking a little in the front, but not with the same abandonment of West's devil-may-care hair. His lips are thinner, too. His chin is a little longer, not as chiseled as West's. It's these little details that help her keep her composure as she scans down and takes in his attire. He's wearing a practice tee with ripped armholes that show off his well-trained biceps and black workout shorts; the outfit reminds her of West. West rarely wore sports attire when they were together, but when he did, it was at home when they were alone and when he was relaxed, being himself. Those were her favorite moments with him. They were the only times when he looked like the real West Rutledge and not the guy he'd been playing for so long.

West never displayed his lingering love of sports to people at school or around town. Instead, he preferred to look the role of the loner in his dark jeans and simple tees. They'd argued about it once, and he refused to admit he was playing a part that didn't suit him. He'd thrown back that she'd given up cheering and wasn't being true to herself, either. She'd started to argue back, and he'd kissed her hard, finding better ways for them to spend their time.

"I haven't had lunch yet. Wanna grab a bite?" she asks once she regains her composure.

"Absolutely." Austin checks his watch, looking around him at the people wandering around campus on a Tuesday afternoon. "Do you have another class or are you done for the day?"

"Done."

"Could we go off campus? I know a small diner a couple blocks away. Best burgers in town."

"Big man on campus isn't much fun, huh?" she pries, stuffing her hands into her shorts pockets.

"Summer semester isn't usually so bad, but I try not to eat in the commons. Especially if I want peace."

Jules agrees and allows Austin to drive a few blocks off campus to Big Daddy's Burgers where they grab a corner table and shell peanuts while they wait for their food.

"Tell me about school. What's your major?" Austin asks after shoveling a few peanuts into his mouth.

"Um, it's good. I decided on sports medicine and OT."

"Really? I thought after the tornado you didn't want anything to do with football anymore?" He sucks in his breath after he speaks. Obviously, almost everything he *thinks* he knows about her he's heard from West. She can tell he is worried about bringing it up.

"That was then," she says pointedly, trying to show him she isn't the same girl his brother had been with anymore. "After the wreck, I had to do a lot of PT. Those therapists and doctors were amazing in helping me get back on my feet again. It made me want to give back, to help someone else who might be in the same place as I was someday."

"That's cool, Jules."

"So, how about you? Business major or sports medicine, just like ninety percent of all collegiate football players in this nation?"

"Ha!" He tips his head and throws an empty shell at her. "Are you making fun of all us dumb jocks?"

"Noooo, I'm pointing out the truth. You don't kill yourself day in and out playing NCAA ball if you're not hoping to make it in the big times. Those who don't make it typically do the basic business degree 'because you can use it for a myriad of jobs.'" She mimics what she's heard so many athletes say. "Or you go into sports med because it's all you've ever known."

"Wow, you're jaded."

"Realistic."

"No. Jaded. Do you honestly dislike athletes now?"

She pauses, thinking about his question instead of spouting an answer that might come across the wrong way.

"You're right. Half the guys on the team take the easy way out in school. If the NFL didn't make us sit out a year, I think the majority of NCAA football players wouldn't even go to school; they'd enter the draft. So yeah, you're talking about a lot of guys who skimmed by high school because all they wanted to do was play sports. So when they got to college, they take the easy route. My dad and Carson both did business, you know."

It was refreshing to hear him agree with her thoughts on jocks and school. She'd always hated the way Stuart would blow off studying for big tests and then miraculously pass them. She knew he was getting passed because of his talent on the field. It wasn't right, but it's the way of the sports world.

"I'm not implying they're stupid," she adds when he mentions Carson and his father.

"Oh, I know. Hell, my dad has done well for our family. He parlayed his short career in the NFL into broadcasting gigs and co-owns a few franchises. He was smart with his money. Carson's smart, too; granted he works for dad. Nepotism at its best," he teases with a wink, and Jules feels herself relax a little more as their food arrives.

"So, your major?" she asks as she squirts ketchup on her plate for her fries. The heavenly smell of burgers and fries make her stomach growl and she digs in, not bothering with dainty bites and manners.

"You guess."

"Sports med or business?" she manages to mumble as she swallows her first juicy bite down. "Oh, my word, this *is* the best burger in town!"

"Told you and no."

"Hmmmm," she ponders as she licks a glob of liquid from the

side of her mouth. "Oh! Broadcasting?"

Austin shakes his head, and she's stumped.

"Accounting, marketing, or communications?"

"Nope, nope, and nope. Also, you do know communications encompasses a lot of jobs, right?" His shoulders shake as she frowns.

"Rocket science!" she spits out after several minutes of quiet contemplation, filled only by the groans of pleasure she takes in each bite of her food.

"Close."

"Close? Really?"

"Don't look so surprised. I'm not as dumb as I look." He laughs, and Jules sits forward and takes a sip of her drink.

"You don't look stupid at all," she says quietly, almost reluctantly, and she wonders why giving a compliment to him feels so strange. *Because he's West's brother, idiot!* her brain shouts at her as she watches his smile. Shaking away the thought, she continues.

"Um, anyway. Rocket science. So you're a science major of some sort?"

"No, more rocket, less science."

"More rocket? What the hell?"

"Do you give up?"

He laughs at her confusion, and she wants to say no, but she's clueless. "Obviously!"

"I'm an engineering major." Her brows raise in surprise. "I've impressed you, I see."

"I have to admit you have. That's very impressive… for a dumb jock."

A peanut shell smacks her in the forehead, and she howls as Austin breaks into laughter. Austin tells Jules about his classes as they eat. The more he talks, the more impressed she is. He isn't another dumb jock and, though he certainly has the talent to make it in the NFL, he confides in her that he is questioning the choice.

"Football is all I've ever known. My parents have shots of my naked butt lying across a pigskin from day one. I can show you a million and one pictures from childhood and the majority will be football. Playing the game, at a game, watching a game. I love it, don't get me wrong, but I get a different feeling when I build something."

"Sure, but you could play ball for a while and always work after, couldn't you?"

"Yeah."

"Have you talked to your dad or your brothers about it?" Jules hesitates when she says 'brothers' because she tries not to speak of West as often as possible, but the Rutledge boys are a package deal. They are a tight knit group and love each other very much.

"Nah. There's no need to worry with it, yet. I don't know what they'll think. Carson wasn't quite good enough to make it, and Wes... sorry." He stops himself from saying West's name and skips ahead. "Uh, my dad missed out on a lot when he played ball when we were babies. You know he coached until mom got sick. That's when he quit; he blamed himself for not being there for her more before she died. Hated the sport for a while, even."

Really? Just like his youngest son. She doesn't say the thought out loud, but the similarities to the way West gave up are striking.

"You're a good player. I remember you back in high school, and I've had the pleasure of watching you play on Saturday's the past two years. You have a shot."

"I know."

He shrugs and Jules feels bad for him. He's lucky he has such an amazing choice to make with his life, but she doesn't envy him with the decision.

"Anyway! Enough of that. How about dessert?"

They share a hot fudge brownie sundae, although Austin eats three-fourths of it, and she balks at him until he orders a second one. Their conversation stays light and carefree for the rest of the meal and, when they finally start to leave, Jules is amazed to see they've been sitting there for over two hours.

"This was fun," she tells him as they slide from their booth. As she pulls out of the tight space between the red leather seat and the table, she freezes as a sharp pain and cramp seize her pelvic area. "Ahhh," she moans, grabbing her hip and gritting her teeth.

"Jules?" Austin leans over her, his hand cupping her elbow as she breathes in deep breaths. "What's wrong? You okay?" His voice is filled with worry, and she nods silently when she can't speak. She's using all of her concentration to breathe through the pain.

Arching her back and pressing her hip out, she tries to stretch. Her sweaty palm lays flat on the table to maintain her balance. The cramps let go some, and she starts to feel relief in her muscles.

"I'm okay. Give me a second."

Austin steps back, giving her a little space while maintaining a light grip on her right arm. When the pain eases to a dull ache, she pushes her hair out of her face with her left hand and stands straight. The whole moment lasted less than sixty seconds, but the pain was acute and she feels the perspiration clinging to the back of her shirt as she rolls her shoulders. She smiles apologetically at Austin's concerned face.

"A little side effect from the wreck. I haven't been getting in enough exercise since June, so when I'm still too long my muscles seize." His face darkens and she quickly adds, "I'm okay, I promise. It's like a charley horse, though slightly more annoying. But it goes away pretty quickly."

"What kind of exercise?" he asks as they finally make their way out of the diner.

"Just typical PT stuff, stretches, running. Things to keep my muscles strong and loose. I even do Yoga." He opens the car door for her, his face thoughtful as she slides into the seat carefully. "Thank you," Jules offers as he closes the door and makes his way around the car.

When he opens his side and falls into his seat, he turns to her. "I could do it with you."

"Yoga?"

"Um, no. But I could run with you or do some PT stuff. I've been put through the ringer enough; I know a lot of exercises."

A small part of her melts at his sweet offer. "That's… well, you have your own workouts to do. You don't have time to work out with me. I appreciate it, and all."

"I have time. I hit the weights and practice, but I have days off, and we could run at night." Jules looks at him skeptically. "C'mon, let me work out with you; at least for the next few weeks until your roommates move in and you have others to work out with. It'll be fun. Besides, if I'm going to be ready for the draft I need all the help I can get."

Jules sits there, taking in Austin's eager face and listening to his explanations. She wants to say no. She needs to say no. But those blue eyes, so similar to his brother's, are pinned on hers and she finds herself giving in.

"Okay, I'd like that."

"Perfect! Let's start tonight. I need to work off that lunch."

Jules wonders what she's gotten herself into.

Six

West

West falls to the ground, sweat pouring from every limb of his body as the scorching August sun blazes down on the field at Freemont. Two-a-days in August, or "hell-on-earth" as most players chose to refer to it, take every last ounce of his energy. Running drills, conditioning, weight training: it's his job, every day. Every football player must take it seriously if they want to play the game, especially West. Since he's been off of the field for so long, he constantly feels the need to work harder, move faster, and lift stronger to prove he belongs.

He knows it's most likely backroom favors that landed him a spot on the team. They already had a quarterback lined up for the season before West showed up, but the promise of a Rutledge was too much to turn down. West almost felt guilty when he stepped onto the field the first time to compete for the starting job against the junior veteran player, Casey Wiggs. Wiggs is a good player. He played all-county in high school, but he doesn't have a future in the league. He's playing for the love of the game, and West walks in and takes his position from him in two short practices. It was like taking candy from a baby. When he first walked on, he was nervous Wiggs and some of the other players might resent him, especially since he missed spring training. He also worried about the perception that he'd bought his way on the team. The guys didn't care, though. Wiggs had been put out at first, but the moment the team recognized West's natural ability they went from irritation at the interloper to seeing a chance at a championship flashing in their eyes.

"Hit the showers!" yells one of the assistant coaches as more players drop to the ground around him. "You boys are lucky you get this weekend off! Monday we head back to hell!"

West is pretty sure Coach takes absolute pleasure in stating that fact, but he sits up and claps with the others as they start to head in.

"Rutledge!"

"Hey, man." West acknowledges his favorite running back as he swings his backpack over his shoulder.

"Couple of guys are heading to A&M territory tonight, trolling for some fresh meat. You in?"

Shaking the excess water from his hair, West feigns interest. "Fresh meat, huh? What's wrong with the ones here?"

"Awe man, c'mon. We're gonna be confined to campus starting next week and this is our last weekend to see how the honies over there taste. Steve-o said the local joints have been ripe for the picking."

"During summer semester?" West's eyebrow raises slightly.

"You know those high-brow sorority girls like to keep close to their mansions all year round, bro."

They walk out of the locker room together, running into a few more teammates loitering in the parking lot. The afternoon sun, finally starting its lazy descent, casts long shadows across the cars. The temperature is nowhere near as hot as it was only an hour before.

"Dude, you get our star QB to come?" Steve, or 'Steve-o' as they like to call him, shouts from two rows back. West looks over to see the team's star tight end leaning against a car with a cellphone pressed to his ear.

"I've gotta pass tonight, but hit me up tomorrow and I might be able to swing it," West responds across the lot, sending him a wave as he rounds on the other guys in his group.

"Sounds like a plan. You got a hot piece waiting on you at home, brother?" asks Acker, one of his secondary linemen.

A few heckles from the other guys follow up the remark. West suppresses the desire to roll his eyes as the mantra *'boys will be boys'* runs through his head.

"Wouldn't you like to know," he shoots back instead, knowing it's all a game to these meatheads.

"C'mon, Rut, hook us up with all the honies whereabouts. I know your bro's gotta have the lockdown on all the willing." One of the offensive linemen jokes, jostling around with a couple players in his vicinity.

"I'll see what I can find out for you. I gotta run. You guys don't get into any trouble now." With a flurry of fist bumps and high fives, West hurries across the lot to his new truck and throws his bag into the cab before his teammates try to stop him.

As he pulls off campus and turns toward home, Austin pops into his mind. He's barely seen his brother since practice picked up the first of August. If Freemont practices are considered hard, then A&M practices can be described as brutal. Knowing Austin will have had a tough day on the field, as well, and thinking he might be down for grabbing some burgers and hanging out, he decides to skip the turn home and head towards A&M instead.

Ignoring the teasing voice in his head, he purposely parks his truck across campus from Austin's building so he can pass by The Century Tree. He's stopped by the tree a few times since leaving Crestdale; typically, he sits on the bench or stands in the shade and wonders if the moment he shared with Jules here last year under the branches of this 'magical' tree was real. Depending on his mood, the answer varies. A few weeks ago, he was still able to swear to Dani and Dr. Steel that what he and Jules had had was real, was lasting. Since leaving CVC and getting back into the "real" world again, he wonders how long he should wait before he tries to see her. He needs to figure out if there is any hope for them, or if it's time to move on.

Move in day for fall semester is Saturday. Two days. Even though he doesn't know if she ended up choosing A&M in the end he clings to the one small slip up Jeff made about Jules when they were talking a few weeks ago. He said something in reference to Katie coming to A&M and Jules being here already, for something. It was a jumbled conversation, and West wasn't able to get him to clarify it, but the slip up told him she was either here already or would be come this weekend.

When he hears the light, familiar laughter he freezes. Lady luck must be smiling down on him because, somehow, he's found himself in the right place at the right time; not fifty feet away, is Jules.

On his brother's arm.

Suddenly he doesn't need to question his feelings; they punch him in the gut the moment he sees her golden strawberry blonde hair. It's darker now, more red tones and less blonde than it was the last time he saw her. He takes a moment, holding his breath as he watches her walk next to Austin. His first thoughts, after the stabbing betrayal he feels from his brother's presence, are of her walking. Walking and whole, not limping, not forever paralyzed as he'd allowed his nightmares to taunt him.

When he left the hospital back in December, he'd known she would make a full recovery. His dad had kept him up to date on that small piece of information while he was at CVC, but seeing it in person is more tangible than hearing about it. He smiles at her long, even gait as she walks away.

The urge to run after them when they turn left and disappear from his view is strong. He takes a step in that direction, then stops himself. His breath is coming out in small pants as his muscles tense. West can barely comprehend what he saw, and yet he can't deny it was her. His brother, his best friend, was walking particularly close to Jules. The way he tugged her hair seemed intimate, personal. The voice of reason tries to calm him. Perhaps Austin and Jules stayed friends after the wreck? Perhaps they ran into each other one day on campus and they're hanging out now? It makes sense, except for one crucial part. Austin has kept it secret. In the seven weeks since West has been out of Crestdale, Austin hasn't said a word about Jules to him. Nothing!

West pulls out his cell and moves swiftly in the opposite direction of where Jules and Austin disappeared. Finding Austin's number, he concentrates on taking deep slow breathes, therapy lessons at their best, as he hits "send" and waits for an answer.

One. Two. Three. Four rings. Voicemail. He ends the call.

"Ohhh, no you don't," he mumbles to himself as he jumps into his truck. He presses "send" again.

"Hey, what's up?" Austin answers, his voice curt and a little irritated.

I bet I know why, West muses, trying to shake the intimate moment he witnessed out of his head. Despite the attempt, there's no way he can get the small glimpse of her out of his mind, especially after nine months.

"Hey, man, I'm on campus and thought we could hang. Where you at?" He tries his best to be nonchalant as he pokes for information.

"You're here?" Austin sounds stunned. "You should have called earlier. I'm on a date. Wanna catch up tomorrow?"

It takes everything West has to maintain his calm. He grits his teeth, thinking before he speaks again.

"West?"

Circling his truck around, West heads toward the parking lot he watched Austin and Jules walk toward.

"A date, huh? You been holding out on me? Who's the chick?" He stalls, his eyes scanning the relatively packed parking lot for a sign of his brother's blue Nissan.

Austin clears his throat and West bites the inside of his cheek at the sound. "Just a girl. Look man, she's waiting. I've got to go."

"Wait, wait. Since I'm already here, why don't I go hang out at your dorm until you get back - ?"

"No! Dude, go home. I'll call you tomorrow." A beep signals the end of their call.

West pulls to a stop, close to the exit of the lot, and waits. Assuming they are leaving campus, there is no way they could have made it out of the parking lot yet. He suspects Austin would have wanted to take West's call privately, so they're either inside somewhere, or he stepped away from her - and maybe she's in his car, and he answered before he got in. His quick thinking pays off a few moments later when he spots Austin's little sports car pulling out of the lot ahead of him.

* * *

Seven

Jules

"Should you get that?" Jules suggests, nodding at Austin's phone as he goes to shut the car door behind her.

"Um, yeah... I guess I should."

She tucks her legs into his small sports car and waits as he carefully closes the door behind her. Pulling his phone from his pocket as he makes his way around the vehicle, Austin stops by the driver's side door to talk. She can't help but be curious as to why he is standing out there in the heat instead of getting in the car. After another minute, the driver's side door opens.

"Sorry," he offers with an apologetic smile.

"Everything okay?" He'd looked tense while on the phone; his eyes would occasionally dart over his shoulder towards her, almost secretly.

"Yeah, it's all good. Listen, are you sure you're cool with tonight?"

His change of subject tells her something's up, but she decides not to press him.

"Yeah, I'm fine."

They're going to what the guys call "The Last Chance At Freedom Party" before football season is officially under way. According to Austin and the majority of the team, they ratchet up the hardcore prep for the season Monday and curfews start to get enforced by the team's captains. Everyone needs to be in top shape to play, so they throw one last end of summer party every year the week before their first game.

Her eyes take in the campus as they drive through it. She's been here for twelve weeks now, yet she's still getting used to it. She barely took the time to explore it during her summer classes, choosing instead to remain in the commons or out on the quad.

She's enjoyed the quiet solitude of her dorm with the majority of students not taking summer semester. She also appreciates not seeing reminders of the past every time she turns around too, but she misses her friends. She's already missed out on so much after the accident and throughout her recovery, and now she'll miss out on that last summer at home before life starts getting real. Not that she particularly needs more real in her life.

They pull off campus, Austin's little baby rumbling and purring as he picks up speed.

"Are you excited for Jess and Katie to finally get here?" he asks after a few minutes of enjoyable silence.

"Yes! Don't get me wrong, the solitude has been nice, but I'm ready to see more of my girls."

"Yeah, I know some guys who would like to see more of your girls, too." Austin laughs at his own joke. "I mean Jess and Katie, not your girls." He teases, flicking his gaze to her chest.

She slaps his arm playfully with a shake of her head. "Katie is taken, as you know, but Jess is dying to party with the team. That girl can't stop talking about getting on campus."

The party they're heading to is at a house in a small neighborhood ten minutes off campus. Many of the homes in the area are rentals for students and she's been to several parties there, both large and small, with Austin in the past three weeks.

"You ready for our last party? For a while, anyway."

The start of school and football also signals the end of so much free time for them. Jules has come to rely on Austin the past few weeks as someone who can make her laugh, and challenge her physically. His workouts are boot camp worthy and his late night company is priceless. She frowns as Austin exits the car and comes around to her side; she's going to miss him and their time together.

"Come on, eye candy, let's go have some fun," he teases, offering Jules his hand so she can climb from the car. She laughs so hard that her toes miss the curb and she slips, almost falling to her knees, but Austin catches her.

"You've got to be kidding me."

Everything fades away as those six words hit her ears and *that* voice registers in her brain. The sounds from the party, the color from the street lamps and moon, everything goes black and quiet as Austin's arms tighten protectively around her. She pushes his arms away, grasping the still open door for support. Standing before them is West, his anger burning a hole through every pore of her body even though he's not looking at her.

"My brother. My own brother! Are you serious right now, Austin?"

Austin's back shields her view of West as he replies, "What are you doing here?"

"Is that the… back on campus, is that the call you took?" Jules whispers, raising her eyes to Austin and avoiding contact with West out of completely irrational fear. If she looks at West, she may break down.

He doesn't have to answer her, though. She can see it on his face and in the tightness of his jaw. She wonders how West found them. It's evident, based on his reaction that Austin didn't tell him they were going to a party.

"You told me you were going on a date… some chick… imagine my surprise when I saw you with *her*." From the corner of her eye, she notices West jerk his head towards her and she grimaces at the way he chooses to not use her name.

"It's not *just* a date."

Austin's voice is smooth and a quiet pause follows. Jules isn't sure if she should punch Austin or hug him for making the insinuation they are a couple. She has to use all her will to force herself to not look at his face. Instead, she watches his shoulders as they rise and fall slowly, the sign of long, deep breaths.

"I'm sorry?" West asks brusquely after a moment. The cool tone causes a shiver to run down her spine.

"I said, it's not just one date. We've been hanging out for the past three weeks," Austin all but taunts, and Jules draws in a sharp gasp of air.

Austin shrugs nonchalantly as he tells West they've been hanging out. It's not a lie, but again she is torn between hugging and punching him. This, whatever they want to call their relationship, is between them and them only. As the scene plays out before her, she feels as though she's in a movie. Everything appears to be moving in slow motion. Her mouth drops open as she sees West's mind register Austin's meaning. His eyes go wide and she staggers back against the car as he jumps forward, his fist pulling back with a curse.

"You son of a -" *Snap!* His fist connects with Austin's jaw in a sucker punch and Jules screams.

Austin loses his footing and falls back into her before standing upright again, while West mutters curses under his breath as he shakes out his fist. She hopes it hurts like hell!

"Are you mad?" she shouts, trying to examine Austin's split lip as he spits blood to the ground.

"He didn't tell me he'd seen you. I've been wondering where you were, how you're doing, and he doesn't bother to tell me he's spending time with you."

"So you punch him?" she scoffs. "A simple 'hi' would have sufficed, you know!"

"You're kidding, right? I just came across you with my brother. My brother!" Jules jumps as West presses forward. "Did you think we'd be one big, happy family?"

"West!" Austin warns, pushing him in the chest to move him back.

"No. Don't." Jules steps forward, her blue eyes meeting West's straight on for the first time in over nine months. She's so close she can smell the cologne he wears. She can see the small indention above his eyebrow where he has a scar. So close to the boy, no, *man* - she corrects herself – that she lived and breathed once. Yet, at this moment, she only wants to hurt him the way he hurt her. At this moment, she wants to see him crushed. She doesn't allow herself even a moment to think about how unfair she's about to be to Austin.

"Believe it or not, West Rutledge, not everything in my life revolves around you! If you'd wanted to know about me you could have called. I have the same number."

"I know -"

"Austin and I don't talk about you. As a matter a fact, I specifically asked him not to." He flinches. "You have no claim on me. You don't get to know where I am or whom I'm with. And you sure as hell don't have the right to punch your brother for dating me."

She steps to the side and holds her hand out to Austin. A triumphant smile crosses her mouth when he takes it. Rolling her shoulders back, she pulls him towards the party.

"Jules?"

"Shut up!" she spits furiously. "You lost the right to ask about me the day you sent your brother to tell me that you were leaving me. Had you had the guts, the nerve, to see me first, maybe things would be different. But you didn't. That's where you and I ended. So leave me the hell alone. Just go away."

The last three words are muttered over her shoulder and she averts her eyes to keep from having to see his anger, or even worse, his pain.

Eight

Jules

As they walk away, Jules feels Austin's slight hesitation and she tugs him harder. They walk past a few bystanders without a word, Austin squeezing her fingers in silent support. The crowd immediately swallows her up when they walk in the side door of the house. A dance mix is beating through the sound system, the deep vibrations rattling her chest, as she forces her way to the kitchen in search of the inevitable keg or makeshift bar setup. She tries to maintain a straight face as she looks ahead and gives small nods to those who wave and say hi to her.

In the three weeks since she'd bumped into Austin at her first party, she's come to recognize the group that typically hangs with the players. The best friends, girlfriends, girls that are willing to bed whoever is interested, she sees them all even as her eyes blur with angry tears. Blinking them back, she turns to Austin when they finally elbow their way to the bar.

"Something strong, Toby," she shouts over the ruckus to one of the guys who helps serve drinks at their parties.

"Uh oh, what did Rutledge do?" He smiles as he pulls the vodka out.

"HA!" she chokes and drops Austin's hand. "Which one?" she mutters and Toby gives her a look.

Austin's hand cups her shoulder, "Jules?"

She shrugs it off and picks up the 'vodka and something' Toby mixed for her. Taking a quick sip, she steps away and gives Austin's lip a glance.

"Hey Toby, give Austin some ice would ya?" she suggests as she walks away.

Austin calls out behind her, and she wants to ignore him, but she can't. She shouldn't. She turns with a sigh, facing him. He doesn't speak; he only raises his brows in a silent question. It's a look she's come to know; it's the same look West used to give her when he was asking her if she was all right. Suddenly, the need to run is overwhelming, and she nods, holding up her hand to let him know she needs a moment. He understands because somehow he always does.

A party full of jocks and their hanger-ons isn't the best place to find peace and Jules struggles through the crowd, looking for a place to be alone. The bathrooms have lines, she finds the bedrooms taken, and there are crowds of people filling both the front and back yard. She finally spots a small shed in the back corner of the yard and finds herself desperate enough to sneak into its dark recesses to hide away. Looking around behind her to be sure she's not being followed, she disappears to the back side of the shed, tucked between a privacy fence and some trees. She leans against the wooden siding and takes deep breaths as she comes to terms with what just happened.

Try as she might, she can't curtail the tears forming again in her eyes. The sound of West's voice had stopped her heart cold. She recalls the sadness she heard in his voice, mixed in with his anger, when he said he'd been wondering where she was. She'd wanted to tell him to join the club. She'd wanted to remind him that she'd sat waiting for him for months, wondering where he was, what he was thinking. Worst, though, was the urge to jump into his arms, to kiss his lips. So she lashed out instead. It was childish, and somewhat prideful, to want to make him think she was okay after his desertion, but she couldn't help how she felt.

A tear escapes, against her permission, and she takes a shaky breath as more follow suit. Each tear is a piece of the facade she's built up over the months; the wall breaking away after one meeting, one moment. Dropping her cup, she covers her face and allows herself to feel the pain she's never stopped living with.

"West!"

Hearing Austin call West's name, not far from where she stands, pulls her head up. She chokes down the urge to shout and takes deep breaths to control her emotions.

"Where is she? I saw her out here from inside." West's voice is strained, angry, and so very close to where she stands.

"Dude, let her go."

A burst of bitter laughter sounds. "Why? So you can have a shot at her?"

"West-" Austin's voice matches his brother's angry tone. "I'm not putting her between us."

"No? You already did."

"No! You did when you sent me into her hospital room nine months ago to deliver that letter."

A slew of heated words fly from West's lips and a desire to peek around the corner to catch a glimpse of him hits her in the gut, but she refrains.

She'd allowed herself one cursory glance when they'd been back by Austin's car and, even then, in that quick look, what she saw made her pulse race.

His shoulders and arms are more defined, broader than before. His dark hair is shorter, still a tousled mess, but not as long and wild. Her eyes traveled up his torso and had barely touched on his jaw, with the shadow of dark stubble strewn across it, when she made herself look away. She couldn't look at his beloved face.

"This isn't over," West warns and Jules bites her lip at the curt sound of his voice.

"I certainly didn't think it was."

"Find her and make sure she's okay, Austin. You and I can deal with us when you get home tonight." He emphasizes 'tonight' and Austin chuckles.

"What if I have other plans?"

"Don't push the bonds of brotherhood."

Austin doesn't reply and Jules closes her eyes, waiting for them to say more and wanting them to leave so she can come out of her hiding spot. Austin clears his throat and Jules looks up to find him standing at the edge of the shed. It's too dark to read his face and she swipes at her cheeks before he gets a closer look at the tear-stained mess she's sure she's become.

"You like hiding out with the creepy crawlers?"

A shiver runs up her spine as she imagines what's possibly chilling out around her right now. "I'm sorry. I needed a moment."

He takes three steps forward and leans his shoulder against the shed, facing her in the dark. "Not the way you expected your first run-in to go, I imagine?" he asks. He's trying to be playful, but she can hear the stress underneath the banter.

He lifts his hand and traces a finger along the seam of her shirt at the shoulder as he remarks softly, "You let him believe we might be more than friends."

After that first night she'd spent with Austin, she truly didn't think they'd run into each other again. She figured they'd maybe pass each other on campus or run into each other at a party, but that would be it. It would be polite smiles and nods wherever they went. However, when he sought her out three days later and took her to lunch, he changed things. She'd known, even back then, it was a bad idea to form a friendship with him. Everything he does reminds her of West. And the few things that are strictly Austin have begun to mend her battered heart and make her hope for love again. It's stupid. She can't possibly date him. It's not smart and it could hurt too many people. Yet, she keeps spending time with him. She keeps letting him take her out, call her, and hold her hand - as a boyfriend would. She's finally starting to get comfortable with that feeling... and now this. All he had to do was show up once and everything she thought she was starting to fit together falls apart again.

She takes the coward's way out, shrugging instead of answering his question and then asks one of her own. "You knew what conclusions he would make by what he saw. Why didn't you say anything?"

The dark silhouette of his shoulders shrug, "I knew it would stop him."

"Stop him?"

"Yeah, we're brothers, Jules. No matter how pissed he is at me if he thinks there's something between us he'll step back. Obviously not without a well-placed punch first." His hand rubs his jaw and she feels guilty.

"I'm sorry," she offers, touching his jaw softly. The tender move causes Austin to straighten up and lean in towards her.

She stands there; her face tips up towards him as he closes the space between them and she wonders if she can do it. Kiss Austin, forget West? The prospect of doing just that causes her to suck in a gulp of air and jump back. Her hand flies to her mouth, covering it as tears spring to her eyes, again.

Instead of a kiss, his forehead touches her and he sighs. "This isn't going to be easy."

"This?"

"You and I," he replies and pulls back so he can look into her watery eyes. "Whatever this is."

"I don't, I -" Jules fumbles with her words.

He shakes his head once and she sees a smile cross his lips in the dark space they're standing in. "Don't. We don't have to figure this out tonight." He steps back and his hand skims down her bare arm to take her hand.

"I didn't mean for this to happen, Austin. We're friends, right?"

His fingers tighten around her and he lets out a loud breath. "Is that all we are? Friends?"

She can't think. Her emotions play tricks on her, her heart and head at war with that question. She never meant for Austin to work his way into her heart. She wasn't looking for anything and she didn't think he was either. It was just so comfortable from day one. A friendship not based on who she was before and yet, if she's truthful with herself, who she'd been has everything to do with their relationship. How can there be a relationship when she was once West's?

"Did you want there to be something between us?" she finally asks.

"You're joking, right?"

She shakes her head, "Then why didn't you say something?"

"I've been taking it slow, Jules." He turns away from her, leaning against the shed and looking up at the branches above them. She's tempted to stop him before he says too much, but instead remains silent as he continues. "I can't lie to you... I'm interested. I didn't plan on it, but you're an amazing girl and we... we just work."

A small cry escapes from her lips and she fights to hold back another rush of tears. *This was not in the plans,* she thinks as Austin curses low under his breath.

"I'm not pushing you, Jules. I'll give you all the time you need. I know this sucks. I know it's not ideal, but I can't help how I feel." When she lets out another soft cry, he pulls her into his arms and tucks her head under his chin. "Hell, what do I know? Maybe this is just a crush. A rebound for us both."

She nods her silent agreement at his suggestion. Standing there with Austin, she feels affection for him, but it doesn't feel anywhere near as powerful as what she felt for West.

"I hate him," she admits in a frustrated whisper and Austin flinches.

"No, you don't. West was a fool for walking away the way he did last year, but he had his reasons. You need to give him a chance to explain them before you decide anything."

She shakes her head vehemently, bumping his chin as she pulls back at Austin's laughter.

"I can't… we're over… there's nothing between us." Her phrases are broken, rambling declarations. Unfortunately, they ring falsely no matter how true she wants them to be.

"Jules, you showed more life in that one-minute tirade you let loose on my brother than you have in the three weeks we've been hanging out. Maybe you're over, but you two aren't done."

"It's the same thing. Stop playing word games."

He drops his arms and moves away from her, his face almost completely in the shadows of the overhead branches now. "I'm not playing. If I made you feel that way, that passionate, we would have happened by now. Hell, I was ignoring the facts, but they're kinda hitting me in the face right now. Literally."

"That passion you think you saw was my hate for him, nothing else," she replies and flinches at her own lie.

"Hey, sweetie?" Austin interrupts. He turns his head her way and she can see the white of his teeth in the dark as he smiles. "You don't have to lie to me, you know that right? We're past that part."

She hears his words, but lowers her face. Staring at the ground, she pictures herself as she was those first few months after West left - a broken body and a broken heart. She'd worked so hard to come back from those things and in walks West as if nothing happened, and she breaks again. Furious with herself for letting her wall crumble so easily, she lifts her shoulders and shakes her head as she stands tall. "We're friends, right?" He stands there silently. "I mean regardless of what happens or doesn't happen with us or West. You and I will be friends. I don't want to lose that, Austin."

"Of course."

"Then let's go back to the party."

"Jules?"

"And, let's not talk about him."

Three weeks ago she'd asked the same thing of him. It isn't fair right now, but she needs it. She needs Austin as her friend, or maybe as something more. She doesn't know yet and, until they know for sure, she's selfish enough to cling to him. Clinging to him keeps her sane as she prepares for the days ahead when she will have to face West and try to make peace with everything that transpired last December.

Austin takes her hand and pulls her out of the dark, but not without hesitance as he repeats the same word he said to her three weeks ago.

"Deal."

nine

<u>West</u>

West slams the front door to the house he shares with his brothers. A million words, none of which are remotely flattering to Austin, cross his lips as he throws himself on the couch to wait for his brother to come home. He'd lingered at the party waiting to see Jules and make sure Austin was with her, but the sight of them coming out from the back corner of the yard, hand in hand, left a bitter taste in his mouth. Three weeks! They started seeing each other after he came home. In secret.

"Son of a bi-," West growls into the dark room, punching the pillow on the couch.

It's the memory of seeing her hand in Austin's that gnaws at him as he waits. He plays her angry words over and over in his head, thinking about what she'd said. He'd made a huge mistake; he never should have followed them and he certainly shouldn't have punched Austin, no matter how much he deserved it. No, he owed her way more than she owed him. He shouldn't have let his jealousy play a part in their meeting.

It's close to midnight when the front door opens. Expecting Austin, West takes a deep breath; he's finally talked himself into remaining calm until he can hear the facts from his brother. *No more jumping to conclusions,* he repeats in his head as the light on the table next to him flips on. Mindy and Carson walk in startled to find him slumped on the couch.

"West! You scared the crap out of me!" Mindy squeals, pressing her hand to her chest. "What are you doing sitting in the dark?"

He sits forward, propping his elbows on his knees and taking his head in his hands. "He's not coming home." There's a pause and West looks at his oldest brother. Carson locks the front door behind him, shrugging as he exchanges a questioning look with Mindy. "Tell me you two didn't know?" West asks.

"Didn't know what?" Mindy asks, as she crosses the room and sits beside him on the couch.

"Austin is with Jules."

"What?" Carson's knee-jerk reaction answers West's question. He'd had no idea.

"No way," Mindy shakes her head.

"Why do you think that?"

West laughs at their denial, "Can't deny it when I saw it with my own eyes."

"Wait, you mean you saw them together? Tonight?" Mindy asks gently, the more level headed one, as usual.

West explains how he saw them on campus, how Austin said he was going on a date, and then he tells them about the punch and Austin's comments.

"Three weeks. He said he's been hanging with her for three weeks... how could he? I told him to come home, that we needed to talk about it." He checks the watch on his wrist. "It's almost midnight, think he's coming home still?"

"Did you call him?"

"Do you think I'm an idiot? Of course I called him!" West snaps at Mindy's question and Carson jumps on his attitude.

"Hey! I know your pissed, but don't be rude," he warns. Mindy pats West's knee when he gives her his best apologetic look.

"It's fine. Of course you're upset. What did Jules say? She must have been as surprised to see you as you were her. Especially after all this time."

"Yeah, I don't think she's my biggest fan anymore." He stands, stretching as he looks at Carson. "Always the screw-up, huh, bro?" he mumbles.

Carson grabs his arm, his large hand gripping it tighter than necessary. They stand face-to-face, West an inch taller than his older brother, and they look at each other. Carson, the mentor brother, who's always tried to be there for his younger brother and blames himself for not doing enough when their mom died and their world fell apart. West, the baby of the family, the one who messes up and brings down the grade curve on the illustrious Rutledge family tree.

"Don't you dare start that again," he orders. His fingers squeeze West's bicep when he tries to look away. "Man, I'm serious. You're not a screw-up. First, no matter what it might have looked like, Austin would never do that to you behind your back. Second, I don't think Jules would either."

"How do you know what Jules would do? I'm not sure I even know."

"The girl I met wasn't that girl, bro. Stop with the puppy dog act." Carson pushes him away as if he can't stand to look at him.

"He's right, you know. She loved you, West, and Austin loves you. Don't flip out until you know what's going on."

"I told myself the same thing as I sat here and waited for him to come up, but at this point," he pulls out his phone and checks the time again. "At this point, I think it's safe to say he isn't coming home. What does that say?"

"That he stayed at the dorms. That he drank too much and couldn't drive." Carson throws the thoughts out and Mindy adds one, "That he wants to piss you off?" Hers is the most believable of the three and West pins his hopes on that.

"You're hitting the gym with me in the morning, right? Get to bed and we'll deal with this later."

"I can't, I -"

"West. Go to bed. You've got other things to deal with right now. You're going to concentrate on your first game next Saturday and let everything else slide. Football needs to come first right now."

He catches his brother's eyes and lets his words sink it. Football over Jules? Suddenly, it's like he's back to being thirteen and making a decision that will change his life.

No, he tells himself, forcing his mind to forget his past way of thinking. They're not related, football and Austin and Jules; one doesn't hinge on the other.

He sighs as Carson nods at him. "Screw it. You're right. I'm going to stay focused on the game. If you talk to him tell him to stay at school. I don't want to deal with him. Not until after my first game."

They say a tense goodnight and he heads to bed, willing his heart to listen to what his lips have just finished saying.

One hurdle at a time.

Dr. Steel has drilled those words into his head. One hurdle, one victory.

Making the team at Freemont, especially after having taken five years off, was a huge victory. The next would be his first game. His first game, which also happens to fall on the one year anniversary of the tornado that started this all.

The next few days fly as West eats, sleeps, and dreams football. Final practices, weight room training, watching game films, and going over his playbook until he knows it backwards and forwards. He attends his first class, a simple Psych 101 class, as if he hasn't had enough psych to last a lifetime over the past five years.

Ten

Jules

"Hey roomies!" Katie's giddy scream echoes through the entire building as she bursts into Jules' dorm room.

"We're in here!" Jules and Jess call out from the other adjoining room. They, along with a new student they've yet to meet, are sharing adjoining suites. Jess and the new girl, Cassandra, are in one room, while Katie shares with Jules.

"We're in here?" Katie's mocks sarcastically coming through the bathroom door. "That's all I get from the welcome wagon?"

Dropping the pillows she's holding as Jess makes the bed, Jules gives her best friend a huge hug. "Where's Jeff, I thought he was helping you move the heavy stuff in?"

"Nah, I don't have much and he wanted to go do some guy thing… besides, that's what you two are for, right?" She smiles falsely and bats her eyelashes at them.

The girls make three trips from Katie's illegally parked car to their second-floor door room instead of waiting for a free cart and assistance from the college moving in crew. All around them, students carry boxes of clothing, bedding and mini-fridges - all of the college necessities - to their new rooms; the excitement is tangible. Their building, named Ward, is situated similar to a hotel with interior entrances off of long sterile hallways. Each floor has two common areas on each end, strewn with couches, chairs and tables, as well as snack machines that work eighty percent of the time. Against her parents' wishes, she's chosen a co-ed building to live in. It seems to be coming in handy for many of the girls in Ward as the majority of heavy lifting is currently being done by a bevy of hot males. Jules pushes the plastic box of clothing in her arms into Jess' back as her friend stops to stare at one of the many shirtless boys sweating on their floor.

"Traffic jam, much?" Jules sings and Jess mumbles a distracted apology over her shoulder.

Once they finish unpacking the car, the girls blast some music, order pizza for lunch, and begin organizing their belongings, decorating and gossiping.

"Oh my word! I forgot to tell you I ran into Candy the other day."

Jules rolls her eyes and lets out a breath of exasperation at the mention of her old classmate Candy Crenshaw. 'Randy Candy' as the boys preferred to call her had ended up at a different high school after the tornado and, with the exception of two hospital visits after her accident, Jules hasn't seen her more than a handful of times in the past year.

"Seems she found herself a man in uniform and she's getting married before he transfers in a month."

"What!"

"Yep, Army boy. Can you believe it? They barely know each other, but she says it was love at first sight. How much you want to bet there's a bun in the oven already?"

"Wow, who would have thought?" Jules says with a sigh and disappears to the bathroom to unpack Katie's pile of beauty products.

"It sounds kind of sweet," Jess pipes in. She's standing on a chair holding up a string of outdoor lights as Katie uses special Velcro hooks to hang them. "Maybe she's in love. Boys in uniforms are mmm, mmm, good!"

"Oh yeah! I'm partial to superheroes... have you seen those uniforms?" Katie teases and both girls swoon over the spandex wrapped thighs of Thor and Captain America.

It's close to three when they're done setting up both Jess and Katie's areas. The commotion both outside their building and inside the hallway is still going strong. Throughout the day, they've been hit with invites to three separate events for the night - a dorm mixer, an informal freshman gathering in the quad, and a mutual friend of Austin's dropped by with an invite to a house party. Katie and Jess beg Jules to attend the house party, but she's hesitant, worried West might show up. She hasn't spoken to Austin since he brought her home after the incident with West Thursday night. The whole situation seems awkward, and she is doing her best to ignore it as long as she can.

"Okay, tell us about Austin," Katie requests.

She gives them both looks of disdain. "There's nothing to tell. We're friends."

"Really?"

"Yes, really."

"You know my 'Jules BS Meter' can smell that lie a mile away," Katie points out.

"Your 'BS Meter' is faulty then and not appreciated right now," Jules counters and gives them both stern looks that clearly state the subject is off limits.

"Fine. Then tell us about West," Katie prods again.

"No."

Katie's eyes go wide. "No?"

"No."

"Jeff said West was pretty upset seeing you two together the other night. He said-."

Jules slides off her bed, "I don't care what he said. Jeff kept his damn mouth shut all summer and all last year where West's concerned. He should continue to do so."

"That's not fair."

"No? Life's not fair."

Katie and Jules stare at each other; Katie's face goes red as Jules starts messing with random junk on the desk that sits at the end of her bed.

Katie slips off of her bed and walks to the bathroom, "You told us not to get in the middle. I thought you meant it, but clearly you didn't."

The bathroom door shuts behind her and Jules lets out a sigh. She looks at Jess, who is still leaning back in the chair with her feet propped on the edge of Jules' bed.

"Don't look at me for support," she says raising her arms in surrender.

"I know," Jules sighs, knowing she's been a bitch. She's always shared everything with Katie who, along with Jess, had been there after the wreck. They'd been there when West wasn't. They'd watched her cry herself into a mass of skin and bones, as depression and misery took over her life. They'd been there and now she is denying them some simple answers. It is wrong.

Jules knocks on the bathroom door and tries the handle, finding it locked. "It's only our first day as roommates, K. Don't you think we should wait until day two before we fight?"

No answer.

"I'm sorry. It's not your fault, and I don't blame Jeff."

Still no answer.

"Fine!" she yells, slapping the door with her palm. "I couldn't look at him."

The door opens and Katie's blonde head pokes out of the crack, her blue eyes somber as she fixes her stare on Jules.

"Jeff is his best friend. He couldn't betray his confidence any more than I could have betrayed yours. We kept your secrets and we kept his. I thought you knew that."

"I did," Jules replies and she means it. "I'm sorry I took my frustration out on you."

"What do you mean you couldn't look at him?"

Jules almost laughs at the way Katie bypasses her apology and goes straight to her original question.

"I saw him standing there and I could barely look above his shoulders. The simple sound of his voice nearly sent me to the ground," she admits as Katie pulls the door wider. "It hurt, K. It hurt and I don't know if I can deal with it yet."

"Awww," her best friend rushes her and pulls her into a hug. "I'm here for you. Correction, *we're* here for you."

Katie leads her back to the bed and Jules explains the entire confrontation at the party Thursday night, but she leaves out the conversation she had with Austin. One boy drama at a time is all she can handle right now.

"You and West obviously still have feelings for each other." Jules shakes her head and Katie grabs either side of her face to stop her. "Don't be stupid. You know it's true."

"He left me. Did you forget about that? He left me; he didn't tell me where he was going, he didn't return my calls, my texts. He told everyone... *everyone*, to tell me nothing. He's been out for what, two or three months now? He could have come after me if he wanted."

"You still love him, Jules."

"Of course I do. He was everything to me. My strength, my love, my first... I will always love him, but-."

"But nothing. Don't close the door for good," Katie begs.

Jess nods and adds, "Not until you know the whole story."

"Austin said the same thing. Let him tell the whole story. What is the whole story? What more could he possibly say that he didn't say in that letter?"

The girls shrug and Jules frowns at them. Their intense conversation is interrupted by a voice in the other room.

"Hello?"

Jess jumps up and rushes through their shared bathroom to her adjoining dorm and Katie and Jules follow behind. Standing at the door, a huge duffle slung over her shoulder, is a small brunette with black glasses.

"Hey," Jess is giddy with excitement and Jules and Katie laugh. "I'm Jess and this is Katie and Jules. They are in the other room."

"Cassandra," the newcomer replies, with a timid smile. Her accent clearly identify her southern roots. "You can call me Cassie. Most people do."

"I took a bed already. Hope you don't mind?" Jess asks, and Cassie shakes her head.

"We've pretty much set up all of our stuff. Can we help you unpack?" asks Katie.

Cassie looks around the room, taking in the color explosion of purple and teal Jess has decorated with. Pulling her bag from her shoulder, she drops it onto the twin bed and smiles. "Well, I guess we will have quite the teal room," she hints, popping the lid from one of her boxes and pulling out a teal and white chevron throw pillow.

They spend the next hour helping Cassie pull things out and organize her side of the small room. Jess, Katie, and Jules had agreed to not decorate their bathroom until they met Cassie so once they're done with the room the four head to the local shopping center. They pick up a few necessities they forgot, agreeing on a vintage 'powder room' shower curtain and shabby chic accessories. Katie, ever the crafty one, drags them into a craft store where she picks out multiple paints, stamps, and other items for projects to complete.

Deciding to skip the parties and mixers for the night, they stop at a local burger joint where they sit and chat.

"So, you three went to school together?" Cassie asks with disappointment in her voice.

"Well yeah, just this last year." Katie explains they're from Tyler and Cassie straightens immediately. She is already aware of the 'Tyler tornado' and recalls the story of the schools being combined.

"I saw that on the news. It was all the talk in Dallas; our club sent supplies to y'all."

"Hey, eye candy!" calls one of Austin's teammates as a group of guys walk into the restaurant and Jules sinks down into her seat as eyes from all over the dining room swing her way.

Cassie's brow quirks at her. "Are they talking to you?"

She doesn't get a chance to answer as the guys stop at the booth; they're all wearing tee shirts and sports shorts, typical jock attire.

"Hey girl, Austin with you?" the tallest of the bunch asks, his eyes scanning over their table and taking in her friends.

"Nope, must be sowing his wild oats before he's on lockdown," she fabricates playfully. "Is that what you guys are up to, too?"

"Ha! You know that's not really the rule."

"Yeah, sure," she teases with a wink. Many of the players try to live and die by the rule that game week is all business. The coaches ask that they adhere to a curfew and stay down as much as possible. Typically, the veteran players, and the ones like Austin who are vying for a spot in the NFL, follow the rules more strictly than the others.

Jess gives her a look from across the table, along with a swift kick to the shin, and Jules offers up introductions.

"These are my roommates, by the way. Jess, Cassie, and Katie. Ladies, some of our fine ball players here. This is Scott, the goofy looking one is Chris, and that's Darren." She points at each guy as she introduces them. Jess sits straighter, puffing out her chest, and smiles flirtatiously at each guy while Cassie looks around with disinterest and Katie nods.

"You're Parker's girl," declares one of the guys Jules doesn't know as he pushes himself next to Scott. "I saw you with him earlier. Damn girl, he talks about you all the time."

"That's my boy."

"JP, huh?" Scott asks, calling Jeff by the nickname Austin told her they gave him in practice earlier in the month. Scott looks at Katie differently. "He's good. He'll be an asset to the team."

She beams, and Jules feels a tug of envy for her best friend. When she dated Stuart people would stop and tell her how talented or awesome he was. It was hard not to let it get to her head, the constant compliments for something she had absolutely nothing to do with.

"Football players, huh?" Cassie asks when the guys leave a few minutes later.

Jules noticed her disinterest while they were talking and wonders if she has a boyfriend at home.

"Nah," she answers when Jules asks her.

"Not a football fan then?" Jess chimes in. Her eyes are still following the guys as they stop at several tables and cause commotion at each one.

Cassie's cheeks tint pink and she shrugs, "Football's okay. It's the players that get on my nerves."

Jess, Katie, and Jules exchange glances and Cassie rolls her eyes. "You're all dating players, aren't you? Well, hell, I guess I can't expect you to be perfect."

"Was dating," Jules says pointing to herself.

Jess interrupts, "I'm single, honey, but I'm not discriminating. These two though," she teases nodding across the booth at Jules and Katie. "They can't seem to get away from the jock strap crowd." Jess giggles and Katie throws a sugar packet at her.

"Hey! Jeff and I have been together for over a year now, thank you very much."

"What about you, Jules? Who's Austin?"

Jules shakes her head, "It's complicated."

"Yeah," Katie agrees. "Way too complicated for our first meal together," she inserts, and Jules could kiss her for helping her get out of that question.

"As a matter a fact, let's toast!" Katie picks up her cup, and the others follow suit. "Here's to the best damn freshman year we can ask for!"

"To old and new friends," Jess adds with a smile.

"To new friends," Cassie repeats, tapping her cup forward.

"And new beginnings," Jules adds as her cup hits her roommates'. Cassie's eyes hold Jules for a moment longer than the others, and there appears to be understanding there.

"New beginnings!" they all repeat and take sips of their drinks.

Eleven

Jules

Jules puts both Austin and West out of her head as the first week of school starts. The motto 'new beginnings' becomes her chant when she wakes up each morning until her head hits the pillow at night.

Wednesday night Jules is sitting cross-legged on her bed fixing her notes from the days lecture in History while Katie rummages through their closets looking for the perfect outfit for the Greek mixer she's attending.

"Are you sure you don't want to come with us?" she asks for the millionth time in the past hour.

Jess and Katie have decided to attend three house mixers this week to determine which house they'd want to rush. Jules knew Katie would want to rush, they'd always talked about going Greek together, but she was shocked when Jess said she wanted to check it out, too. Jules' mom is a Delta Zeta and she's been fielding requests from their chapter all summer.

"Which house is tonight?" Jules asks, feigning interest to placate her best friend as she walks into the bathroom.

"Kappa Kappa Gamma and Delta Sig, and then you are not backing out of going to the Delta Zeta house with me tomorrow, right?"

Jules sighs.

"Promise me, Jules," Katie calls out, poking her head out of the bathroom and glaring at Jules.

"Ugh, I promise."

Jess steps out of their shared bathroom right before Katie and they both pose, waiting for approval from Jules on their outfits.

"Perfect southern belles," Jules offers as she looks at their little sundresses and cute sandals.

"Here, here… take a pic for us?" Katie asks, grabbing her cell phone and handing it to Jules, all giddy with excitement.

"Okay, but no duck faces!"

They snap ten pictures before Jess and Katie decide on one that is social network acceptable and then they're off in a flurry of air kisses and laughter. Falling to her bed once they're gone, Jules takes a deep sigh of relief. Just then, her cell goes off.

Austin: Hey, candy girl. Dinner in the commons?
Jules: Rain check? I really wanted to chill tonight.
Austin: You can't avoid me forever.
Jules: Have you seen your brother?

She deliberately doesn't say 'West' as if using his name is bad luck. When he doesn't reply right away, she sends another text.

Jules: You can't avoid him forever…
Austin: smart ass
Jules: yeah, we're both kinda screwed, huh?
Austin: maybe. Rest and meet me for coffee in the am. Whats your schedule?
Jules: communications at 9:25
Austin: 9:25!!! AM? Overachiever
Jules: Us 'regular' students actually have to schedule classes.
Sleep in slacker and we'll catch up for dinner tomorrow before I have to go to a rush mixer.

Austin: deal.

Plugging her phone into her docking station and turning on some low music, Jules crawls back onto her bed and loses herself in her classwork. Two hours later, Jules is pouring herself a second bowl of cereal for dinner when she hears Jess and Cassie's door open and close.

"Hey, Cassie, is that you?"

Keys jangle and a thud is heard before Cassie appears in the bathroom door. "Hey, Jules. You didn't go to the party, huh?"

"Nah, I just wanted to chill tonight. What about you? Where have you been?"

"Library. I know it's antiquated these days to study at a library, but it's what I'm used to. I find peace there. Or I usually do."

"Usually?"

Cassie groans in disgust and takes a seat in Katie's chair. "Yeah, it was packed and seemed more like a meat market than a place to study."

"Welcome to college," Jules deadpans, remembering good and well how the first week of summer semester felt like one giant dating game until people settled in. "It'll calm down."

"I hope so." She eyes Jules' bowl. "Cereal for dinner, huh?"

"Welcome to college," Jules repeats with a laugh. "Have some."

"Are you kidding? I need to eat real food, thank you very much." Cassie leaves the room, telling Jules she'll be right back. A few minutes later she returns with her own bowl and Jules' curiosity gets the best of her.

"Real food?"

"Yep," she replies smartly and tips the bowl low enough for Jules to see the orange-ish colored pasta.

"Mac N Cheese?" she asks incredulously and both girls break into laughter.

"So," Cassie speaks up some time later once they've finished eating and Cassie has moved her laptop into Jules' room and sets herself up on Katie's bed. "Can I ask about your complicated situation?"

"Complicated?… Oh, Austin." Jules recalls their dinner conversation on Saturday.

"Yeah, I mean if you don't want to talk about it…"

"No, no. I mean, it's just a lot to explain. Um… he's a friend, but maybe kinda more. I don't know."

"You don't know?"

"He's my ex's brother."

"Oh! Ouch for the ex," Cassie points out, looking back down at her screen.

Jules is wary of her tone and doesn't want to start off the year on a bad foot with her roommate, so she tries to explain further.

"It ended pretty badly. With the brother, West, I mean," she fumbles. "A lot of things happened last year after the tornado and I had a hard time. West and I had a hard time, coping. Things happened. He left. I ended up here this summer and Austin showed up. We've been hanging out and I thought we were friends, but he might want more and I… well, I like him, but I'm not over West. I want to be, but I'm not. I'm just scared and Austin deserves the truth and -"

"Whoa, whoa! Jules," Cassie moves her laptop aside and joins Jules on her bed. "That was the Cliff Notes vomit explanation and I'm rather confused," she teases lightly with a smile.

"You're confused? I'm living it."

"Ha. Okay, tell me about West."

"Non-Cliff Notes version, but still abbreviated… we were trapped together during the tornado and formed a close bond after that. I dumped my longtime boyfriend, because I have to say it was pretty obvious pretty quickly that I didn't have strong feelings for him anymore. Plus, his family moved away only a few days after the tornado. They couldn't take living there. His mother comes from money and Tyler had lost its small town charm."

"Wow, okay."

"I'm sorry, the Daniels are honestly nice people. Just a little stuck up, that's all. Anyway, Stuart was good about it and so West and I started seeing each other right away and it was perfect, it felt meant to be. We were both dealing with a lot more guilt and grief than I think either of us knew, though, and we didn't know how to talk about it. I don't know. Whatever was going on came to a head when a guy who'd had some problems with West in the past ran us off the road back in December."

Jules shows Cassie the scar and explains her injuries and how when she woke up West was gone. Cassie's face looks appropriately shocked at her story so she continues.

"It was Austin who delivered a letter from West to me. Austin had been a senior when I was a freshman and so I knew him a little before. Of course, growing up in a small town I knew him from afar my whole life, granted he was always on the field. After that, I rehabbed, got better, came here and thought I was on my way to a new life, and then I ran into Austin and now things are sticky again."

"So do you like Austin?" Cassie asks once Jules tells her about the party they ran into each other at and the lunch date they went on after that.

"I... I'm grateful to him. He worked out with me all of July and brought me to parties, introduced me to his friends...."

"Yeah, but do you like him? Are you interested in him?"

Jules smooths her brow with her finger and shrugs.

"How about West, do you still love him?"

With a sheepish grin, Jules shrugs again. "I need closure with him. I was so angry when I saw him at the party the other night. But then, after my anger I hid in the bushes and cried. I hate that he still has any effect on me at all, but he does."

"This is why I stay clear of relationships," Cassie blurts out, and Jules eyes her suspiciously.

"Speaking of, I noticed your reluctance to join in any of the conversation the other night when the guys stopped by our table at dinner. Is there a story there? You said you don't like jocks."

"I'm not particularly fond of most guys, truthfully. But jocks and privileged guys do tend to irk me the most."

"Why?"

"I'll spare you the messy details of my life and all of my issues."

"Hey! I spilled my guts to you," Jules points out.

"Let's just say my momma has had men issues all my life and I don't particularly want to follow in her footsteps."

Jules wants to poke for more information, but she can read the look on Cassie's face and it's not one of full disclosure. Not yet.

"Don't look at me that way. You know it is possible to go to college and not get all hormonal and boy crazy, Jules."

"It is?" she retorts playfully. "Don't tell Jess."

"Nah, Jess is hopeless! I think she's already fallen in love with three different guys and it's only the third day of classes."

They both laugh at Jess' boy crazy ways as Cassie moves back to her laptop on Katie's bed. Katie and Jess return from their mixer not long after and fill the girls in on all of the gossip they learned.

Later, after calling it a night with Cassie and Jess, Jules and Katie lay in bed with the lights out, the sound of Katie's nighttime playlist filling the silent room. After a few minutes Jules gathers the courage to ask Katie the question that's been on her mind.

"K?"

"Hmmm?"

"If Jeff had left you, the way West left… could you forgive him?"

"I can't… Jules, I don't know if I can answer that truthfully."

"Why not?"

"I've tried to stay neutral, because you asked me to, but Jeff did tell me a few things. I feel like I'm biased to the situation now."

Jules sits up and tries to make out Katie's form across the dark room. "What did he tell you?"

"Oh no! I'm staying out of it."

"But…"

"But what? You asked us both to stay out of it. It's only fair that I not spill his side, unless you want us to spill yours to him."

The months after West's desertion were extremely hard for her. She let herself become a pitiful shell of a woman. She doesn't want West to know how much he hurt her.

"Look, I've told you on more than one occasion you need to let him tell you the story. Give him a chance and remember before that night how much he loved you, Jules. That's all you really need to know."

"You know I don't know what I would have done without you, right?"

"I know, Ju-ju, I know."

"Night."

Twelve

<u>West</u>

Austin doesn't come around during the first week of school and West is both angry and relieved. He uses the time to do what Dr. Steel urged him to do - study hard, practice hard at football, and work on himself. He does, and the hard work pays off when he's standing on the sidelines for his first game in five years. He's glad he did the right thing this week by not going after his brother, or Jules. Because standing there, he feels at home, he feels like himself again. A football field had been his playground his entire life until he walked away. The cheering of the crowd, the chanting of the cheerleaders, the student section, seeing his picture and name on the small scoreboard - it's not the Division I game he always dreamed he would play in as a kid, but it's football, and damn! he's missed this.

West drives the three hour drive to Tyler with adrenaline from his first college game, a landslide victory, still coursing through his veins. Being on the field again today felt amazing; he is sure he has a smile plastered on his face as the music blares in his truck and the fields go by. The drive into Tyler feels different, though. It is the first time he's come home since leaving in December. When he got out of Crestdale in July, his dad surprised him with a fishing trip for the fourth. 'Some much needed bonding with my boys,' he'd called it, as if they were still young kids. After that weekend he'd needed to report to Freemont for training and workouts, all unofficial because NCAA regulations hold athletes to specific rules for how much time they can be forced to train and practice in an official capacity. He'd reported to the weight facility daily and hooked up with a few local players to practice and work drills. The extra work paid off since his team had demolished the Bulldogs. The victory is a bittersweet one though. Today, on the field, he'd felt like a king. Tonight, as he comes closer to his hometown, he is reminded of why he is there. One year ago, he'd driven to The Ice Shack and his whole life had changed in a moment. One year ago tonight, this town had lost forty-eight people and he'd lost his heart. It's a sobering thought as he passes the 'Welcome to Tyler' sign and the last of the sun's bright rays touch the sky ahead of him.

Center city is packed with people and he pulls his truck into the first parking spot he can find along the street that won't earn him a parking ticket. Hands in pockets, he makes his way with the rest of the crowd towards the park where the vigil is taking place tonight. He stops to talk with former classmates and friends, joining a large group of the slackers he used to party with on the outskirts of the crowd. Things unfold the same as they did at the first vigil he went to: they pass out candles, the mayor says a few words, and a prayer is offered up from a local pastor. It's a poignant and somber event, but also one with more hope for the future. The new high school is almost complete and the main street businesses that were destroyed have been rebuilt. Tyler is getting back to normal and he smiles as the crowd breaks into clapping at the rousing 'we will be stronger and better' speech someone is giving. It reminds him of the corny 'today we celebrate our Independence Day' speech Bill Pullman recites before the big climax in the movie 'Independence Day.'

"Hey, big shot football player."

The smooth voice turns West around with a surprised smile. "Lauren!" He pulls her into a tight hug.

"Why didn't you call to tell me you'd be here?" she asks after he releases her.

"It's been a long day, sorry."

"It's okay. Big shot QB doesn't have time for his loser friends anymore."

"Whatever, you're not a loser."

"I'm still in Tyler, aren't I?" She frowns.

He hadn't talked to Lauren since leaving Tyler last December. He'd shut her out, as he did everyone. The only reason he finally talked to her was because Austin had relayed a message from her about how guilty she'd felt about the wreck since it had been her ex that caused it. He held no ill feelings towards her. It isn't her fault Rick was a crazy drunk and he'd told her so.

"Why are you still here? I though you wanted to get out of Tyler."

"I do, but you know school wasn't really my first priority." She shrugs and he understands. "I'm going to cosmetology school, though. Plus, I'm working at the mall. It isn't much, but it's a start for me."

"That's great, Laur. You'll be okay."

"Yeah, I will be. The local news made a big deal out of your game today, by the way. Between you, Austin, and Stuart Daniels, Tyler has a lot more than a tornado to talk about right now."

The name Stuart Daniels makes his muscles flinch. Jules' ex, the one she'd left for him. He wonders if she regrets that choice now, after all they went through.

"She's here, you know."

"Jules?" He figured she would be, but hadn't wanted to pin his hopes on it.

"Yeah. I saw her earlier. She actually gave me a big hug and told me she didn't blame me."

"What? You talked about the wreck?"

Lauren gave him an apologetic glance. "Actually, I kinda cried all over her the moment I saw her. It was rather embarrassing, but I couldn't help it. I can't tell you how much guilt I've carried over that night."

"There's no need to tell me," he deadpans, completely aware of the guilt.

"She's a better person than I ever gave her credit for, West. I should have been nicer to her last year."

West nods absently, his eyes already scanning the crowd as the event comes to an end.

"I'm gonna let you find her, then." He barely hears her voice and gives her a half-hearted hug as his eyes wander the crowd. "I'm proud of you Rutledge boys. Tell Austin he owes me a call soon, kay?"

He nods in reply and shifts as the larger crowd closer to the center of the park breaks up. There, standing alone by the tree where a year ago a makeshift memorial had popped up, stands Jules.

Memories from a year ago assail him as the familiar pull that has always brought him to her side pulls him her way. He recalls the mounds and mounds of flowers, pictures, letters, and stuffed animals that surrounded the large tree at center city when the town had gathered for the first vigil in honor of the dead. He remembers taking her hand and pulling her away from a pushy reporter who was bugging her for an interview. That moment had been so pivotal. That was the night he'd told her he would be her strength, that she wasn't alone.

He comes up behind her, the urge to slip his fingers into hers

makes his hand hurt, and looks over her shoulder to see what is
holding her attention. There's nothing. She's standing there, her
candle burnt out in her hand, simply looking down at the empty
ground.

"I still feel alone sometimes."

Her voice startles him and he steps forward hesitantly agreeing
with her. "I know the feeling."

Her shoulders rise and fall with a deep breath, but she doesn't
look at him and he doesn't know what to say. Nine months of
wishing he could make things right between them goes out the
window every time he's around her because, no matter what he
learned in counseling, he still feels as if he's not worthy. He feels as if
he might screw it all up again, and hurting her isn't something he
wants to do ever again.

"It's hard to believe it's been a year already," he says.

She laughs lightly and he closes his eyes, savoring the sound. "It
feels like a lifetime ago to me."

The comment digs into his heart, cutting deep, and makes him
want to drop to his knees to beg for forgiveness.

"I'm sorry."

"You're sorry?" She finally looks his way.

His eyes hold hers before he shrugs without a word and Jules'
face falls after a moment. She's getting ready to step away. He can
feel it; she's about to leave because he's said nothing to make her stay
and he breaks. His hand reaches out and takes hold of her wrist as
her body leans away from his.

"I'm sorry this past year was so painful."

Jules' head tips to his hand on her arm before she gently tugs it
away, nodding and scratching her forehead in agitation.

Taking note of her mood, he changes the subject. "The town
looks good, it seems like most of the shops and offices downtown
have been built back."

"Yeah, it won't be long before everything is back to normal. Or to the way it used to be."

"Nothing will ever be normal again."

"I suppose you're right." Her hand rubs her arm as she looks about. "You know what, I should go."

Terrified of her walking away, he tries to bare a small piece of his soul.

"I thought it all happened for a reason, remember that? I believed there was a purpose to the madness of the pain we were going through." He takes a breath before continuing and Jules wraps her arms around her midriff.

"West-"

"I used to believe in happy endings, Jules. I'm not so sure if I do anymore." He interrupts her, pushing the words from his lips and shocking himself as he admits the thoughts his mind teases him with so often. "You're right, it does seem like a lifetime now."

"I can't... West, I-" she falters, her mouth opening and closing. She reaches into her shorts pocket and pulls out her cell phone. "It's Katie, she's waiting for me. I need to go."

"I can give you a ride home," he offers quickly.

Her hands rub together, making fists as she shakes her head. "Um, thanks, but we're heading back to campus tonight. I was supposed to meet her at her car, so I better go."

"Why aren't you staying here?" He kicks himself for prying. "Sorry, it's not my business."

She doesn't answer him, which is technically her way of saying it's not his business, and he grasps at one last straw.

"Can I-" He wants to offer her a ride back to school, three hours in his truck for them to talk and work things out, but he stops short. *Baby steps, West. Baby steps,* he reminds himself. She's waiting for him to finish his sentence and he swears she looks tense, expectant to hear what he will say.

"Can I call you sometime?" he finally asks lamely, feeling as if he's back in middle school again.

She frowns slightly and shakes her head, "I don't think-"

"Please. I owe you an explanation, Jules."

Her trim shoulders shrug as she takes a deep breath. Her voice is barely audible when she answers him, "I have the same number. Why don't you text me."

West nods his head.

"All right then, goodnight," she offers, turning away, and his eyes follow her as she gracefully leaves him behind. She's almost twenty feet away when she stops, her back straight, and she wipes her right palm down her shorts at her hip.

"Hey, West?" she calls out, not bothering to turn and face him. "Just so you know... I will never stop believing in the things you find so unbelievable." For a moment he's confused and then she adds, "Maybe happy endings just take time." She starts walking again and West's mind reels.

Is she giving him a door to make things right? He doesn't stop to think. He doesn't want to.

"Jules!" he calls out, getting ready to jog after her. She spins around, her red hair following her movement and swinging around, falling over her shoulder as she looks at him with her brow arched in question.

"Text me," she replies with a nod, not letting him get a word in before she speeds up to find Katie.

Thirteen

Jules

The smile on her lips remains long after she leaves West standing at the tree in town. Katie doesn't ask questions when she meets her at the car and they drive back to campus with the radio singing to them. A week ago, when West found Austin and her outside of the party, she couldn't look at him. Tonight, she still couldn't look at him. It took all she had not to throw herself into his chest and beg him to hold her. She resisted not because she doesn't want him, but because she's scared.

"I saw you and West talking," Katie mentions, pulling Jules from her thoughts.

"Yeah."

"Yeah… annnnnd?" Katie drawls.

"And what?" Jules shrugs and tries to play it cool.

"Oh Juliet, my dear," Katie breaks out in her best Shakespearean accent. "You know you can't hide that smirk from me. What did Romeo have to say?"

Jules rolls her eyes at her best friend. "He asked if he can call me."

"Well that's good, right?"

"I guess." Jules didn't take much time to think about it when he asked. His admission that he isn't sure if he believes in happy endings anymore had taken her by surprise. His asking her if he could give her a ride, even more so. When thoughts of West enter her mind, the need to protect herself overrides all other thoughts she has. She can't go through it again. She can't do it to her family or her friends. No, if he wants to patch things up, and after their meeting it seems likely, he's going to have a lot to prove. "Actually, I told him to text me.," she admits. The headlights from the car behind them reflect in the rear view mirror barely enough for Jules to see Katie frown.

"Text?"

"It's a start, K. Don't give me crap about it."

"I'm not! I'm just surprised, that's all. I mean, a week ago you wanted his head on a platter after his fight with Austin. This week you've acted like everything was great and now you're telling me you gave him the okay to get in touch with you. I just want to know where your head is at."

Jules laughs sarcastically, "I'll let you know when I know."

They're pulling back to campus around midnight when Katie's phone goes off. The A&M fight song clearly identifying Jeff as the caller.

"Hey, baby! Are you guys back to campus yet?"

Jules picks up her phone to scan her social media as it vibrates in her hand.

Austin: Almost back. How was the vigil?

They'd both been busy with their first week of classes and Austin with practices and last minute game prep that they'd barely spoken more than a few text messages. When they did talk they stayed away from two subjects: West and their feelings for each other.

The team played a West Coast game this afternoon and is en route back to school by bus. Katie and Jules were able to catch most of the game at home before heading to the vigil. Thankfully at that point, A&M was crushing the other school and there was no contest.

Jules: Hi! It was nice. Different. It felt strange to be home again.
Austin: I bet. I haven't been to Tyler much since senior grad. Wish I could have been there.
Jules: I know, I would have liked you to be there.
Jules: Um, West was there.
Austin: He was? I didn't know he was going, sorry! I would have told you if I did.
Jules: So you haven't talked to him about the fight?
Austin: No.
Jules: I don't want you two fighting bc of me.
Austin: no worries
Austin: k?
Jules: ok
Austin: Hey, I'm starving. Wanna grab some breakfast?

They've both become pros at changing the subject lately. Jules laughs as Katie parks in the first vacant spot they can find in the dorm lot.

Jules: Breakfast, huh? It's after midnight
Austin: and??
Austin: <—football player!!
Jules: lol... fine.
Austin: pick you up in about thirty!
Jules: kk

Getting out of Katie's car, she grabs her overnight bag from the backseat and walks back to the dorm while Katie chats with Jeff.

"See you in a bit. Love you," Katie says, finishing her call and smiling at Jules.

"The busses are just off campus. Jeff is coming to grab me for a while."

"For a while or for the night?" Jules teases, as they enter Ward. The common area is littered with a few students hanging out talking and eating pizza, and Jules smiles at one of her friends from Bio.

Katie presses the elevator button, "We'll see."

They pass Jess and Cassie's door first and Jules notices the note on their white board. "At party, text me -J." Cassie's side is empty and she wonders if her new suite mate is in. When they enter their own room, she drops her bag by her closet and strips her dress off, quickly pulling on the first pair of comfy yoga pants and tee shirt she can find. Katie does the same thing and they share a laugh. Using the restroom, Jules checks and finds the bathroom door to Jess and Cassie's room locked. Typically, they leave their bathroom doors open unless they want privacy, so she decides against knocking to see if she'd want to go out with her and Austin. Instead, she flops down on her stomach and allows herself to replay her moments with West at the vigil as she waits for Austin to get there.

Feeling hot and cramped, Jules wiggles as the sound of something vibrating goes off near her ear. Slapping the shelf at the head of her bed, she feels around for her phone while trying to pull herself fully awake.

"Hello?" she grumbles sleepily into the phone. She tries to shift in her small bed, her arm bumping into something, and she yelps when she realizes that some*thing* is a some*one*.

What the…!

She practically falls off the edge of the bed as Austin grunts from her elbow and an achingly familiar voice speaks into her ear.

"Uhhh, sorry. I'm looking for Austin," West says, and she yelps again. "Jules! What? Did I dial you... nooo, holy shit! I dialed Austin. Are you...?" The line goes silent and time stops as she takes in Austin's sleepy face and listens to West's hurt voice. "I'm sorry. Shit, you know what... forget I called! Forget everything!"

The cell phone beeps, signaling the end of the call, and Jules drops it to the bed as Austin sits up slowly.

"Jules?" he asks, his voice thick with sleep. "What time... oh man. It's morning," he confirms as he looks at his watch. The heavy curtains she and Katie hung block almost all of the light from the room. His confusion, mixed with sorrow, pulls Jules from her frozen state and she rubs her face hard.

"Oh my God... oh my God," she mumbles, scooting to the edge of the bed and turning to slip off.

"Whoa!" Austin's large hand grabs her shirt and she stops. "Nothing happened. I just-"

Twisting, she hits at his arm and pushes at him until he's backed against the brick wall. No wonder she was hot and cramped when the phone starting ringing. Austin's body had been pressed up against her side.

"Nothing happened? Nothing!" she shouts, standing and rounding on him. Her hands rake through her mass of knotted hair. "That was West! WEST! He thinks... oh God... he thinks we're sleeping together now. Damn it, Austin! What are you even doing here?"

"Jules, hun. Calm down," he asks patiently, moving to his knees and inching towards her.

"Keep calm?" Hysterical laughter explodes from her lips as she falls onto the oversize beanbag on the floor by her bed. The swooshing sound of her weight hitting the bag fills the room and she throws her head back, looking at the ceiling of her room.

The bed creaks under Austin's weight and Jules closes her eyes. Her mind races at the disaster they've created. *Forget everything.* Those are the last two words West said before he hung up. *What does that mean?* she wonders.

"Come here," Austin asks, leaning down and grasping her hands to pull her to her feet. Reluctantly, she allows him to help her up. "Do you really care what he thinks?"

"Do you honestly not? He's your freaking brother, Austin. Even if we were together, in any capacity, I would never flaunt it in his face." She huffs, frustrated that he doesn't get why she's so upset. "And I certainly wouldn't want him to find out like that, by phone."

A knock at the bathroom door startles them and Jules jumps back.

"Jules?" Jess calls through the thin door, not opening it.

Giving Austin a firm look, she walks to the door and opens it allowing Jess to peek in.

"Oh, hey Austin." Her eyes grow as wide as saucers as she takes in the scene and draws conclusions. "Sorry, I heard fighting and I just wanted to be sure you were okay."

"Yeah, we're fine. Sorry we woke you."

"No biggie. Sure you're good?" she asks again, arching her brow.

"Mmmhmmm," she answers with an eye roll and closes the door on Jess.

Stifling a yawn, Jules shuffles back to her bed and bumps into Austin as she climbs onto her small mattress. "How did you get in here anyway?"

Sitting on the edge, he explains himself, "Jeff and I came over at the same time. Katie said you'd just closed your eyes and she let me in. I figured I'd sneak up behind you and wake you, but once I laid down beside you-" He shrugs, his cheeks turning pink. "I didn't have the heart to bother you. You looked so peaceful. I should have left, but damn it was comfortable and you smell really good."

She tries not to laugh, but his compliment makes her giggle. His answer is so endearing and completely understandable. She taps the bed and scoots over meaningfully.

"I'm sorry I yelled at you," she offers once he's lying beside her. He lies on his back with his head turned towards her as she lays on her side facing him. She moves slightly, her head touching his shoulder, and wraps her arm around his and hugs it to her chest lightly.

"Jules?"

"Let's get a little more sleep and then we can have that breakfast you wanted, kay?" she asks, trying to ignore the plea in his voice when he said her name.

"I'm going to need you to make a decision. Soon. I can't keep doing this."

She closes her eyes, feeling ten kinds of horrible for not being able to give him an answer.

"I know. I'll figure it out, I promise," she offers and closes her eyes, praying she'll be able to make good on that promise.

Fourteen

West

Sometimes the best way to get over hurt is to lose yourself in something that hurts more. West isn't sure where he ever heard that, but after the six a.m. call he'd made to Austin three days ago he's been following that faulty logic. His brain is cluttered with every last piece of information he can absorb between Psych 101, a lit class, and a highly ambitious playbook for his game against the Bearcats on Saturday. His body feels abused to no end due to team practices, his solo weight training, and all of the long runs he's been taking. If he's not sleeping, he's moving or studying. This is his brilliant idea for getting Jules' sexy morning voice out of his head when he'd expected to catch his brother.

It was stupid, beyond stupid, to call Austin at six in the morning on the day after a game. Especially a late night one where he knew Austin was coming back from the West Coast by bus. He couldn't help it, though. After seeing Jules at the vigil and exchanging a few pleasant words, he was pumped up. Adrenaline pushed him to call her the moment his eyes flew open. He'd barely slept at all that night, thinking of all the things he wanted to say to her, but first he wanted to speak with his brother. He needed to know what was going on with them.

Carson and Mindy swear it has to be friendship. Jeff pleads the fifth, as he always does when it comes to Jules. 'Hoes before bros' is apparently alive and kicking, much to his displeasure. Austin has avoided him since their fight two weeks ago, so he picked up the phone to call, knowing he would wake his brother up, and honestly not caring. When the voice answered, it took him by surprise. He didn't place it as Jules until he heard her little yelp. He knew that yell immediately. It was the surprised shout that she made when he'd startle her. The moment he heard it, anger rushed through him. Pure, hot, murderous anger. He'd hung up the phone and admittedly punched the pillows on his bed more than a few times before he allowed himself a bout of angry tears. He's cried four times in the past five years - his mother's death and funeral, the night of the tornado in the hospital with Jules, and the night of the wreck in December when he thought she wouldn't make it. And Sunday morning, the moment when any thought of getting her back went out the window with the idea that she'd slept with his brother.

Damn her! he shouts in his head as he tightens his shoelace and slips on his headphones, readying himself for another run to cool his emotions. Pressing play on his iPod, heavy guitar riffs assault him, and the noise temporarily drowns out his thoughts of Austin and Jules.

With nothing else to occupy his mind, he will concentrate on the game, on school, and on getting over her. He is done. Whatever they want to do with each other will be their business. His therapists had been right. Dr. Steel had told him he needed to concentrate on himself before trying to work on his love life. That's what he will do now.

As he runs, he plans out the next few weeks. He can get by without seeing Austin for another three weeks before he has a free weekend and his dad will expect him to support A&M and attend a game. Three weeks to come to grips with his new reality. Three weeks before he might have to see them together, if they're even together.

The thought of finding some girl to take the edge off crosses his mind, but he quickly discards it. He has no interest in meaningless sex anymore. Not yet anyway. 'Give it time,' Dani suggested when he talked to her. She'd listened to him cry into the line and pour his heart out and she'd offered him the only advice she could. *Time.*

Fifteen

Jules

Jules finds herself too busy over the course of the next few days to worry about the ramifications of her night with Austin. With her full load of classes, clubs to look into, and Katie and Jess dragging her to rush week - even though she still isn't sure if she wants to rush - she keeps herself busy. Delaying the inevitable decision she needs to make. She meets Austin a few times, always with friends for meals or coffee. They talk and cut up, like they did back in July when they first bumped into each other, and Jules carries the hope that perhaps the awkwardness is gone between them. Then, each time the thought enters her mind, she notices the way Austin's eyes follow her around. He doesn't ask about her feelings at all, though; and as much as she misses the comfort of being closer to him, she stays back. Maintaining a friendly distance until she can figure out what she wants or, more accurately, how to tell him what she wants. Game day Saturday, two weeks after the call with West, things work themselves out on their own.

"I can't believe I let y'all talk me into going to a game," Cassie groans as she and Jules make a coffee run on campus before meeting up with friends to tailgate.

They weave around groups of students and visitors as they make their way across campus. The pre-game excitement is in effect and Jules laughs as Cassie frowns at the rabid fans in their school gear, cheering and partying all before ten a.m.

"It's all part of the college experience." Jules teases looking around at the chaos.

"So are mono and the freshman fifteen, but we're not running out to sign up for that now, are we?"

"Ha, ha. Besides, it's time to get your hottie self out of the library and into the mix."

"Jules, you know I'm not looking for a guy," Cassie needlessly reminds Jules.

They pass a group of shirtless guys playing a game of touch football in the courtyard and Jules nudges Cassie's shoulder, nodding their way.

"I know, I know. If any of the mega hot, ripped frat boys bother you, just tell them you have a boyfriend at home. No pressure."

"Mega hot and ripped, huh?"

"Girl, this is Texas. You know we breed them nice and strong." She winks and Cassie almost trips over her own feet as she laughs.

They reach the coffee shop and Jules opens the door and runs directly into Mindy, who is leaving, a tall frappuccino in hand.

"Jules!" Mindy's voice is overly loud as she steps back. "Hi. Um… you look good. How are you? All healed and back to one hundred percent?" She trips over her words awkwardly and while Jules had liked Carson's fiancé when they met last fall, this is just uncomfortable.

"Hey, um… yeah, I'm better. Thank you," she offers, standing half in and out of the coffee shop as Mindy blocks her entrance. "Oh, this is Cassie, my roommate. Cassie, Mindy."

The girls smile at each other timidly, but Mindy looks uneasy and fidgets with the sunglasses on her head.

"I'm sorry I didn't come and see you at the hospital, I wanted to… but after the fight your dad had with West, we all figured we should stay away."

"Don't be silly, you didn't owe me a visit-" Jules replies. She starts to tell her she holds no ill feelings for them not coming to see her. She'd spent one weekend at their house; they didn't know her all that well. "Wait. What fight with West?" she asks as Mindy's words register in her mind.

"Excuse me," a student behind them grumbles and Mindy steps back and to the side to allow Jules and Cassie to enter and let the person by. Once in, Jules levels her gaze on Mindy, waiting for an explanation.

"Right," she answers slowly. "You still don't know everything, do you?"

"If there was some kind of fight with my dad and West at the hospital, then no. Apparently, I don't know everything."

Mindy's face scrunches as she eyes Jules thoughtfully.

"Ummm, why don't I grab our drinks," Cassie offers, stepping away.

"Look, I have no right to ask you this… but what's going on with you and Austin?" Mindy asks when Cassie leaves them alone.

The change of subject irritates Jules more than it should and she replies back with a bit of a bite in her tone, "You're right, you don't have the right to ask me that."

"Fair enough," she replies with a curt nod. Stepping around Jules, her hand grasps the door to the shop and she adds, "Do yourself a favor and get all of the facts before you all get hurt, again."

She walks through the door and turns at the last minute, pushing the door back wide. "Jules, please don't pit those two against each other. They're brothers to me and I love them." Jules stands there, Mindy's plea like a spoon digging into her fragile heart and scooping away pieces. "I know you care for them, too, and for what it's worth,

I'm glad you're okay. We were worried about you."

Jules stands at the window of the shop and watches Mindy walk away. The moment leaves her both confused and resolute in what she needs to do.

"You okay?" A tall mocha is waved in front of her face and Jules looks at Cassie. "Wanna talk about it?"

"You just gave me coffee. I think I'll be okay."

They push through the crowd without another word. The scene never leaves Jules' head as she tries to smile and make small talk with the other students grilling outside and drinking before the game. Cassie throws worried glances her way now and then, but Jules smiles and nods, trying to prove she's fine.

A few hours later, she's passing boxes of Chinese back and forth with Austin in his room after a rainy victory against an out of conference rival. She's bundled in his over-sized sweatpants and huge sweatshirt to ward off the permanent chill in her bones from the elements and her own wet clothing. The steady rain that moved into the area during the second half of the game is still going strong outside; the wind drives the water into his window as they eat. They originally had plans to hang with their friends, but after her run-in with Mindy, Jules asked Austin if they could be alone. They've been eating in silence for twenty minutes with a random assortment of Austin's music playing in the background as they stare at their chopsticks and out the window at the mess outside. The early evening sky is darker than it should be with the weather, and the room is dimly lit by only a string of beer can Christmas lights above his bed and the bedside table lamp.

"I ran into Mindy this morning," she remarks nonchalantly as she picks out a chunk of chicken from the chicken fried rice.

"Yeah?"

"She had some interesting things to say," Jules hints, and Austin smiles. She reaches for the box of broccoli chicken at the same time as he does and their hands fight for the container. "You haven't talked to West about us, have you? Or Carson either?"

He gives up the broccoli and leans back crossing his arms over his chest.

"Well?"

"Well what?" he asks innocently and she tips her head. "No, okay? No, I haven't talked to them. I've been busy and I was waiting for something to tell them."

"So, he still thinks we spent the night together."

"We did spend the night together," he points out and she thrusts the broccoli chicken at him in anger.

"Not what I meant and you know it."

"What else did she say?" he asks as he takes the food from her and sets it on the bedside table. He moves the plate of eggrolls and box with spicy chicken, as well, until there is nothing left between them. Jules wipes her hands on her napkin and stretches her legs over the edge of the bed.

"That's the interesting part, actually. She said that my dad and West had some fight. That that's why she and Carson didn't come see me."

She watches his face closely; the small flinch he makes at her words proves something had indeed happened at the hospital between her parents and West. Something she knows nothing about.

"Come here," he says, scooting forward towards her and cocking his finger at her.

"Why?" she asks as she does what he requests.

"Kiss me."

"What!" Jules jerks back incredulously.

"You heard me. Kiss me. Let's figure this out."

"Let's figure this out? Do you hear yourself? If that's how we are approaching this, then I think we've already figured it out, Austin."

A long sigh falls from his mouth as he collapses back onto his pillow. "Damn it," he grumbles and cover his face with his hands.

She can't help but smile a sad smile at his frustration because she feels it, too. She curls up next to him, careful not to touch him, as she props her head up and looks at him.

"I met this girl."

That was the last thing she expected to hear. "You what?"

"There's this girl... I don't even know her name, but she's different and she seems to hate me which is-"

"A first for you." Jules laughs lightly when he doesn't seem to know what else to say. No wonder he's been distant this week.

"Different, frustrating," he concedes, dropping his hands and rolling to his side. "I didn't want to hurt you."

"You're not hurting me. Oh, Austin, this is our problem. We've both danced around the truth for two months now because we're too damn scared to admit our feelings."

He nods.

"You and I sounded nice to me. It sounded safe. I'm sorry I led you on like that."

"C'mon, Jules, don't blame yourself. I knew better. We both know nothing was going to work between us, even if we had tried. Neither one of us could hurt West that way."

Jules tries to shake off his mention of West, but Austin's hand touches her chin. "Don't pretend like he doesn't care. You know he did... he does. Stop acting like what you two had isn't something worth fighting for."

Her eyes blur as tears invade them. "Then why hasn't he tried to fight?"

"He has." She starts to argue and he stops her. "He followed us to that party where you told him to go away. Then he spoke to you at the vigil. He asked to call you, didn't he?"

"Yeah, but."

"But nothing, I've told you all this time you needed to let him tell you what happened. Do you think you're the only one who is scared? What he did wasn't easy either, you know." Austin sits up. It is the first time she's seen him defend his brother to her so forcibly and she wonders where this has been all this time.

"I've been a shitty brother," he says out of the blue. "You know, he gave me his phone when he left. He wanted to cut all ties and figured I could keep up with any calls that were important and relay the messages to him."

Her eyes go wide and he nods at her understanding of what he is saying. All the voice mails and texts she sent West those first few weeks run through her mind and her stomach turns at the memory.

"Jules, I had to listen to your calls and your pain for weeks. It was hard as hell to hear that. You were so broken and I began to hate West for what he did. I…"

"Is that what this has been between us?" She waves a shaky hand, pointing from her chest to his. "You felt pity for me?"

"No! Not at all. I admired your strength. That last message you left him, the one where you said you were done waiting for a boy to come back for you, that you didn't need a guy. I admired you for that. For what you'd been through and what you were overcoming," he explains and Jules recalls the day she left that message. It was the first time she'd taken steps again without assistance. It was the day she knew she would truly heal physically.

"He cut me out, too, you know. He would barely speak when I'd call him. So here I was listening to your hurt and getting nothing but silence from him. I let what you were going through overshadow what he was dealing with."

She takes a shaky breath and sits up beside him on the edge of the bed. "What was he dealing with Austin? What am I missing here?"

She waits, sensing his reluctance to fill her in on West and she wonders how she is supposed to work towards forgiveness if no one will tell her the story.

"He loved you, Jules. Everything he did, he did because he wanted to make things right for you."

"But you're not going to tell me."

"I don't know it all. I don't know where he was coming from. I know parts. I know it wasn't easy for him to leave Tyler. He had demons to deal with just like you did."

Her head slips down to rest on Austin's shoulder and she sighs at the heaviness in her heart. "I don't know what to do anymore. I don't know what I want. I miss him so much, Austin… and yet-" She bites her lip, sucking in a deep breath at the pain she still feels from his abandonment. "Yet, I don't know how to forget the hurt he caused."

"I know," he offers and pats her thigh. "No one said love was easy, huh? It confuses the hell out of me."

A small chuckle escapes her lips at his disgruntled sigh and they spend the evening listing all of the reasons the world would be better without the confusion of falling in love.

Sixteen

<u>West</u>

Four wins down, eight more to go! West thinks to himself as he exits the athletic building and heads to his truck. Ignoring the come hither stares of the football groupies hanging around the gates, he nods politely as he makes his way across the parking lot where he spots Austin. He's leaning casually against his car, which is parked next to West's truck. When he'd planned the three weeks he would have before he thought he'd have to attend Austin's game with his family, he'd completely forgotten that A&M had an off week before he did. It didn't occur to him that his traitorous brother would be here for this game. His fist tightens as he looks at him standing there, his best friend, pretending all is good between them.

"Good game, bro." Austin smiles as West walks by and unlocks his truck. He tosses his bag into the passenger seat, slamming the door behind him before he faces Austin.

"I have every right to kill you right now."

"Dad would probably disagree-" Austin starts.

"Don't screw with me, Aust... if Dad knew what you're doing he'd hold you down while I pound on you."

Austin stands straighter, stepping towards West and West's fists clench and unclench again; the itch to punch Austin is stronger than it has ever been.

"Really, little brother?" Austin challenges, his face no longer filled with humor. "You want to fight me, over this, over a girl?"

The fact that he would call Jules 'a girl' both infuriates him and makes him laugh at the same time. It's not the first time they've stood five feet apart, both flexed up and angry as hell, but it's the first time he's ever truly wanted to do physical harm to his brother.

"She's not just some girl, and you damn well know it. Are you with her?" He watches his brother's face closely. "I don't have a lot of patience when it comes to this subject, Aust, so don't screw with me here."

"Ha!" Austin barks out a harsh laugh, catching West off guard. "No patience, really? You've been sitting on this for three months. You could have gone after her. I would say you have the patience of a saint."

"That's not the deal here and you know it." He looks at Austin with his arms crossed over his chest and suddenly he doesn't have the energy to fight. "Forget it. I can't deal with looking at you, much less talking to you." Skimming his fingers through his wet hair, he steps back and waves his arm in disgust.

"Running again? I thought you fixed that at Crestdale?"

"Are you…" West's words mumble out incoherently as he spins on his heal and launches himself at Austin. His forearm pushes across Austin's chest as he pins him to the side of his small sports car. "What is your problem, man?" he shouts into his brother's face. "You think this is a joke? I was serious; I want to kick your ass, Austin. I'm trying to contain it, but damn you! You have your pick of any girl you want and you went after mine. Mine!"

"She's not yours West."

"Like hell she's not! I just needed a little more time. I need to follow the plan." West pushes Austin against the car once, and steps back throwing his hands up. "Stay the hell away from me, got it?"

West looks up, finding several curious stares from teammates in the parking lot and he curses softly. He leaves Austin standing there and walks around to his door. One of the linemen parked a few spots down points behind him and shouts out a warning at the same time as Austin pushes him from behind. Spinning him around, Austin throws his body into West's and pins him forcibly against the truck door.

"Tell your buddies to back off. Now!" Austin sneers into West's face as the sound of people rushing to them beat against the parking lot pavement.

As pissed as he is, he doesn't want his teammates involved, so he shakes his head their way. "Back off guys. You should recognize this guys as my brother.

If you're a football player in Texas, you should know what Austin Rutledge looks like and, as they come closer and Austin turns his head offering them a slight sneer, they slow up and confirm his identity.

"Now, you listen to me, little bro," Austin growls menacingly into West's face. "I let you get in one hit a few weeks ago and I let you pin me to my car without a fight, but that's it. Got it? We're done."

"Are you sleeping with her?" West growls back.

"What if I am?"

The visual those four words give West makes his stomach churn and fuels his rage. He pushes off his truck with a Herculean effort, freeing his arms and throwing Austin back. They grab at each other, grappling for position, as fists are thrown randomly at each other.

"Are you kidding me? How could you? What were you thinking?" West chokes out each phrase between punches. The pain of knowing she's been touched by anyone is overwhelming, but his own brother? That's unbearable.

"We haven't."

"It's like you've taken a knife and stabbed me in the back!"

"We haven't, man."

"You don't love her. You don't need her like I do -"

"West! I haven't," Austin shouts again, elbowing West in the ribs to get out of the headlock he's currently in. "West! We're not together."

Austin's arguments reach West's ears and his grip loosens. "What?"

Spreading his arms wide, Austin lets go of West and steps back. The move is one of surrender and they've done it millions of times growing up. It lets West know he is safe to back off, as well, and he drops his arms. Austin shakes himself out as he falls against the side of the truck straightening his crooked shirt.

"Nothing to see here people, just a little brotherly love," he quips at the small crowd gathered around them. He prays nobody has a phone out to record their little episode. All they need is for it to end up all over social media.

West ignores the crowd, "You're not together?"

"No, we're not. I was just pushing you."

"Pushing me? You were just pushing me! What the actual fu-"

"Dude, unless you want to end up on ESPNU tonight, I suggest we take this conversation elsewhere," Austin mutters, his face still wreathed in a smile for the curious on-lookers.

Sure enough, they are the main attraction right now and, as much as West would prefer to tell them all to go to hell, he is well aware of how important a players public image means come draft and recruiting time. With his trying to get a spot on A&M next year and Austin entering the draft, they can't screw up any more than they already have today.

"Hug it out," Austin whispers under his breath and the two play nice. Austin tells West to follow him around the corner and ruffles his hair for good measure.

The move infuriates him, but he smiles anyway and calls out to his teammates. "See you boys bright and early in the weight room on Monday, right?" Grumbles follow him as he climbs into the truck and follows Austin out of the football facility.

They're not together? The statement replays in his mind the entire five minute drive from the stadium to a shopping center located right off campus where Austin pulls in and parks in a vacant corner of the lot. Austin signals for him to stay in the truck and he jumps in.

"It's hot as hell out there. Can we talk in here and not be tempted to punch each other?"

"That depends on what you have to say."

He watches his older brother shake his head, a smile tugging on his lips. "I ran into her at a party back on the first of July. Actually, I ran *to* her." West glares and Austin explains. "Groupies were on my tail all night, so I finally gave into this one chick, but after twenty minutes I was in dire need of saving. In comes Jules. She was shocked when she saw me, but she was a good sport. She covered for me and then proceeded to give me all kinds of hell for using her."

"Have you touched her?" West asks quietly, looking out the windshield.

"Let me explain the situation-"

"Did. You. Touch. Her?" he asks again annunciating each word clearly. Until this one question is answered, he can't concentrate on anything else.

Austin shook his head. "Not in any way that should worry you."

"Austin."

"I've held her hand, I've slow danced with her, hugged her closely. That's it."

"Then why'd you lead me to think differently? What about that damn morning I called and she answered your phone? At six-thirty in the morning."

"Can I explain it now?" Austin asks and West nods as relief floods him knowing they haven't slept together.

"I started to fall for her, West. I didn't mean for it to happen, it just did. She chatted with me at that party and I took her to lunch a few days later and we clicked." West bites his tongue as he listens to Austin explain. "She liked me for me and we could talk football and school. We had a good time together. I started helping her with some workouts and we spent so much time together. I couldn't help it."

West doesn't need Austin to explain his reasoning where Jules is concerned. He has first-hand experience in how easy she is to fall in love with.

"What do you mean you helped her with workouts?"

"She hadn't been doing her PT here when we first started to hang out, so I offered to help her. What's another work out, right?"

It's exactly something West would have done and he found himself begrudgingly glad his brother had been there for her when he wasn't.

"So why are you here now? What happened?"

"The inevitable. We both knew it wasn't going to happen between us. I knew I wasn't the Rutledge she wanted. Even if she were over you, what were we going to do? Rub it in your face? Neither of us wanted to hurt you, and as much as you've tried to tell everyone you're okay, I know you're lying."

"We haven't spoken or seen each other in weeks," West points out, irritated with Austin's insinuation that he knows everything about West's feelings.

"I have my sources. You think running yourself into the ground is fooling anyone? None of us buy the act. Besides, I didn't have to see it to know it was fake. Remember when Lauren cheated on me in high school?" West nods. "I did the same thing, remember? I threw myself into the game and school. Anything to get her off my mind. When Carson told me about your three runs a day, I knew exactly what you were doing."

"So, you were never with her? At all?"

Austin chuckles lightly. "Not at all. It was more of a comforting relationship than a romantic one. Here's the truth though, bro. I love her, too. I love her enough to give her what she wants."

"You love her?"

"Yeah, I love her, but I'm not in love with her. I was confused and tired and she came along. When I say I love her, I mean I care about her. As a friend, as someone who I want to see happy. You need to call her, West, before you lose her for good."

"I lost her a long time ago."

"No, you haven't. Not yet. Your mind has entertained the idea of getting her back all this time. I know it has, we all know it. But, you're scared."

He opens his mouth to argue and Austin stops him. "Don't bother trying to convince me I'm wrong. Dr. Steel has you putting all your energy into football. How much did you tell her about Jules? Does she know Jules is the only thing since mom's death to make you truly smile?"

"She knows… but I can't build my happiness on a person."

"Is that Doctor speak?"

"Mumbo jumbo? Yeah it is," West relents and he can't help but ask, "Does she hate me?"

"We don't talk about you. From the first night, that was her rule, and for the most part we followed it."

"For the most part?"

"There were a few fights. The morning you called being one of them." West's eyes narrow and Austin smiles. "Did I not just tell you we were never together? I fell asleep in her room. Nothing else."

West accepts his explanation as Austin types a message into his phone. He checks the clock on his truck and realizes he's already late for dinner. "You're coming to dinner with us, right?"

There's hesitation in his brother's face that speaks of secrecy, but he doesn't ask when Austin declines. "Nah, I've got a thing to go to." He pops open the door. "You've been playing one hell of a game on the field Rutledge. A&M should be impressed."

"Thanks, man." He smiles, pride filling him at his brother's words.

After the door closes, he hits the window down button before Austin opens his car door. "Hey Austin, will you keep an eye on her tonight?"

Austin doesn't deny he'll be seeing her and they exchange glances.

"What do you think I've been doing, bro?" He moves back to West's window and leans onto the frame. "I won't be able to hold the wolves off for long, though. You need to make a decision."

Make a decision. West doesn't have to ask what he means by that; he knows. Put up or shut up.

"I know," he says with a sigh. Then, swallowing his pride, he admits, "You're right. I'm scared."

"You're a Rutledge. We're not scared of anything."

And that's the truth. Except for one extremely important detail.

"Not until her, man. Not until her."

Seventeen

Jules

"There's a rumor floating around that you're not actually dating Austin, Is that true?" slurs the frat boy who's been bumping into her side as he leans up against the wall next to her. She recalls his face from the last time they'd met, but doesn't remember his name and doesn't bother to ask since she could care less.

"Really?" she drawls, feigning interest in all things rumor-related.

"Yep. So, why won't you dance with me?"

"Nah, I'm good, thanks though." She's declined his request at least five times in the last ten minutes and yet he keeps asking between taking swigs of whatever fills his cup and elaborating on his summer adventures.

"C'mon, are you just a tease, like all of those other chicks?"

She resists the urge to outright laugh in his face and maneuvers herself out of the corner he's backed her into. "I'm not a tease, I don't want to dance. I'm gonna go get a drink."

His hand catches her forearm, his fingers digging in perhaps a little too forcibly. "Let me," he offers and she opens her mouth to argue before conceding and watching him drift into the crowd.

The moment he disappears, heading toward the kitchen, she hurries from the corner and loses herself in the crowd. Pulling out her phone, she shoots another message to Austin as she slips by a couple going at it against the wall that leads to a hallway and out the back door. His first text had indicated he was on his way nearly forty minutes ago, yet he is still MIA.

Jules: WHERE ARE YOU?

She steps outside and finds the patio crowded with people standing around chatting. Jules smiles at those she recognizes, and lingers to make small chat, all the while looking at her phone waiting for a reply. The end of September Texas air is muggy, as usual, and she secures her long hair in a bun to cool off her neck.

"What's with the shouty caps?" Austin's voice teases in her ear and she whirls around taking in his casual A&M athletic shirt and shorts. He grins as his eyes watch her fasten her hair.

"Can't reply back? Where have you been all day?"

"I was driving. It's illegal to text and drive, you know that." He pokes at her ribs while her hands are occupied with the lose strands of hair around her neck. "Why? You miss me that much?"

"No, I just need you to keep the wolves away," she replies, giving him the same reply he gave at their first party together.

His face darkens subtly. "Having trouble with your harem, princess?"

Jules breaks into laughter, "Uh, I don't think girls have harems. Or at least this girl doesn't."

"You don't swing that way, huh?" He winks, a devilish grin taking over the frown that was there a moment earlier.

"Wow, um… no, I don't. Although boys are way more trouble than necessary. Maybe I should reconsider?"

His arm slings around her shoulders and he presses a kiss to the top of her head. "First, I'd pay good money to see you swing just *that way*. Second, maybe you've been dealing with the wrong guys?"

"Well, the last one was a Rutledge, so you tell me… do you think

I'm dealing with the wrong guys?" The question slips out and she curses herself for mentioning West.

"Do you honestly want me to answer that?"

Yes! her heart screams. "No," she replies instead and shakes her head knowing she already knows the answer to her own question.

"Then take me to find your roomies. I need to meet Jess still."

"You're not hitting on Jess," Jules warns, tugging his arm off of her shoulders. "It's so hot. You've got to get off of me."

"Hey, wait," he calls after her as she starts to walk back to the house. "Why can't I hit on Jess? She's single, right?"

"Yes, and she's my friend and I have enough problems with you Rutledge boys without you breaking her heart and having to listen to her cry."

"Ye of little faith. Do you not trust me?"

"No."

It's hotter inside than out and Jules struggles to breath. The scent of beer, sweat, and heavy perfume fills the house. A dash of sex rounds out the aroma and she's ready to leave. Austin's hand is resting lightly on her shoulder as she leads the way through the melee of students enjoying the party.

The summer parties she'd been to had nothing on this one. They were typically smaller crowds, local students or the very few who were taking summer courses. She's sort of sad to see how much the new influx of students changes things. Nothing about being at this crowded party feels fun to her. She starts to feel claustrophobic as she squeezes through.

"Jules!" Jess' shouts reach Jules over the din and she looks about to pinpoint Jess' location. Jess is winding through a break in the crowd leading to the open front door and they reach the exit at the same time, escaping the inferno together.

"Phew! It's like a sauna in there." Her cheeks are red, her dark hair damp and stringy around her face.

"Where's Katie?" Jules asks.

"Jeff showed up and she left with him. She told me to tell you to look for the sign." Jess waggles her brows, making air quotes around 'look for the sign'.

That bit of news effectively means Jules is kicked out of her room for a few hours. She gives Jess a pleading look.

"Don't look at me that way. Of course you can come back to my room. I've got extra blankets." She turns to Austin, standing behind Jules, with a flirtatious smile. "And I finally get to meet the legendary Austin Rutledge."

"That's me."

"Cocky, like your brother, I see."

"It's a Rutledge trait," Jules hints as she fans herself. The heat is oppressive and she feels miserable. "Lord have mercy, we need an ice bath tonight."

"You going soft after all the workouts in the air conditioned student gym, Blacklin?" Austin teases.

"Hey! I remember all too well what cheer camp in August felt like and that is why I choose to be inside now."

"Oh… me too," Jess adds, tugging on her own shirt and fanning her stomach. "You want to head out then?" she asks, and Jules has to admit that she is more than ready to head back to the dorms and take a cold shower. The need for the shower is not strong enough to balance out the need for not wanting to hear Katie and Jeff though.

"Think we should give the lovebirds a little more alone time?" she replies instead, waving at a girl from one of her classes behind Jess' back.

"You want to cool off?" Austin asks them, and he nods in that way of his that says he has a plan.

Jess and Jules exchange looks. "What do you have in mind?"

"C'mon, I've got just the thing. Let's drop your car back at the dorm and I'll drive."

"Drive where," Jules asks skeptically as Jess jumps at the cryptic offer.

"Jules Blacklin, have I not taught you anything in the past few months? You want to cool off, we're going to cool off."

Jess claps her hands with a squeal and Jules almost dies of a heart attack right there. Jess is not a squealer, or a clapper. Half the time she's shocked Jess was even a cheerleader when they met. She gives in to her friend's enthusiasm, with a warning for Austin, as they leave to find their cars.

"This better not be illegal."

Less than ten minutes later, they're in Austin's little sports car cruising down the back roads towards the house he shares with his brothers. The radio is blaring and Jules, being the good friend she is, is sitting in the back seat to allow Austin and Jess to chat and get to know each other.

She listens over the music as they make some small talk. She was only half serious when she asked Austin not to hit on Jess. Truth is, he's a great guy. She's not worried he'll screw her over so much as him not having time for her. He's been immersed in football twenty out of twenty-four hours a day for the past three weeks. The NCAA might have limits on how much time players can train during the week, but players do not have any such limit. She understands this, Austin told her himself before the season started how crazy things would get for him. A&M is expected to make a run for the championship and Austin has a good chance of being drafted if he decides to enter a year early. He doesn't have time to work on a relationship right now; most collegiate players don't.

Twenty minutes later, Austin's car pulls down a dirt path and they're bumping their way along a small road. Wayward brush hits the side of his car every once in a while and he curses under his breath as he tries to avoid it. Something reflects in his headlights up ahead and they pull to a stop in the middle of the road.

"Ladies." Austin purposefully draws out his southern accent as he jumps out of the vehicle and opens Jules' door for her. Offering her his hand, he adds, "Welcome to 'The Hole'."

"The hole?" She squints in the darkness, the bright moon and stars are the only light they have. All she sees is a tangle of brush and trees surrounding them as Jess comes around and joins them on the driver's side.

"You'll see." He pops his trunk and pulls out two lanterns, handing one to each girl and a blanket of some sort.

"Austin? You didn't bring us out here for a misguided attempt at an orgy, did you?" Jess mumbles. The lantern lights half of her face and Jules cracks up at the trepidation written on it.

"Awww, honey, contrary to popular belief not all jocks are pricks and I'm a one woman man." He shuts the trunk smoothly and takes the lantern from Jess' hand. "I like to be prepared, that's all."

"Yeah, you're a real boy scout," Jules groans as they traipse into the brush.

The path isn't well worn, but she can tell others have trampled down some of the vegetation and she hears a few shouts and some laughter in the distance alerting them to the presence of others.

They break through the thicket to discover an assortment of lights hanging from trees and abandoned on the edge of a large dark hole. As her eyes adjust to the new scene and lighting, she realizes they are at a swimming hole with a crowd of about twenty. A rope swing is tied to a branch and hangs limply over the water. Several people are floating on top of the dark pond in inner-tubes, and a few more are standing around the edge of the pond wading up to their knees and waists as they talk and laugh without a care in the world.

"Hey, Rutledge!" an excited voice calls out, and Austin turns to Jules and Jess with an expectant face.

"So?" he asks, clearly not sure what they might think of such a place.

Jules, who'd been grasping Jess' arm as they weaved their way through the branches to this spot, squeezes her friend and locks her eyes on her with a smile.

"Oh, hell yes," agrees Jess when she sees Jules' face and they drop their arms. Making quick work of her clothing, Jess strips down to her bra and panties and hightails it into the water with a loud squeal as she dives under.

Austin pulls his shirt off and looks at Jules. His body is finely sculpted from all of the workouts and football, but she doesn't feel anything when she looks at him. The feeling comes as a relief and she nods, telling him silently to go jump in the water and cool off. He leaves his athletic shorts on and, after setting the lantern on the ground and spreading the blanket, he runs into the water and jumps at Jess, who is floating on the top.

Jules drops Jess' clothes to the blanket and watches Jess and Austin splash around playfully for a moment and she feels a tug at her chest. She glances around, half expecting to find someone watching her, but no one is there.

"Don't make me get out of this pond to get you in!" Jess yells from the bank. The moon is shining down on her wet skin just enough to cause several of the guys who have moved closer to them to stop and stare. "Get in here Ju-ju!" she teases, using Katie's nickname for her.

The last request breaks down her wall and Jules jumps up to strip to her underwear quickly before she can get too embarrassed and back out. Thankfully, the garments cover as much as her bikini would, especially in the dark. She plans to jump in when she sees a guy pulling the rope up to the incline next to the tree that sits over the water. She watches as he pulls back, leaps up, and dives in when he swings out into the center of the pond, and an idea forms.

Go big or go home! she tells herself, walking along the dark edge of the water and ignoring Jess and Austin's calls asking her what she's doing.

"Hey," a handsome guy about her age says when she meets him at the tree. "Want a turn?"

"Do you mind?"

"Not at all. Ladies first."

"Um, I've never done this. Any instructions?" she asks shakily as she nears the tree and reaches out for the thick rope that he is holding.

"Here," he says, holding the rope to her and pointing out where to stand. "It's easy. Just stand here and when you're ready you jump up and forward, lifting your feet and swinging out. You let go once you're about half way out or further."

"It's plenty deep? I'm not going to break my neck or something?"

"Do you think I'd let you jump off this thing if it were dangerous?" he asks, a playful smile crossing his face and Jules is momentarily struck dumb with how good looking he is.

"You don't know me," she points out diplomatically

"Oh? Well, what's your name then?" he asks and Jules laughs.

"Jules. What's yours?"

"Levi." His shoulders shrug in the moonlight. "See, now we're like best friends. You ready to jump?"

She looks back at Jess, who waves before splashing her arm towards Austin's body. He retaliates in kind and Jules rolls her eyes at their flirtatious manner.

"I'll jump first and catch you. How's that for a knight in shining armor?" Levi asks, pulling her gaze from her friends.

"I'm sorry?"

"I'll jump in and prove to you it's totally safe and then you can give it a whirl. No worries. I'll be there to save you if you need me," he adds with a wink before tugging the rope from her fingers and flying out across the water. His body hits the water with a splash and a few people clap and laugh around the pond.

Jules leans forward, reaching for the swinging rope as it comes back to her. She steps back and brings it taut, taking a deep breath.

"Nothing to be afraid of, Jules. Just jump in!" Levi yells.

Jess' voice joins in, "Jump!"

The moment feels larger than it is and Jules wants to laugh and cry as she stands there half-terrified of jumping and half-terrified of not. It mirrors her life right now. She laughs at the crazy thought; she has no idea why her heart feels so heavy and strange tonight. Taking a deep breath, she closes her eyes and wills herself to make the most of this situation. The reminder to live tickles the back of her mind. She said she would live for Tanya and now is her chance. Tanya would have jumped three times by now.

"Here goes nothing!" she tells herself as she launches her body into the air and then smacks the water feet first with a crisp *swoosh*.

As she floats under the chilly, yet refreshing, water her mind chooses that moment to picture the symbolism of a baptism. A rebirth for one's soul and the moment strikes her. She's started fresh, she's worked things out with Austin, she's making new friends, and she's starting to get over the past. The sentiment is probably crazy, but it sticks in her mind anyway and the moment she comes up for air, Levi is waiting not five feet away.

"Ready to jump again, daredevil?" he asks, his southern drawl charming, as he wades the deep water.

It doesn't take her more than a brief second to think before a large smile creeps across her face.

"Abso-freaking-lutley!"

Eighteen

<u>West</u>

After talking with Austin, West's head whirls with thoughts and ideas of Jules and how he can approach her. He's meeting up with his family for dinner at a local steak restaurant, but all he wants to do is drive the thirty minutes to A&M and make things right. It's rare he gets time with his dad these days, though, so he pastes on a smile and tells himself that he will figure it all out tomorrow.

"There's the star quarterback," his dad's booming voice carries across the dining area as the hostess shows him to their table. The pretty blonde gives him a once over when she hears this and smiles seductively as she tells him to enjoy his meal. West nods and shrinks into himself, still not used to the looks he's been getting because of football.

"Really, dad?"

His dad stands up and greets him, "What? I'm a proud dad." He gives West a quick hug and a slap on the back. "Great game, son."

West bends down to kiss Mindy's cheek and fist bumps Carson as he takes the empty seat next to his father.

"The masses are starting to rumble, West," his dad mentions once they've placed their orders and are all eating their dinner salads.

"The masses, huh?"

"I'm fielding more and more questions each day about why you aren't wearing maroon and white. You keep your game up and the boosters will be clambering to get you."

"Dad, the boosters aren't the ones I'm trying to impress," West reminds him as he butters a roll.

"Don't you worry, son. The coaches notice, too. Your arm is amazing, your timing and precision. If only you'd never quit, I can only imagine the offers you would have received."

"Dad," Carson mutters as West looks down and concentrates on his salad.

"Hey, you know Austin was there today!" Mindy blurts and West snaps his gaze to her face.

The level of awkward at the table increases and West cracks a small smile at his family. His dad harping on his quitting the game is something he's gotten used to, so the comments don't bother him as much as Carson seems to think they do. Mindy blurting Austin's name is her obvious intent to fix what she thinks is still a messed up situation between Jules, Austin, and himself. He looks across the table at Carson and then to his dad and the feigned concentration they are taking to eat their food. Right when he is ready to ease the tension, their waiter appears to check on them and offer refills.

After he leaves, West chuckles. "Austin and I talked after the game."

"You did?" The three of them echo, breaking the silence.

"Yeah, he was waiting at my truck for me. It's why I was late, we had a little skirmish." He adds that part for fun, to get a reaction and he isn't disappointed. All three of them reply with vastly different comments.

"Damn! You two couldn't wait for me before throwing down?" Carson grumbles.

"Please tell me you two made up?" asks Mindy, her eyes pleading with him as she drops her silverware.

His dad who only knew he and Austin were arguing about "something" shook his head. "You two need to get a grip and put whatever this is behind you."

"I dunno, dad. I think Austin has a good punch coming to him," Carson confesses, locking his eyes with West and letting him know he supports him. Mindy slaps his arm in frustration.

"He doesn't actually," says West, to the surprise of everyone.

His explanation is cut short as a server shows up at their table with their food. Once their waiter has checked on them once again, West is able to explain.

"They're friends and have been hanging out, but nothing has happened." When Mindy and Carson look at him with wide eyes, West nods, knowing they are recalling the night Jules spent with Austin and the phone call. "Nothing."

"You want to explain this cryptic conversation?" his dad asks and West decides to fill him in now that he knows he won't have to deprive his father of his middle son.

"I thought you were over her, West? Or at least, I thought you were moving on and concentrating on school and ball and letting that go for now?" his father points out.

"I don't think we have to discuss this right now, do we?" asks Carson. "Anyway, Mindy and I have news."

Mindy chokes on her drink and his dad stops mid-bite. Before his brother can speak, West sets his knife and fork down and turns to his dad.

"Dad, I love her. So, no, I'm not going to let it go. I can't let it go and, unless Austin is wrong, she can't either and all we are really doing is slowly killing ourselves."

"Weston, I don't want to see you fall back into old patterns again." His dad using his full name is so rare that it actually softens West's attitude.

"I'm fine. I promise. Everything in my life is making me happy, except for one thing, and that's Jules. I need to make things right with her."

"And if she isn't interested? If she's moved on?"

"Then I know I explained what happened and I wish her well." He shrugs. Those words were not quite true, but his dad doesn't need to worry about him anymore than he always has.

"So! What's this big news, you two?" he all but shouts at Mindy and Carson as he throws a smile on his face. "Did you knock her up, Cars?" he teases with a wink.

Mindy and Carson laugh, Mindy rolling her eyes and smiling at West as his father shakes his head.

"We've decided to set a wedding date, actually. It's kinda soon, but we don't want to wait anymore. I graduate in December and we're ready to start our life together, alone." Mindy says pointedly as West shoots a sneer at her.

"Not that we don't love having you and Austin in our hair all the time, bro."

"Hey, man, I get it. I put a damper on the sexcapades."

"Can we please leave the sex out of this conversation, son?" his dad mutters. "So, what's the date?"

Mindy and Carson exchange looks, and West smiles at the way his brother's entire demeanor changes as they smile at each other.

"We were thinking New Year's Eve," Mindy says, "a destination wedding?"

"In honor of mom," Carson adds and West's dad goes still.

New Year's was always a favorite of his mothers. She used to make a big deal of getting snacks and sparkling grape juice, and they would stay up all night dancing and playing games until the giant ball would drop in Times Square. She'd say the new year was a time for new beginnings and they could be whoever they wanted to be now. The slate was clean. West recalls how she would spend the month of January always yelling at them about how they couldn't hold grudges, reminding them it was a new year. Eventually, the advice worked and they learned to never hold grudges with each other. A quick roll around on the floor, or punch to the gut and a sincere apology, and it was water under the bridge.

He pulls out of his memories to hear his dad's remarks. "She would have loved you Min, honey."

Mindy sniffles and runs her finger under her moist eyes. Carson agrees with his father and slings his arm around the back of Mindy's chair.

"I like the idea," West chimes in.

The dinner discussion turns to wedding plans and thoughts of the future. West is sitting half-listening to Mindy gush girly things and thinking about Jules when his cell phone vibrates in his pocket. Pulling out his phone quietly he finds a text from Austin that floors him.

"I'm on the way to the hole with Jess and your girl. Meet us there, I won't tell her."

Shit! Shit! And triple shit, he screams in his head as he re-reads the message. The hole. It's fifteen minutes from the restaurant. He shoves his hand through his hair and yanks it with a groan.

"Everything all right?" his dad asks, and West looks up to see three sets of concerned eyes on him.

He growls low. "Yea, I… just. Austin just sent me a text. He's bringing Jules and another friend to the hole. Told me I should meet them there."

"So go!" Mindy orders, as if it's that simple.

"What if it pisses her off? She's not expecting me."

"How long are you going to pull the what-ifs, man? Just go," says Carson.

Feeling bad about skipping out on their family time, he looks at his dad, who's leaning back in his chair. "Dad?"

"What the hell are you asking me for? If you love her and you want to win her back, then go win her back."

"I'll see you in the morning, then?" he asks, making sure his dad is still staying at the house, instead of heading back to Tyler.

"Yep, now get out of here, boy! That's an order."

Mindy's call of "good luck' puts a smile on his face as he leaves dinner to go win his girl back.

Forty-five minutes later, West finally works up the nerve to walk through the brush into the clearing surrounding the swimming hole. He's been frequenting the spring fed hole for years with his brothers and the locals. The place flies under the radar due to the heavy brush and shade. It attracts teens and college students who crave seclusion from crowds to play loud music, drink, and make-out with their dates.

West can hear the sounds of laughter as he uses the flashlight on his phone to maneuver the thick roots. When he makes it to the edge of the brush, he takes in the spring, his eyes slowly adjusting to the darkness. The moonlight reflects off of the water slightly, but the area isn't bright by any means. There are about seven lanterns lighting up the edge of the water and one hanging by the tree swing; that's where West spots Jules. It takes him a moment to see she is talking to someone, and then a face shows up in the light and his heart clenches with jealousy before he can stop it.

It's just a guy, he tells himself as he watches. He hears Jess' voice shout from the water and he catches a glimpse of Austin and Jess splashing around in the shallows. He returns his gaze to Jules in time to see the guy she was talking to jump from the rope swing. The swing flies back towards the tree and Jules catches it. From his vantage point he can make out her profile, the lantern on the tree hanging at the right spot to shine a yellow glow of light on her face. Even from this angle, he can see her hesitation and he waits to see what she will do. The guy in the water yells for her to jump and Jess chimes in, as well. That's when West sees it - that look of determination she used to get on her face when she wanted something. Suddenly, she jumps and flies through the air, breaking through the water with her body.

He's jumped off that rope thousands of times over the years, but when Jules goes under he can't help but hold his breath until she comes through the surface. The guy with her swims her way, saying something that makes Jules laugh. He's about to step forward and show himself when he looks closer and realizes the guy has a hold of her arm and is pulling her towards the edge of the hole. And Jules is smiling and laughing all the way there.

He stands there for another few minutes, watching as Jules laughs and talks with the nameless guy before they climb up to the tree and jump again. Once they've they landed in the water, they're approached by Austin and Jess and a massive splash fight breaks out.

West turns, deciding to leave them to their fun. The sound of Jules' laughter, mixed with the sounds of the others', chasing him to his truck.

West takes a seat at a small burger joint halfway between Freemont and A&M to wait for Jeff. It's been three weeks since they've hung out and he's looking forward to talking crap and gorging himself; then Jeff walks in with Katie. He's always thought Katie was cool, but she's Jules' roommate and best friend. It makes it hard to talk shit when the best friend of the girl you're in love with is sitting across from you. From the moment they sit down she subjects him to meaningful glances until he can't take it anymore and he asks what her problem is.

"Do you plan on trying to win her back?" she asks, to his surprise. "I thought for sure once you knew she wasn't with Austin, you'd jump at the chance to see her."

With the subject now on the table, West opens up; as much as he doesn't want to admit his faults, he decides to explain the situation at the hole Saturday night. When he finishes, Katie looks at him in shock and Jeff rags on him.

"You said nothing?" Jeff says as their food is delivered.

West's only reply is a shameful shake of his head. He busies himself with adding ketchup to his burger and fries, making a production of getting his meal together.

"Seriously, dude. Nothing?" Jeff asks again. "Why the hell not? You should have run and jumped in and crashed their party. Or jumped in and grabbed her."

"She looked happy. Truly happy and I couldn't screw that up."

"What about you?" Katie asks, popping a french fry in her mouth.

"What about me?"

"Oh, West." She blows out a slow breath and gives Jeff a knowing look. "You finally get the chance to make amends, and you don't. What is wrong with you?"

"Hell if I know, Katie. You tell me. You seem to know it all," he snaps back.

"Dude!" Jeff warns with a frown, and Katie shakes her head at him, visibly telling him it's fine.

"You spent months when you were together telling her you'd screw up and being afraid. And then you left. I know you left for a good reason, but she doesn't. She's scared. She's not going to come to you, you know," she points out softly.

"I'm still scared of screwing up. I don't want to hurt her again. If she's happy now, maybe it's best I leave her alone?"

"Hell no, man. Would you please talk to her so we can quit all this whining?" Jeff groans.

"Thanks for the support, bud." West replies sarcastically.

"She needs to know you've changed and she needs to know you love her." Katie points out. "Tell her that her parents and the shrinks were wrong. That your love wasn't a product of the tornado or the grief of losing Tanya; or even because of your mom… Tell her you love her because of her."

"Does she think our entire relationship was fake?" he asks, remembering the few times people had tried to make him feel like they'd only been together because of the stress they were under after the storm.

"She refused to believe it when they told her that. She swore up and down you cared, but when you cut her out you hurt her deeply. She was a mess for months."

He grimaces at the thought of how much pain he's caused her all because he thought it would be best for her.

"I love her, Katie. You know that don't you? It was always real and has nothing to do with that damn storm, or my mother. It has everything to do with her. I'd been watching her for years, waiting for the chance to speak to her. I loved her… I love her, still."

"Then tell her. That's all girls want, West. They want to be loved irrevocably by a man for who they are. You tell her that, you remind her how amazing you two were together, and she will forgive you. I truly think she will."

Nineteen

Jules

Jules is sitting on the kitchen island talking with Toby as he mixes drinks, when one of the guys nearby shouts.

"Hey, eye candy! Throw me one of those beers, would ya?"

She reaches across the counter, grabs a beer, and tosses it across the kitchen to the whistles of the crowd. They'd been asking for her help all night and at some point it was Toby who realized every time she stretched behind her to grab a beer from the cooler she was showing off a little thigh as her skirt rose. She doesn't bother pretending to be offended. Most of the crowd is made up of Austin's friends and they still assume she is off limits since Austin hasn't bothered to tell them otherwise. They are guys being guys, so she laughs and shakes her head at their antics.

"Hey, when are you gonna dump Austin and let a real man have a chance?"

"Well… if I saw a real man around, I might consider it," she calls back and looks at Toby with a wry grin. "No offense."

"None taken," he laughs, winking at her. Suddenly, his face turning comical at whatever he sees over her shoulder.

"Awe, c'mon, candy girl. Don't you need someone to keep you warm on the nights he's away?"

"I think I'm cutting you off, Brenden."

"I think if Austin were here, they wouldn't be hitting on you like that."

The sarcastic voice behind her causes her to jump and her pulse to race. West seemingly appears out of thin air and skirts his way around the counter, where he leans casually against the island next to her dangling legs. The shirt he wears hugs the muscles in his arms tightly and she's struck, again, by how much he's changed since she saw him last.

She sits there, her mouth open wide, as he looks up over his shoulder and smiles at her. His black hair looks damp at the ends and he smells fresh, as if he recently got out of the shower and came straight to this party.

"Hey man, it's been a while," Toby nods and throws his hand out. She watches them in silence as they do a high-five handshake combo thing. "Hey, asshats," he calls to the guys Jules had been throwing beers to all night. "I'm guessing you haven't met West yet."

From the corner of her eye, she sees West's brows rise and the guys standing around stare at him with confusion. It's obvious to her they don't know who he is.

"Austin's brother," she finally tells them when neither West nor Toby bother to explain.

The laughs and "no way" comments that typically accompany a group of college-aged guys ring out. Introductions go around and they chat about the away game this afternoon.

"I missed it, unfortunately," West offers and Jules can't help but gape at him. He didn't miss a game when they were together last year. What would make him miss one now?

"So, brothers away and you're checking up on his eye candy?" Brenden asks, and she wants to vanish.

"Something like that," he mutters, returning back to leaning on the counter at her side.

Jules sits there, a casual observer, as the guys continue to talk and Toby continues to mix drinks for newcomers. She considers slinking away, but her position in the middle of the kitchen and right next to West means she can't get away unnoticed. When a bunch of sorority girls enter the house twenty minutes later, Brenden and his gang finally excuse themselves and Jules finds herself alone with Toby, West, and the liqueur.

She's studying her manicure when West clears his throat and finally speaks again. "The bartender always gets the prettiest girls hanging around, huh, Toby?"

"No doubt, man."

She looks up and bites back a smile at West. His face is so close to hers, she can smell the woodsy scent she recognizes as purely West Rutledge.

"Let me grab you a beer," she offers, leaning over as she did for Brenden and the guys to dig a can out of the cooler. Her left arm reaches across her body as she goes to hand him the beer and he shakes his head.

"No thanks. I don't drink anymore." His eyes flick down to the beer in her hand and then back to her face.

"Since when do you not drink?" she asks at the same time as his face changes. It's like he's seen a ghost and he grabs her wrist before she can pull away. His touch makes her insides go crazy.

She realizes, too late, what he's seen. His thumb rubs over the small tattoo at the base of her palm and she swallows hard at the caress. Her blue eyes divert away from his dark ones as he looks over the permanent reminder she wears.

It's a small anchor, nothing fancy, but there's no way he can deny knowing exactly what it means to her. To them.

He leans infinitely closer, his thumb still moving over her skin, and she makes a fist to keep from shaking. His hand slides up her arm; his thumb finding the long scar running the length of her forearm and he drops her arm as if it were a hot coal.

"Since I almost killed you the last time I did," he whispers and it takes her a moment to realize he is answering her question.

• • •

Standing straight, he steps away from her; holding his hand up before his mouth tightens and he walks away. Just like that. He steps out of the kitchen without a backward glance and Jules is left with shaking limbs, a confused head, and one very shocked Toby staring at her.

She runs her fingers through her hair as Toby stands there. "It's complicated."

"I'll say. Your scar, he's the reason you got it?"

The kitchen is starting to fill up again, but Toby ignores them as he asks Jules the question.

"I didn't know anyone paid attention to it." She slides off the counter and pours herself a small shot. Throwing her head back, she lets the liquid fire burn down her throat and into her stomach; the warmth knocks out the chill West left behind when he walked away.

"Did he cause it?" Toby asks again.

"No. It wasn't his fault." Her hand moves to the bottle again and he stops her.

"He seems to think it is."

Toby looks at her and she agrees silently, tears pricking her eyes as she nods. Toby moves the shot glass away from Jules. He turns, looking at the path where West exited the kitchen.

"Go after him."

"What!"

He laughs, "Jules, seriously you think I don't know you and Austin aren't a couple? He calls you 'eye candy' and never touches you. I'm a bartender; I'm trained to notice this stuff."

"I hate to break it to you, Toby, but you're a frat boy drink server. Not an actual bartender." She tries to be cute, sarcastic even, but the stress of the moment has left her voice shaky.

"So what? I'm not wrong. Go after him," he says again, more forcefully.

"Why?"

"Because you care."

Jules heart races, her mind toys with her. "It's not that simple."

Toby levels a look on her. It's daring her to move.

The look in West's eyes when he saw her tattoo flashes before her. That warm melting chocolate gaze that had seduced her more than a few times in the past is seared in her memory. She wants to be over him, and yet, she's not. She never was and everyone's been right. They need to talk things through.

She's been angry, and let her pride get the best of her by refusing to let him back in; but it's been a lesson in futility. They need to iron things out once and for all.

"Thanks, bartender," she teases, pressing a friendly kiss to his cheek and then begins elbowing her way through the crowd in search of West.

She scans the house, looking for his tall dark head among the sea of people dancing and hanging out around the large open space. She notices Jess tucked into a corner talking with some guy and she makes her way to her friend's side, excusing herself as she slides between them.

"Have you seen West?" she whispers and Jess straightens from her lazy position against the wall.

"West?" she asks, surprised. "No. He's here?"

"Yeah, he's here," Jules says as she looks over the heads in room. "I'm looking for him now. You're the DD tonight, right?"

"Yep. Promise I haven't had a drink." Jess crosses her heart with her index finger as she asks, "What's your plan?"

Jules looks at her friend and shrugs. The girls have been after her for weeks to work things out with West and now she finally can. She can see the hopeful look in Jess' eyes as they stare at each other.

"If I don't come back before you're ready to go call my cell; I'm going to try and find him."

"And if you find him, might I be heading home alone?" Jess asks with a wink and a smile, giving Jules hope.

She doesn't want to go that far, but she acknowledges the possibility to Jess. "I don't know. Call me."

Jess pulls her into a quick hug, whispering 'good luck' into her ear as she lets her go.

Thinking West might have intended to leave, Jules rushes out the door and down the drive to look for him. She doesn't know what type of car he drives anymore and the driveway and street are lined with vehicles. She walks to the street and looks both ways down the road. Seeing nothing, she considers going to the back of the house when a car alarm beeps twice.

A light goes on in a large truck on her left and she rushes towards it when she sees his silhouette leaning against the driver's door.

"You're leaving?" she cries out, drawing the looks of a few bystanders.

His right hand is on the driver side handle, his left is draped up across the top of the door, and his head drops at the sound of her voice, the top of it resting against the window as if to brace himself when he speaks.

"Yeah, I need to go."

She stops at the hood of the black over-sized truck. "Why did you come here tonight? You knew Austin wasn't going to be here, so why bother?"

He doesn't move from his spot and she knows he's grappling with something.

"It's been four weeks," she points out, recalling the amount of time since the vigil and his phone call to Austin that morning.

He groans and pushes away from the glass and turning to lean his back on the truck. He looks straight ahead instead of at her as he answers her. "I know."

"Four! So why did you come?" She's angry now. She tries to hold it in, but suddenly she can't. He could have called her and asked her about Austin. He could have fought for her, instead he ran. Again.

"I wanted to see you. Katie said you were here."

"Katie? How'd you-"

"Austin told me what dorm you live in and I went by earlier hoping to talk. Katie told me you were here."

She mentally curses both Austin and Katie for not sending her any type of warning signal. "So, then why are you leaving?" she asks again.

"Jules - I need to go. I shouldn't have shown up without calling you, I'm sorry." He opens his door and she slams her palm down against the side of his gorgeous shiny black vehicle.

"Sorry? Wow, so sorry that you're not even going to bother to stick around and talk, huh? You're just walking away... again." Her hand tugs at her hair, scooping it away from her face and to the side. "I don't know why I'm surprised; you didn't care enough to stick around the last time. Not even to see if I was okay."

She spins to leave and the truck door slams behind her. The loud clatter of keys dropping to the ground sounds as West grabs her from behind and pulls her back. He releases her, spinning her to face him, and he pushes her up against the truck.

"Now wait a damn minute. Is that what you think? That I didn't care?"

She shrinks inwardly, momentarily taken aback by his anger, before she straightens up; throwing punches with her words.

"You left me with nothing, West. Only a letter. That your brother delivered. I woke up from a coma broken in a million places, and then you broke me again."

His grip loosens as she stabs him with each word. "I did what I thought was right."

"How convenient for you," she replies, trying to ignore the pain in his brown eyes.

"Convenient? I lost seven months trying to make it up to you. I gave up everything for you!"

His admission hurts and she whispers, "I didn't ask you to."

"You didn't have to!" He steps back with a curse, his eyes avoiding hers. The nearest street lamp casts them in a spotlight and she relishes this moment. Being this near to him again, even while fighting with him.

"I almost killed you! Don't you see? It was the least I could do. I had to make it right."

"No! No, you didn't have to make it right. That night wasn't your fault."

"It was. I'd been drinking. I was screwing around-" His defense of his actions fall on deaf ears because she never blamed him and she needs for him to know this. Now.

Jules grabs the fabric at the edge of his dark shirt and tugs on it, to keep his attention as she speaks. "You were careless, West. We all were. It wasn't your fault alone and I didn't want you to take the fall for it." She starts to reach for his face, but forces her hand to stop. "I never would have asked you to do that for me."

"You wouldn't have to." His voice is thick as their gazes meet. His dark eyes cutting straight through her heart and she flashes back to the night of the twister when he'd met her gaze and gave her his signature sly grin over the picnic table before all hell broke loose. "I will always do whatever it takes to make sure you're happy, Jules. That's what it means to love someone."

Her breath catches at his declaration, even as her mind screams at her to run before he breaks her heart again.

"How do you do it?" he asks as he backs away to give her room.

"Do what?"

She notices his eyes flick to her arm. The sadness in his face is unbearable. She recognizes the guilt in that cursory glance, because it's the same look she used to wake up to every morning after the tornado when she blamed herself for 'allowing' Tanya to die.

"You live with the physical reminders of that wreck every day, and yet you stand here and talk to me. You have every right to punch me and hate me, yet you're asking me to stay?"

The tension of his question is broken by the sound of someone calling her name. "Jules?"

She turns to see Levi walking up the street with a few friends in tow.

"Damn it," she mutters to herself at his poor timing. They'd made plans a few days ago to meet up at the party tonight. She never thought for a moment she'd run into West.

"Everything okay?" Levi asks, his steps quickening and West stiffens as he steps aside, his face already adopting that blank façade of someone who doesn't care.

She waves towards Levi to stop him and responds hastily, "Yeah. I'll be right there."

"West?" she asks as he bends to pick up the keys he dropped earlier.

"You should go, your date is waiting," he hints. "I'll see ya around."

She stares him down for a moment and he crosses his arms across his chest. "Just go, would you?"

She nods and lifts her left arm, her finger tapping her tattoo as she speaks.

"You see this? I did this when I thought I hated you, months ago. When I was so angry I thought I needed something to help me forget. Except, the truth is, I didn't do it to forget you; I did it to remind myself that I never once hated you." Her voice breaks as she adds, "Never."

Spinning on the sole of her shoe she hurries to the sidewalk where Levi is waiting, a curious look upon his face, and they head back to the party together without a backward glance.

West

Watching her walk away with another guy, after the conversation they'd just been having, feels as if someone has ripped the heart from his chest and is stomping on it.

Stupid! he chastises himself as his gaze follows her and her friend, Levi. Levi slows his pace, placing his hand on her lower back as she walks in front of him, and they disappear around the corner of a house.

The moment West saw him, he recognized him as the guy from the Hole last week with Jules.

You're such an idiot, he yells at himself between curses as he climbs into his truck. Her last words are like nails on a chalkboard; they make every nerve in his body itch and curl. They irritate his soul because she doesn't hate him. She never hated him and he let her walk off with another guy.

He spends two minutes contemplating going after her. He allows himself to visualize telling Levi to get lost and dragging her to a dark corner to beg her to listen. The scene morphs to one where, instead of talking, he kisses her senseless first and then begs her to listen to his explanations. He smiles, this visual a much more accurate scene of what he would do if he had the guts to get off his ass and go after her.

"Damn it!" He slams his palm on the steering wheel and throws his truck into gear; his tires squealing as he peels off down the road.

Twenty

Jules

Jules is sitting in the commons area on the second floor of Ward when Katie steps off the elevator, her hands filled with packages and mail. Sliding her books to the chair, she jumps up to help her best friend.

"Thanks," she murmurs, nodding at the white box in Jules' hand. "That's for you, actually. It was at the desk downstairs."

"For me?" She looks at the return address and sees that it's from home. "It must be the shirt and books I left at home last time I was there."

She follows Katie to their room and tosses the box on the bed. "What do you have in those?" she asks, nodding to the grocery bags hanging from Katie's fingers.

"Provisions."

"Provisions?"

"Movie night, remember?"

"Movie... oh shoot! It's Tuesday. I totally forgot."

The girls had agreed they would start implementing Tuesday night movie night in the room. Just the four of them - Cassie, Jess, Katie, and Jules. Tonight was supposed to be the first night, but Jules' mind has been so occupied with West and Levi the past few days that she's forgotten all about it.

"Dang, K, I'm sorry. I wasn't supposed to get the movie, was I?"

Katie shakes her head, her blonde bob bouncing to and fro as she dumps the popcorn and candy onto her bed. "Nope. Cassie is getting it tonight. Although," she looks about and lowers her voice, "I'm a little worried what she might make us watch. That girl barely ever cracks a smile; I imagine she is going to make us watch some black and white Indic film with sub-titles about saving baby sea lions or something."

"Sea lions?" Jules laughs at the absurdity and returns to the commons area to grab her books.

It's early afternoon the next day before Jules remembers the package she'd thrown on the floor last night as they piled on her bed to watch 'Ever After.' Katie and Jess had been shocked at Cassie's pick, their chins dropping to their chests.

"I figured you two must love all this fairytale BS," she explained, giving Katie and Jess a disgruntled look. Jules had only groaned a little on the inside. Sweet perfect love was something she wanted to watch about as much as Cassie she guessed, but she smiled and giggled at all the appropriate moments and thankfully when her tears started to roll, she was able to cover them because Katie and Jess were crying right along with her.

The silly sentimental saps! she thinks as she tears the cardboard strip from the box from home.

Emptying the contents on her bed, she's confused when a large envelope falls out along with her favorite shirt and a book she'd meant to grab last time she was home. Picking the sealed envelope up, she registers the weight in her hands as she flips it over, seeing the postage and how it's addressed to her. Her eyes flick to the return address and her pulse quickens.

Crestdale Victory Center, Houston.

Her hand trembles for no reason at all as she stands there and stares at the burgundy logo and then back at her name and address. The script is feminine and not one she recognizes. Shaking her head at her silly behavior, she grabs a pair of scissors and cuts through the clear packing tape the sender used to seal the top of the envelope. As if she's expecting something to bite her, she pops the mouth of the envelope wide and looks in before sticking her hand in. When nothing jumps out at her she pulls out a bundle of paper. The sheets are ragged at the edges, some with the torn edges of a spiral notebook, and they're stacked together with a rubber band around the center. On the top of the stack is a sheet of clean, white computer paper with the simple words:

You should know.

Sweat breaks out above her brow as Jules flips the envelope back over and matches the penmanship of the note to that of the sender. Crawling onto her bed, she leans against the wall and pulls the rubber band from the pile, removing the top sheet. The moment her eyes take in the first page, she no longer wonders where this package came from. West's bold script is right there for her to see.

Jules,

Tomorrow I meet with Dr. Steel one last time. It's my get out of jail meeting.
Finally.
I have to admit, I'm scared as hell.

She stops reading, tucking her knees up to her chest and setting the stack on her thighs. As she sifts through the stack, she sees each piece of paper is a different letter to her, some short paragraphs and others spanning the course of multiple pages. Some of the pages have dates and a few are folded and crumbled, as if he stuffed them in his pocket, or had thrown them away.

A quick glance at the clock reveals she has another hour before any of the girls will be back from their afternoon classes, so she flips to the first letter again and takes a deep fortifying breath before she dives in.

I'm scared as hell of going back home and what I will find when I get there. Are you still there? Do you understand what I did? Why I didn't respond to your calls?

Do you miss me, love me, hate me...

Do you feel indifferent and we'll be like old friends who once knew each other and now just pass on the street?

Please say no! Tell me that no matter what happens we will never be like that. I don't want to pretend I don't know you, that I didn't love you once and hold you in my arms... that those months, as short as they were, weren't the best of my life.

I can't do it, Jules. I just can't. I can't pretend I don't love you. I will always love you. It's impossible to not love you. Impossible to think of what we went through and chalk up every kiss, every smile, every touch to a so-called normal teenage crush.

A freaking crush, a traumatic experience... this is the crap they've tried to feed me in counseling. Bullshit!

I don't care if you ever tell me you love me again, I will love you... I'm coming home and I'm going to prove it to you. I just hope you will give me the chance...

West

Jules sets the letter next to her and immediately begins the next. It's dated March and goes into random details about the weather, about a counselor who won't listen, and how much he wants to come home. Page after page, word after word, she reads through West's thoughts; both clear and rambling. The stack is out of order numerically, but it's clear that no matter what date he wrote she was always on his mind. There are a few that are void of anything but scribbled lyrics and doodles and then there are longer, tortured letters where she can feel his hatred towards himself for the wreck. None are quite as full of declarations of love as the first one she read, until she gets to one dated December seventeenth. That would have been a few weeks after he left. There's no salutation and the words are messier, the thoughts jumbled together, unlike most of his other letters.

> I think I made a mistake, Jules. I'm sorry! I was stupid, I should have stayed, and I should have seen you before leaving. I should have fought for us. I should have told your parents the truth, but I wanted to protect you.

> I miss you
> I miss you
> I miss you

The words are written in blocks down the page and Jules heart clenches.

> You're everything to me. Everything and I walked away. I walked away, but I did it for you. I hope you

know the truth by now. Carson told me you're awake, that you're going to be okay. Jeff gives him all the details. It's the only time I take a call from them, you know. Updates on you, that's all I care about right now.

Six months and I'll be home and hopefully you will listen to me explain.

The letter only confuses her. *Tell her parents the truth? What truth?*

"What am I missing?" she mumbles out loud as she shifts and lays the letters on the bed. She starts spreading them out looking for dates or words that stand out to get the whole story.

Tears are streaming down her face when Katie walks in sometime later.

"What's wrong?" she cries, rushing into the room when she spots Jules hunched over the bed still pouring through the letters. "What are you doing?"

Jules lifts the first letter she read, the last one West wrote, as she wipes her face with the back of her hand.

"West wrote me letters."

"Wrote you letters? When, where did these come from?" she asks, falling to the floor and kneeling next to Jules.

Jules thrusts the letter at her best friend and tries to explain through her shaky breaths. "He wrote them at Crestdale, the facility he went to, and I got them from home today. Someone mailed them to me two weeks ago."

"I -" Katie starts to speak and then closes her mouth as she reads the letter Jules handed her. "Oh, this is … wow," she admits, her face melting like Jules heart did when she reads the words.

"All of them, K. It's like he wrote to me every day. Some are completely crazy and random notes about the strange patients there and the trees in the courtyard, but others are beautiful. He never stopped thinking about me all this time." She stops and Katie pulls her into a tight hug, causing Jules to cry harder.

"You tried to tell me -" she hiccups into Katie's hair. "You and Austin. God, even Mindy tried to tell me to let him tell me the whole story and I wouldn't listen."

"Hey, don't do that." Katie pushes her away lightly and gives her a stern look. "Don't blame yourself. He never had to cut you out, Jules. He could have called. He could have mailed these. He should have mailed them. What you did is understandable."

"But he loved me!"

"And you loved him! You loved him and he cut you out when you needed him." Katie's points out again and Jules nods.

She felt the same way about what West did until the moment she saw his words pleading her to forgive him. Those words washed away all of her anger and now she wants nothing more than to see him. She wants to find him and tell him she needs him and loves him, too.

"Where's Jeff?" She jumps up excitedly and grabs her phone. "Or Austin? I'll call Austin."

Katie gets up slowly. "They're at practice. They won't answer."

"Damn!" Jules checks the time, knowing practice will most likely run for another hour.

"Jules, calm down. You're acting like a mad woman. What do you want to do?"

"I need to see him, Katie. I need to talk to him and I don't have his number."

"Can't you wait? I can get it from Jeff in an hour or so when he gets out. We were gonna get some pizza anyway. Come with."

"Come with? Are you kidding me? I can't wait another day!"

"Fine, fine. Chill out and let's wait an hour. You can wait an hour, can't you?"

Throwing her bag over her chest and grabbing West's letters, Jules sorts the stack and stuffs them in the over-sized purse. She goes to the bathroom, as Katie tries to talk her into sitting down, and she runs her fingers through her long hair. Her eyeliner is smeared under her eyes and she wipes at her face knowing that nothing short of a good face washing is going to help sort her splotchy, tear-stained face.

"Jules!" Katie finally grabs at her arm and hauls her to a stop.

"Don't you get it, K?" She pulls her arm free and holds Katie's gaze. "He tried to talk to me at the party that night I was with Austin, and then the vigil, and then he called Austin and I answered. God, he tried to talk to me Saturday, then Levi showed up and he shut down. We keep getting our signals crossed and I don't want to wait another minute to make this right. I need to know what happened with my parents and I need -"

"He's playing football at Freemont." Katie admits, interrupting Jules.

"He's what!"

"The guys made me swear not to tell you. I figured you'd hear by now or West would tell you himself. I never thought you'd be able to get almost five weeks into the season without knowing."

"How? I don't -"

"It's why he's at Freemont instead of A&M. They picked him up and he's starting QB. He's good too, Jules. Just like back in middle school."

"And you didn't tell me?" Jules accuses her best friend, irrationally angry at her for keeping something this huge a secret.

"He didn't want you to know, I promised."

Stepping back, Jules shakes her head. "Keep Jules out of the loop - that was the goal from day one. If someone had told me the truth after the wreck, all..."

"I know, I'm sorry. He's probably at practice, you know. It's only thirty minutes. If not, you know where he lives. Stalk him." Katie shrugs, offering an apologetic smile.

"Seriously, Jules, I'm sorry I didn't tell you. I really didn't think it would take him this long to tell you himself."

"He did it for me." All the conversations she's had with West since she first saw him, the way he stepped back because of Austin. Even the way he stepped back the other night when Levi showed up. It was West doing what he thought she needed. She knows this irrevocable truth without even speaking to him, because just as his letters said, he did everything for her. "He did what he thought I wanted. He still thinks I should hate him." She opens their door, grabbing her keys from the hook and turning to Katie with a smile. "I guess it's time I make sure he knows that's the furthest thing from the truth."

Twenty-One

<u>Jules</u>

The thirty minute drive to Freemont's campus is unbearable as Jules' head keeps replaying the words she read in West's letters. She thinks back to their time together, back to the stolen moments they used to share when they were both still in shock from the tornado and neither of them knew how to deal with it. She remembers the way he would walk up behind her at the funerals and slip his hand into hers without a word. As she drives she wonders how he could seemingly give up on a love like that.

She follows the signs pointing to the small stadium on campus when she pulls in. Freemont isn't a bad school, but it's much smaller than A&M and soon she's parking her car in the lot next to the gym facilities on campus, two rows behind a shiny black truck she is pretty sure belongs to West.

It's close to three in the afternoon and she sees a crowd of players standing in a huddle on the field from where she sits. Smoothing her hair one last time, she slips out of her car and crosses the parking lot keeping her eyes on the players.

Most of them have pulled off their pads and their helmets are on the ground at their feet. Jules nears the open gate to the field and looks into the stands by the entrance to see a small crowd watching the players. She's surprised. Practices at A&M are closed and entrance to the field is virtually impossible since all of the gates are locked; you have to be a player, coach, or assistant to get in.

"Thank you, junior college security," she mumbles, stepping into the stadium and moving to take a seat on the first row benches.

The coach's deep voice can be heard issuing a few orders before one loud coordinated group shout and the team breaks up. Jostling with each other, the players grab their helmets, pads, and other gear and start her way. She glances around for the entrance to the locker room and sees she's on the team side.

Perfect.

As the guys disperse, she notices West's tall, dark head standing above a few other players still talking to a coach. He's wearing a sleeveless muscle shirt, his pads and helmet both at his feet still. His white pants fit him to perfection and her throat goes dry at the sight. West Rutledge belongs in a football uniform. A smaller student wearing khakis and a team shirt grabs West's equipment and West lifts his head. She sees his mouth forming words when suddenly he stops and she finds his gaze staring straight at her.

She is fifty yards, or more, away from him, but he sees her and she can't control herself any longer. Standing slowly, she takes a few steps forward and stops, watching as West returns his focus to his coach and starts talking again. She waits for him to stop, and when the coach gives him a fist bump she moves again. To her left, several players are already talking with the girls that were sitting on the bleachers when she arrived, but she ignores them focusing solely on West. He stops halfway to her, running his hand through his messy hair and lifting his shirt to wipe his face.

His pause makes her still for one moment and then thinking of all of those big moments in movies where the couple is reunited at last, she speeds up. She hurries towards him with abandonment until a crooked smile cracks on his gorgeous face and then she is running. His arms reach out for her as she flings herself at him. Her body flies through the air and her legs wrap around his waist as she weaves her hands into his hair. Within moments, she is holding his face in front of her as his hands hold her rear and lower back, pulling her close to his body.

"What are you doing here?" he gasps, a wide smile playing on his lips.

"Shut up and kiss me," she demands, swooping in and kissing him hard.

Whoops and cat-calls sound around them, but she doesn't care. The salty taste of his sweat is Heaven to her after almost ten months. Tears stream down her face as he kisses her with the same abandonment she is using.

He lets out a groan as their mouths tangle together and Jules wants nothing more than to kiss him for hours; instead, she presses a few final soft kisses to his lips and pulls back slowly to look at him. West's arms tighten protectively around her and she gets the feeling he isn't planning on letting her go anytime soon.

"Hi to you, too," he whispers softly, his brow arching over his warm brown eyes before he drops his forehead to her chest. Jules sets her chin atop his hair.

"Sorry, I got a little carried away," she speaks over his head.

"You can greet me that way any day, Buffy," he declares as he asks her again why she is there.

His voice saying 'Buffy' makes her breath catch and it takes a moment before she can speak.

"I got tired of waiting for you to fight for me," she admits on a low sigh and he pulls back, bumping her chin.

"I've been a damn idiot. That stupid party. I let you walk away with Leroy -"

"Levi."

"Whatever." He grins and she gives him a watery smile. "Point is, I wanted to talk to you and I chickened out. I kept letting myself think you were happier without me. That you were better off."

"You made decisions without asking me. You never asked me

once what I wanted, what I needed.

"Baby, I know. I was stupid. I screwed up."

"Don't," she warns, tugging at his hair so she can meet his eyes. "We've both done some stupid stuff."

West grins. It's the sly grin that can make a girl drop her panties in two point six seconds flat and Jules' pulse quickens. "We need to talk."

"Talking is overrated." Jules smiles, leaning down to kiss him again when a deep voice interrupts them.

"Rutledge! Off the field."

A few claps sound in the background and Jules laughs against West's lips as he curses and acknowledges his coach.

"Going!"

West calls out to his coach and Jules wiggles preparing to jump from his arms, but he holds tight, his fingers digging into her upper thigh and pressing against her lower back. As he walks off the field, she hugs him tightly, pressing her face against the sweaty side of his neck. His stride is smooth and strong and he carries her as if she is as light as a feather. West stops at the bleachers, where she unwraps her legs and allows him to stand her on the bench in front of him so they are face-to-face.

"How did you know I was playing ball?"

"How could you not tell me?" she counters. She tries not to sound hurt, but she can see by the fall of his face he can tell she is bothered.

He cocks his head to the side almost sheepishly. "Yeah, we have a lot to discuss, don't we?"

She nods and his hands slide from her hips to cup her face and he presses a soft kiss to her lips before moving back. "Wait here while I shower and change? I'll be quick." he asks hopefully, and she smiles at the anticipation in his voice.

"Of course. I'm not going anywhere."

"Promise?"

"I swear."

Twenty-Two

<u>West</u>

Ignoring the ribbing he receives from his teammates, West takes the fastest shower of his life. Within twenty minutes, he is heading out of the locker room and down the tunnel back into the stadium, water still dripping down his back. The entire time he was away from her his mind asked one question - *Is this for real?*

When he looked up from the conversation with Coach and saw the glow of red hair in the seats, he knew immediately it was her. After everything they've been through, he never expected her to run into his arms and throw herself at his body, let alone his lips; not without a lot of explanations. He recalls her words Saturday night before she walked away and left him at his truck:

"*I've never hated you, West. I wanted to.*"

When he was in Crestdale meeting with Dr. Steel several times a week, he thought he'd finally gained the strength he needed to stop blaming himself for the things that happened to the people he loved. However, Saturday when he saw the ugly scar running the length of her arm he faltered. He ran. Again.

She deserves better, and yet he knows with every fiber of his being that he isn't going to walk away from her tonight. He can't, he tells himself as he walks onto the field and looks to the bleacher where he left Jules.

She's gone.

His pulse races in a moment of panic when he doesn't see Jules waiting for him and he quickens his pace as he heads toward the exit gates. He rounds the corner of the stadium, his heart racing in his chest, and comes to a stop when he spots her. She is leaning against the door of his truck, with her legs crossed at the ankle and her head bent as she fiddles with her cell phone. That copper colored hair he loves so much hangs down the side of her face and he lets out a sigh of relief.

West takes his time walking to his truck, watching her as he goes and waiting for her to look up. He wonders if she regrets running to him. He can't help but think it's grossly unfair that she came after him when he should have been the one chasing her.

She looks up when he's almost there and a warm smile appears as she tucks her hair behind her ear.

"You scared the hell out of me. I thought you left."

"Sorry." Jules looks down and plays with her phone before waving it at him and finishing her sentence, "I left my phone in the car."

"And... you had an important call to make?" he asks as he drops his duffel on the asphalt next to her feet.

"Something like that."

He smiles at her diversion. "Did Katie tell you I was here?"

"Sort of." She plays coy again and he shakes his head.

"Ummm, I received your letters today," she says and his face screws up in confusion as she rushes to explain. "My parents had them and I guess they didn't think to tell me I had mail, but they sent them with some other stuff and so I was reading them and Katie -"

"Whoa, wait!" West blurts, still trying to understand what's happened. "My letters?"

"The ones you wrote while you were at Crestdale," she explains and his mouth goes dry.

"Dani," he hisses. Dani must have sent them to her recently. Damn her for sticking her nose in his relationship.

"Dani?"

"I didn't mean for you to see those. I mean, I wrote them, but didn't plan on sending them. I gave them to a friend, Dani." He trails off as Jules' eyes go wide with understanding.

"Oh," she breathes. "Were you never going to tell me how you felt? Were you not planning to fight for me?" She pushes her hair back with her hand and West catches a glimpse of her anchor tattoo as she starts to chuckle. "God, I'm so stupid, I just came running to you."

"No!" He leans in and blows out a breath, heavy with emotion. "I didn't mail those letters because I didn't want you to feel pity for me. I wanted to win you back on my own."

He takes her arm and lifts it to his face to inspect the beautiful black anchor she put there. Studying it, he lowers his lips and presses a kiss to the tattoo, her arm stiffening under the touch. Now that he's had a small taste, he can't stop there and he leans forward slightly, his mouth grazing over her skin to the scar.

"I'm so sorry, Buffy." The words are faint as he murmurs them over and over while his lips leave a trail of kisses along the length of the damage. "Every time I'm around you, I'm at war with myself. I want to fight for you and keep you as mine, and then I want to run and hide because you deserve better and I swear I will screw it all up again. I'll hurt you, I'll break you-"

He raises her arm, pressing it against the glass next to her head as he kisses it. His body is mere millimeters from hers and his fingers grip her wrist, as his thumb presses into the anchor, rubbing it softly.

She hasn't moved or spoken since his lips touched her skin and he lifts his face from her arm, fully expecting to see an angry girl.

What he finds instead breaks his control. Inches away from his face is Jules' beautiful one. She's watching him with silent tears running down her lovely cheeks and he wants to die.

"Don't cry," he pleads as his free hand touches her cheek. "You know how I hate it when you cry."

Jules right hand wraps around the back of his neck and she pulls his face to hers, their mouths so close he can feel every shaky breath she takes blow across his lips.

"I want to hear the whole story."

"You what?" he whispers, restraining himself from swooping down and kissing her.

"The whole story," she repeats. "Why you left. What happened between you and my parents when I wasn't awake."

"Jules?" He hesitates, not wanting to give her the full story for fear of putting a divide between her and her family.

Her fingers slide into his hair and she tugs his face back slightly so she can look at him. There's fire in those eyes as she pins them on him and repeats with more force. "I want to hear the whole story."

"Why?"

"You loved me. I know you did, West. I laid in that hospital bed and I waited and waited for you to come back or to call and explain everything because I *knew* you wouldn't just walk away. Then when you didn't come, I pretended to hate you. I tried to convince myself that what we had wasn't real or was puppy love or brought on by the stress of the tornado and everything else going on… but that was stupid. You know it and I know it. We were stupid to think we could walk away from this. You loved me and -"

West doesn't allow her to finish her sentence before he kisses her. His hand moves from her cheek up into her hair and pulls her forward, his tongue sweeping into her mouth, claiming her for himself.

It's the sweetest madness he's ever known.

And he never wants to lose this feeling.

When his hips make contact with hers, it's a mind-blowing pleasure only surpassed by the more intimate act of having her beneath him. Every part of him wants to throw her in the back of his truck, rip off her clothes, and show her the depth of his need for her. To use his body to beg hers for forgiveness. Instead, he slows down. He pulls back, even as she fights with his mouth to keep kissing him, and presses several small kisses to her lips as he allows himself to consider what this moment might mean.

"LOVE, Jules Blacklin," he finally says when she lets him leave her mouth. "I love you. I never stopped."

Her arm is still pressed against the glass next to their heads and she opens her fist, splaying her fingers wide as she watches his face. Words aren't necessary as he let's go of her wrist and runs his hand up her arm until he winds his fingers between hers. The feeling of holding her hand again is indescribable. He takes in the girl before him, her cheeks flushed pink from their kissing, her chin red from the scratchiness of the stubble along his jaw, and he finds a peace he's been missing since that cold December night when he almost lost her.

"I've missed that so much," she sighs and her head swivels against the window to look at their hands. "I missed you. I missed your strength."

"You didn't need my strength. You had your own."

Her faces scrunches up, her brows furrowing in protest before they relax. "You're right. I found my strength, but I needed yours, too."

"No, baby, you didn't. I knew you were strong enough to get through what happened without me. I never would have left if I thought differently -"

A shout of laughter interrupts West as more of his teammates trickle out of the stadium. The commotion reminds West they have an audience not twenty feet away and he steps back and pulls Jules away from the truck. Their hands remain connected as they fall to their sides.

"Do you want to go talk?"

"Will you tell me the whole story?"

He smiles, a small laugh leaving him at her stubbornness. "If you want me to, then yes."

"Okay."

Walking her to the passenger door, he looks about the parking lot. He has no idea which vehicle belongs to her. "We can pick up your car later, if that's okay. It'll be safe here."

She climbs into the truck with a smile, "That's perfect."

"Do you mind if I take you somewhere?" he asks when he climbs in next to her and starts the engine.

She tucks her hair behind her ear, shyly sending him a glance from the corner of her eye before offering sweetly, "I'll go anywhere you want."

The small fear of the past kicks him gently in the gut when her big eyes look at him that way. He wishes he had time to call Dr. Steel or Dani, or even one of his brothers, so someone could tell him to stop worrying, and being afraid to screw this up and live in the moment.

"Okay, Buffy," he teases lightly, pushing the doubt away as he's learned to do and throwing the truck into drive. "I know the perfect place."

Twenty-Three

Jules

Jules pinches her arm discreetly as West pulls onto the street and heads away from campus. *I must be dreaming because this is too easy,* she tells herself as she sneaks a peek at his profile. His cheeks are splotchy and red from the heat, a Russian trait he inherited. She recalls how she used to tease that he looked like he was blushing. His dark hair is damp still, and while it is shorter than it was in high-school, the thick mass still sticks up and about in its normal careless way. The most prominent change she can see is his jawline. It's more chiseled, something she didn't think was possible, and harder looking. He looks like the man he is, instead of a teenage boy. His shoulders and arms bare the same resemblance. Everything about him screams mature, hard, and she feels somewhat mournful of the months she missed out on. The months that made him into this man.

"You're staring," he remarks without looking her way and she flushes with embarrassment.

"You've changed." As soon as she says the words, she wants to take them back. She feels silly remarking on his physical appearance.

"How's that?"

Jules' mind scrambles for something to say. "Your muscles," she blurts out, pursing her lips and shaking her head as she turns to look out the window.

West laughs gently. "My muscles?"

She lets out a deep breath, "Forget it. I was just thinking stupid thoughts."

"Nothing you think is stupid," he points out, reaching for her hand and pulling it across the cab so he can press a kiss to the top of it. Their fingers stay entwined and she sighs inwardly.

This is too easy.

Jules knocks the thought away and smiles at him. "I was admiring them, your muscles, that is," she finally explains after a brief pause, grinning as he flexes a little in the driver's seat. "Football's had a positive effect on you, physically speaking."

"You've changed, too."

"I have?" Jules straightens and preens, her fingers automatically touching her face and smoothing her hair, causing West to chuckle at her again.

"You're more beautiful, if that's even possible -"

"Oh, stop."

"It's true. Plus, your hair is a deeper red... darker."

"Oh, well that's L'Oreal," she laughs as she tugs on the strands. "Katie was bored and wanted to color my hair."

"It's still you. I like it."

"Thank you."

They drive for twenty minutes south of campus before West pulls down a road to a local park. The area is crowded with stay-at-home moms watching their kids play on the playground. A trail that runs around the edge is spotted with joggers and people out walking their pets. Jules admires the area as West drives past the crowd and down a small road leading to another, more secluded, section of the park. There's a lake and an older playground across from tennis courts surrounded by woods.

They park in the corner of the lot and West turns off the engine and sits there staring out the front windshield at the smooth water in front of them.

"Austin and I were never a couple."

"I know."

Surprised, she turns and unbuckles her seatbelt, to face him. "You know?"

"He stopped by to see me after my game last Saturday and told me. I'm sorry I didn't give you the chance to explain-" He stops and runs his hand through his hair. "Not that you owe me an explanation, but I should have let you tell me what was going on."

He snaps his seatbelt and pops open his door, "Come on."

They jump out of the truck and walk side by side to the playground. When they reach the swing set, they both take a seat and Jules kicks off with her toe letting the slight breeze cool her as she swings. West remains still, his eyes following her as she moves back and forth.

"How do you like Freemont?" she asks as she pumps her legs and moves through the air.

He laughs out loud and she giggles at herself. "Too simple?"

"I think we're past small talk, Jules," he points out. "But, to answer your question, it's okay. I'd rather be at A&M. It was always my plan to be there."

She assumes he didn't make it into A&M based on grades and missing the last half of senior year, and she feels guilt rising up. "Sorry."

"For what? It's not your fault. I could have gotten in."

"I just assumed with your leaving school-"

"Jules, I finished school at Crestdale. Believe it or not, I was a good student."

Her eyes flick to him before she pumps her legs harder, propelling her swing higher. "I always knew you weren't the bad boy you pretended to be."

"You always knew me better than I even knew myself."

"So why Freemont?"

"Football. My counselor at Crestdale decided I needed to play again and they let me walk on." He shrugs.

"Surely with your dad's pull and your name you could have gotten a walk-on at A&M."

"Sure, as a bench warmer. Roberts is a beast and a fifth year senior," he says about A&M's starting QB. Jules nods in agreement at his assessment, having seen him play. "I wasn't ready to walk-on and play when we approached them in June. We were a little late, anyway. So Dr. Steel pulled some strings with friends and got me an interview with Coach. Freemont was happy to offer me a spot."

"And you're getting to play?"

He laughs, "Yeah, Jules. I get to play."

"You missed it, didn't you? Playing football."

"There's only one thing I've ever missed more," he replies. The warmth and intensity of his eyes as they lock onto hers and make his point for him.

Jules takes a shaky breath and drags her foot along the ground to stop her swing. She takes a small hop off as it slows down and she lands perfectly in the sand, the swing hitting her backside as it continues to move back and forth. Looking around, she decides to sit on a nearby bench so they can talk more seriously. West follows as she moves a few feet over and takes a seat. He stands in front of her and stuffs his hands into the pockets of his loose cargo shorts.

"You're ready to talk, huh?" he asks and she nods.

"I feel like I have so many explanations to give you. Not only from that night, but before that too. I don't know where to begin," he admits.

"I think we both have a lot of explanations to make. Let's start with what happened that night after the wreck. I woke up a few days afterwards and you were already gone."

"I'm so sorry. I can't imagine how that felt for you." West falls to the bench and takes her hand. He clears his throat and explains, "I swear, Jules, I never would have left if I thought there was another choice. I was there for days. I didn't just leave. If you believe I would just walk away then there is no reason to explain what happened."

"I have to be honest," she pulls her hand from his and tucks it under her crossed arms. "Honestly? I don't know what I believe anymore and I don't understand what happened to make you think you had to leave."

"Austin said he explained the situation to you back then." She frowns, not quite sure what he's referring to. West runs his hands through his hair in agitation. "Okay, you know the people in the car we hit? That other couple? They were pressing charges and threatening to sue. They were going after my dad, your parents, Rick and Aubrey; they weren't even injured, but they claimed mental distress and -" He shakes his head, clearly disgusted and cuts himself off. "Anyway, Rick fessed up pretty quickly once Aubrey was able to tell the cops about the incident. Lucky for us, she called 9-1-1 and was on the phone with them when it happened, so they had proof from the call records."

West sits forward, leaning his elbows on his knees and folding his hands; Jules moves forward with him, mimicking his pose.

"Problem was, I'd been drinking. I wasn't drunk by any means, you know that, right? I never would have driven if that had been the case. I had two drinks."

"Of course. I know you wouldn't have gotten behind that wheel with me if you were." Jules acknowledges honestly with a nod of her head. West was never careless with her, it was one of the reasons she fell in love with him.

"I wasn't drunk, but there was alcohol, and of course I was underage. My dad probably could have smoothed things over, but something happened."

She holds her breath and waits for him to explain.

"Your parents rushed into the hospital that night and the fear in their faces -" West stops abruptly and Jules wants to touch his shoulder; she wants to console him as he hunches farther forward.

"I remember when my parents sat my brothers and I down to tell us about Mom's cancer, how it was terminal. The pain, the hopelessness hidden in the creases along their mouths and eyes; even while they tried to remain optimistic." Jules eyes sting with tears as West's voice cracks.

"That's what your parents looked like when they came in that night. They spotted me standing there in the ER covered in your blood and I swear your mom almost fainted on the spot. She ran to me, scanning over my face and arms, asking if I was hurt. She was crying and she hugged me so tightly, like my own mom would if she'd been there. Your dad, on the other hand, gave me one grim look and went straight to the desk for answers. They were still running tests and doing whatever it is they did with you... there was nothing to do but wait at the moment.

"I hadn't been seen yet; I only had a few scrapes and cuts, but they wanted to take me back to run a few x-rays. They were worried about internal injuries, I guess. When I returned, your parents were sitting in the corner and I approached them, trying to explain what had happened. Your dad asked me to wait until they'd seen you. I tried a few times to talk to them after that, but your mom seemed to be in shock and your dad was, uh."

He sits back, turning to Jules with a wry smile. "Let's say he was scary calm and scary angry and leave it at that. My dad finally pulled me away from the area and down to the cafeteria. By that time, Mindy and Carson had arrived and we left them in the waiting room to wait for news."

"They didn't tell me any of this. I can't believe they would shun you like that, they really liked you." Jules says, feeling physically ill with her parent's actions. She leans forward, shaking her head, as West continues.

"Well yeah, that was before you ran out on them, went to a party, and drove with your drunk boyfriend," he points out sarcastically.

"Once they knew you were going to be okay, though, that's

when things got uglier. Your mom took pity on me after you were finally put in a room and she allowed me to see you the following day, but when your dad walked in he went ballistic. He blamed me for your behavior, said you'd been drinking and partying ever since we'd met. How you'd never snuck out before, how your grades were slipping, you were short tempered and too clingy… I forget what else he said, but he laid all the blame at my feet."

The tears in her eyes quickly dry up as anger begins to build up. Jules leans into West's side lightly, trying to give him what little comfort she can, though it feels like too little too late.

"He ordered me out of your life."

"I can't -"

"I let him believe I was to blame, Jules."

"What! Why?"

"I guess I let myself believe it for a while, too. I shouldn't have been at that party that night. I should have stayed home when you told me you couldn't go out or I should have met you back at my place when you did call me."

"I begged you to go to that party. It's not your fault."

"Jules, I could have said no to you." He bumps her shoulder with a small laugh. "It was possible, upon occasion, to say no to you."

"So what happened to make you leave and go to the facility?"

"It doesn't matter, does it? In the end it was the right decision for me," he waffles, pushing off the bench and taking a few steps forward.

Jules examines his back and replays all he's said while sitting here. She recalls the warning of how she doesn't know the full story and the aversion her father had to talking about West, or the wreck, with her. Knowing her parents most likely played a role in him leaving hurts. She steps up behind him and leans into his back, her head resting right under his shoulder blades, and she feels him stiffen at the contact.

"I missed this," she murmurs as she feels his muscles rise and fall as he takes a deep breath. "I missed the way you always felt so strong when I needed you to be strong."

"You make me stronger," he whispers low. He turns slowly and she falls away from leaning against him until they are facing each other. His hand brushes her cheek and her arms wrap around his waist automatically, as if she'd been doing it daily for the last ten months. "Here's the thing, Buff, I don't want to hurt your relationship with your parents, I swear I don't. But, I'm going to put us first here. I can live with them hating me, but I can't live without you."

She melts against him and looks up into his face as he continues to explain the past.

"When the cops told our parents about the alcohol and the other couple wanting to sue us all for liability, I flipped. I didn't want you to get in any more trouble than you already were, so I asked my dad to work out whatever deal he could to get you, and your family, off the hook. He was pulling strings with a judge and talking with the couple, asking them to back off. Things seemed as if they might actually work out and then..."

West blows out a breath and gives Jules a sad look. "Then your dad paid mine a visit. At this point, your parents weren't seeing or speaking to me. They'd actually asked me not to come to the hospital at all."

Disbelief at their behavior floors Jules. "Why did my dad go to see yours?"

"He raised serious doubt with the judgment my dad made at getting all the charges dropped against us, or me more specifically. He didn't want me to go to juvie, but he told my father he should consider getting me help. I guess he convinced my dad I was unstable. I was a mess, filled with guilt and worry for you, and add that to what your parents thought was PTSD from the tornado, and then reminding him of my lingering depression from mom's death...

They built a strong case about my mental health. He suggested dad get me help, and whatever he said worked. The judge friend of my dad made it a court order. Six months in rehab for mental health."

"So you left."

"The truth is, I wanted to leave." She frowns at his words. "I couldn't face you at that point. The moment I almost lost you is a moment I will never forget. Remember when you told me about how seeing me with Aubrey that day at lunch had taught you how easily I could break you?" She nods, recalling the moment easily.

"After my mother's death, I was able to walk away from everything in my life, Jules. I didn't form attachments; I didn't care about people or things anymore. The night of the wreck hit me like a ton of bricks. It brought back my mom's death all over again.

"You asked me at Carson and Mindy's engagement party why I quit football, remember?"

"Yeah. You said you had practice that day and it pissed you off, so you quit."

"Ha, well that's partially true. The truth is, the day she died I'd promised her I would be there for her. She was getting weaker and weaker and we knew the time was getting closer. I wanted to be by her side when she went. I'd taken to sleeping on a pallet on the floor so I wouldn't lose her."

"God, West," she whispers as tears roll from her eyes and she tightens her arms around his back.

"I promised, and then I went to football practice. Football! She ended up dying without me there and I couldn't forgive myself. I couldn't fail someone like that again, so I decided to close everyone off."

His hand swipes a tear from her chin. "Everyone, until you came along in that damn little cheerleading outfit and the tornado hit."

"I couldn't walk away from you then, and I can't walk away now. I've tried, God knows I've tried, to forget you and move on, but I can't. I want to... but I can't."

West pulls her into his chest, resting his cheek on her head as they hug each other tightly. He strokes her back as she grips his shirt in her fists and swallows back the flow of tears and emotion trying to push its way out of her chest.

"Why do you want to forget?" she's able to ask after a few moments.

"I don't want to see you lying on that pavement covered in blood anymore."

"Then don't think of me that way. Think of me in your arms watching movies on your mom's chaise in the game room, or the way we danced in the corn field on my birthday," she suggests, pulling back and looking up into his face. "Or think of me and all the new memories we can make now."

"You want to make some more memories?"

"I think we owe it to ourselves to try," she offers with a small shrug. "Do you want the same thing?"

He pauses, and she takes in the way his brown eyes melt when he looks down at her and his signature sly grin overtakes his face.

"A wise girl once told me if you want something in life you need a reason for wanting it, or else you will give up when it gets too hard. She said a person with motive and reason will work harder than someone who wants something on a whim."

She laughs lightly, "Wow, that's pretty smart. She must have heard it on *Law and Order*."

West groans, bringing her to his chest and pressing his lips to the top of her head.

"I love you, Jules. That's my reason. The moment I left Crestdale I wanted to come after you, but I let my insecurities eat at me. I promise you, I'm not walking away again, because I have a reason and a purpose for being here. I want to love you forever. I want to hold you again, and I never want to let you go."

"That sounds like a damn good reason, Rutledge. Now kiss me," Jules orders, leaning up on her toes and offering him her mouth.

* * *

Twenty- Four

<u>West</u>

When West cannot keep his hands from wanting to roam all over Jules' body it's time to stop kissing her. Pulling away from her willing mouth, he sighs and looks around them. Several cars have pulled into the parking lot and there are a few people on the tennis courts now. He noticed none of this as they stood there wrapped in each other's arms, and lips.

"We should take a step back," he suggests reluctantly, sliding his hands down her arms slowly until he reaches her hands. West weaves their fingers together giving them a squeeze as he looks down at Jules.

"Okay." Jules voice is feathery light as she looks up into his face with a winsome smile and he can't help but bend down to press another peck to her mouth.

"God, you're so beautiful."

Jules giggles under his lips and West steps back again.

"Dinner," he blurts out and she shakes her head. "We should get some, you hungry?"

"I could eat."

"Mindy likes to mother me and feed me well. Want to come back to the house with me?" Jules' face scrunches up and he slows down. "If you're not comfortable going there, we don't have to. I can take you out."

"No, no. I just. When I saw her last week -" she rambles off.

"Jules, they don't hold anything against you. I swear. They know nothing happened with you and Austin, and even if they didn't, they wouldn't judge you."

"I just feel as if I betrayed you or something."

"Betrayed me? What are you talking about?" She shrugs nonchalantly and West tugs on her hands. "Baby, come on."

He steers her to his truck and waits for her to climb in before he closes her door and moves around to get in himself. Starting the engine and cranking the air on high, he turns to her and reaches for her hand.

"Let's get past this now, okay?" She nods. "How can you possibly feel as if you betrayed me?"

"We're talking about your brother, West."

"Yeah. Whom you did nothing with."

"But I could have, we could have."

He blows out a deep breath and runs his free hand through his hair. The truth hurts, but he can't blame her for it and he tries to come up with a way to make her feel better.

"First, I left you. Cold turkey, babe. If anyone should feel bad, it's me. Austin is… Austin. He's a good guy and he tried to take care of you. I can't get mad at you for that."

"Can we try to agree to forgive each other for what happened?" she asks, her eyes sending him a soft plea.

"I want to be with you. I will do whatever it takes for us to get past this. What do you need from me?"

"I need you to stop blaming yourself for that wreck. And for this," she holds her scarred arm up. "I lived with the guilt of what happened to Tanya for months for no reason, so I know what I'm talking about here. We have to stop placing blame for the things that have happened and we have to move forward."

West chuckles. "I think our shrinks might have gone to the same school."

"You've heard this all before, huh?" She smiles and joins in with him laughing at the poster children for guilt they've both become.

"Okay, so I stop blaming myself for the wreck and you let go of any guilt you have about hanging out with my brother."

"And, we'll be open and honest about our feelings." She adds that with a slight raise of her brows.

"Can I be honest now?" he asks, stretching to the side to get closer to her in his large cab. His fingers comb through her hair as he smiles at her. "I never stopped loving you, Jules Blacklin. Those letters, I wrote you every day and sometimes twice a day? I wrote those all the while pretending I was on a vacation somewhere and you were waiting at home for me. I'm going to be nothing but honest with you and everyone else from now on. I know I kinda suck at this love thing sometimes, but I'm going to keep working on it until I get it right. You are that important to me. I won't give up again, I promise you."

West blinks his eyes hard, the sudden emotion that swells throughout him taking him by surprise as Jules touches his cheek with tears flooding her own eyes.

"That's all I needed to hear," she offers sweetly, bringing him in for another kiss.

It's close to six when Jules and West finally arrive at the house. Carson's and Mindy's cars are both in the driveway and Jules clears her throat when West turns off the truck.

"Ready?"

"As I'll ever be."

Jules pushes West to enter the house first, only to find it empty. They walk through the den and to the kitchen where they catch sight of Carson and Mindy sitting at the table on the back porch. Grabbing them each a water bottle, West pulls Jules to the glass doors and, with one last breath, they open the door and walk back out into the hot air.

Carson sees them immediately and his face twists in confusion as his eyes trail down West's arm to where his hand connects with Jules'.

"It's about time you came home, we actually waited for you to eat," Mindy, whose back is to the house, calls out. She twists in her chair to look over her shoulder and freezes as she spots Jules.

"I brought a guest," West points out, squeezing Jules' hand.

The high pitch frequency of Mindy's squeal could bring dogs running as she jumps up excitedly and hurries forward.

"Jules! You're here! You, with West, and you're here! What?" She pulls Jules into a hasty hug and pushes her back. "What is this? West, why didn't you tell us! Oh my gosh, I could stab you with a butter knife. You keeping this from us."

The craziness of Mindy's outburst causes Jules to laugh as she tries to respond.

"Don't smother her," Carson warns, standing and approaching them.

"I need details. What are you doing here?" Mindy asks, grasping Jules' hand and pulling her past Carson and to the table. "I mean, I'm happy you are. I just, I didn't expect it."

"Hey, Mind? Can we dispense with the third degree for now? Please?" West finally asks, ignoring his brother's look and putting his hands on his future sister's shoulders. "I know we are all excited to see Jules here, but can we give her a little time to acclimate?"

"West, it's fine, I'm fine," says Jules and Mindy smiles at her.

"Well, I'm starving. Can we eat first?" he asks, thinking that might spur Mindy to get up and be a good hostess to their guest.

Instead, Mindy surprises him when she pats his hand that's still sitting on her shoulder and replies, "Sure! You two go make our plates. Jules and I will wait out here and chat.

* * *

"Well, um…" he stammers, looking at Jules and trying to communicate without words. She smiles his way, looking comfortable, so he leaves the girls be and steps into the house.

"What the hell, man?" he asks Carson who laughs as the door shuts behind them.

"You know her, she gets over-excited. I could ask the same thing, though, bro. What happened? Two days ago you were moping around the house again and now she's here."

"Dani happened." He tells his brother about how Jules received the letters and how she came to him to talk. Without going into all the details, he explains how she'd been waiting for him to fight for her.

"I told you in July to go back to Tyler."

"I know, I know. I was stupid." He looks out the window over the sink as Carson fixes plates of spaghetti for them. Jules is sitting on the edge of her chair, but she's talking animatedly and she looks at ease. "I'm not screwing this up again."

"Can I give you some advice?"

West has always looked up to three people - his dad, Carson, and Austin. They are the four musketeers, always there for each other no matter what, especially after their mother died. He doesn't hesitate to nod his head in hopes of some sage advice.

"Date her."

"Date her? That's your advice?"

"Yeah. You two jumped into this serious mind-blowing relationship the last time and it ripped you both apart. Savor it this time. Woo her, date her, fall in love with her slowly."

"I'm already in love with her, man."

Carson shakes his head slowly. "I'm sure you think you are. West, you two are different people now than you were then. And even then you didn't know each other. Take it from a guy who almost lost the girl of his dreams once, too. Make her fall in love with you again. The new you."

West vaguely recalls when Carson and Mindy split up for a few months. He remembers hearing Carson give him a good ribbing a few times, when they were together for a game, about all of the crazy things he was doing to win her back. West looks at Jules once more from the window before picking up the plates to take outside.

Date her. A plan forms in his head and suddenly he is more than willing to follow Carson's advice.

"I still can't believe how easy that was," Jules remarks as West drives her back to the stadium parking lot at Freemont to get her car.

"I told you, you had nothing to worry about."

"They were perfect. Thank you for asking me to the house."

He pulls his truck into the spot next to her car and he flips the headlights off as he lets the truck idle.

"That's my home so I don't have to ask next time, okay? Anytime you want to come over you just show up."

It's close to ten and she covers her mouth as a yawn escapes her lips.

"I hate letting you drive home by yourself. You could stay here, you know. I could take the couch."

"No way. You have a game this weekend; I can't be blamed for you playing poorly because you ended up with a kink in your neck. You do get to play, right?"

West smiles. When she'd agreed to come to his game this Saturday, he'd decided to be vague about his spot on the team. He wanted to surprise her with how far he's come. Mindy agreed excitedly, already relishing being able to stand in the bleachers and watch Jules' face for her reactions.

"Yeah, I'll get some snaps. You don't have to come if you don't want to," he teases.

"Not come? Of course I'm going to be there. I can't wait."

Opening the door to the truck, she gives him a sad look as she slides down. West comes around the truck and finds her leaning against her door, the frown still pinned on her face.

"Call me when you get back to your room?"

"I still don't have your number," she remembers and pulls her phone out.

West takes the phone and pulls up her contacts, his heart clenching when he sees his old number next to the name 'Spike.' He edits the entry and hands it back, looking at her shadowed face.

"Now you do. Call me, promise?"

"I will."

He presses a quick kiss to her lips before pulling away, thinking of Carson's plan to take things slow, and says goodnight. Jules takes the cue and climbs into her car. As she starts her car and turns on the headlights, she takes a moment before she looks out the window at him; the blue dashboard lights cast a mellow glow on her face. She's pulling away and West takes another step back planning to go to his truck when she stops suddenly and her window slides down.

"Hey, West," she calls out with a huge smile on her face and he stops walking. "I love you."

His heart explodes as she says those three words and he walks to her car full of purpose. "Put it in park," he orders as he approaches.

He hears the transmission sound as she shifts into park and he pulls on the door handle yanking her car open. Swooping down, he kneels at the seat and presses an urgent kiss to her lips as his hand fumbles with her seat buckle. He pulls her from the vehicle, all the while kissing her with his hands digging into her hair and pressing against the small of her back. Carson's words, about going slow, fly out the window as his mind replays those three beautiful words. *I love you.*

"I couldn't leave without saying it," she murmurs against his mouth when he runs his lips from hers across her cheek and down her neck.

"I'm glad you did. I love you, too, Buffy."

It's a good twenty minutes before he lets her go again and she drives off. West drives back to the house and sits in his truck, waiting for her to call. He's half asleep when his phone goes off.

"I'm back in my dorm, safe and sound," she tells him when he answers.

"Good. I know it's barely thirty minutes, but all of a sudden it feels like you're across the country."

"I know it does. When do I get to see you again?"

"Saturday," he throws it out there, wondering what she'll think.

"Saturday? Really?" He can almost see the pretty pout she used to make to get her way with him.

"Yes, Jules. I'm asking you on a date for Saturday. I'll be the one on the field and we can get dinner after the game?"

"What's your number, anyway?"

"Twelve."

"Okay, Number Twelve. I will be the girl in the stands anxiously waiting to have dinner with you. I look forward to seeing you on the field."

"I look forward to having my own personal cheerleader in the stands."

"Goodnight, Spike."

He sighs at her using her nickname for him again. "Night, cheerleader."

Twenty-Five

Jules

"You told him you love him!"

Jules jumps at Cassie's shout as they make their way to West's game. Neither Katie nor Jess could come, so Jules had begged Cassie to go. Cassie had agreed, under one condition; Jules had to tell her about her conversation with West Wednesday night.

Jules had kept most of what had happened to herself when she made it back to her dorm that night. Jess had nearly broken down the door in her excitement to get the whole story; Katie had filled them both in on where she'd gone and they were all eager to know what transpired.

"You told him you love him, yet you haven't really talked to him in what, nine months? How do you know you love him still?" Cassie asks and Jules throws a quick glance at her friend.

"I never stopped loving him." Cassie's face is full of questions as Jules tries to explain the connection they have to no avail.

"I guess I don't get it. I've never even been close to falling in love." She says it as if she's brushing a speck of dirt off her shirt.

"Really? Never?"

"Nope."

"So you weren't kidding when you said you really don't want to have anything to do with guys, huh? Have you never had a boyfriend?"

"Nope." Cassie laughs when Jules frowns. "Don't look so sad about it. You don't know how much crap I've dealt with from my mom and men. I'm not kidding when I say I have no interest."

"One of these days some guys is going to sweep you off your feet." Jules points out as they inch along the highway with the rest of the traffic heading to Freemont's game. "I just hope I'm around to see it."

"Don't hold your breath."

Jules drops the subject as they pull into the parking lot.

"I'm pretty sure I told you I had no desire to go to another football game, I can't believe I let you drag me here," Cassie grumbles as they park and Jules pulls out her phone.

She sends Mindy a text letting her know they've arrived before they get out and make their way to the ticket gate.

"So, Mindy and West's older brother, Carson, will be here right? What about his dad?"

"His dad? You know Mr. Rutledge does commentary for A&M games for the school, right?"

Cassie gives Jules the most 'are you kidding me' look she has ever seen and Jules slaps her own forehead.

"Duh," she laughs. "I guess that was a no-brainer. Their dad played for A&M and went on to play in the NFL, too. He coached until their mom got sick. After that, he stayed home for a while and took care of the boys. I guess he's been broadcasting for the past three years or so," Jules explains. "So he travels to all A&M's games."

"Did you know their mom? I mean, you knew their family growing up, didn't you?"

"I did. I cheered for the pee-wee teams and all the way up until senior year. I remember cheering for teams West was on a few times. His mom was amazing. She always brought cookies and hot chocolate thermoses on cold game nights. That's all I really recall about her, though."

"I guess I can see how you can love him. You've grown up with him. It's sweet."

"Yeah. Well, between you and me there was a time there when he was all bad-boy-recluse after his mom's death that I didn't speak to him. At the time I thought myself above him. I kinda hate myself for that now."

"I can't see you as one of those people."

"A bitch?" Jules asks as she spots Mindy and Carson and waves at them.

"Ha! No, well, I mean, yeah. You don't strike me as a mean girl."

Jules looks at Cassie with a serious face. "I wasn't really, but I hung out with them. My life was all about social stature and having *the* perfect boyfriend, and the perfect look." Jules shakes her head and takes a step forward. "Let your whole life flash before your eyes and you'll be amazed how much you change," she adds as she greets Mindy and Carson with hugs.

"Hey, Jules." They're sitting in the stands waiting for kick-off when Carson leans around Mindy to grab Jules' attention. "Send West a text."

"A text? What's wrong?" She asks confused as she pulls her phone from her back pocket.

"Nothing. It's tradition. Dad has the game down to a science. He always sends one last text before game time. If you do it now, West will see it when he checks his phone one last time." He winks at her, "Trust me."

The thought of sending him a word of encouragement fills her heart with joy and, just as quickly, her head with fear. The pressure to send him the perfect note is thrust upon her and she waffles, looking around at Mindy, Carson, and then Cassie.

Cassie shrugs, "Got a nude pic on there?"

"No!" Jules cracks up and Mindy chokes on her drink. Fortunately, Carson is talking to the guys on the other side of them and doesn't hear the suggestion. Thinking hard of something inspirational, she types him a message:

Jules: We've been on a boat, you and me. You were my anchor when I needed someone to keep me from sinking into my guilt. You were my strength, my compass, when I needed someone to help steer me through the roughest parts. And now you're the sails. Your very presence lifts my spirits and propels me forward to a place I know we both want to be. I'm in the stands cheering for you, Number Twelve. Good luck! xoxo

"I think I just threw up a little in my mouth," Cassie whispers into Jules ear as she hits send.

"Shut up!"

"That was some sappy shiz-"

"Another word and I'll start sending every frat boy and ball player I know to your door for dates," Jules interrupts Cassie with a playful sneer effectively cutting her off.

Looking over Jules, Mindy laughs and adds to the conversation. "Those two have always been full of sappy romance. Did she tell you how West took her to The Century Tree?"

"Noooo, she didn't tell me that."

"It was cute…" She budges closer to Cassie so she can fill her in on the one visit Jules had with them last year when she and West went to the campus and walked under the tree; legend has it that if a couple walks under the tree they will get married. As Mindy is finishing up and the marching band is finishing the opening song on the field Jules phone goes off.

Sinking to her seat, as everyone else remains standing and cheering, she reads a text from West:

Spike: I expect a victory kiss in about four hours! Fence behind team bench, be there.

Jules laughs at his order and presses her hand to her chest to slow her racing heartbeat. It doesn't slow once the entire game. Her biggest shock comes when she watches number twelve take the field for Freemont's first snap.

"Um, Carson?" she shouts over the crowd noise around her as she slaps at Cassie's arm and grabs her in excitement. "Why is West on the field? He's getting the start?"

Mindy and Carson laugh, pulling her gaze from West for a brief moment.

"He's been the starter -" Carson informs her with a nonchalant shrug.

"He's the what? He didn't tell me, he... he said he might take a few snaps."

Mindy smiles at her. "He wanted to surprise you."

"Surprise me-"

"He's amazing, Jules," Carson interrupts her. "He was always the most talented player in the family."

As a kid, playing pee wee football all the way into middle school, Jules recalls how gifted West was. Everyone wanted him on their team and everyone said he'd be the next big thing. Jules can't help the tears of pride that fill her eyes as she listens for West's strong voice to shout out the play call. As he hands off the ball for the first snap, she holds her breath and cheers as the receiver rushes for seven yards.

She blinks swiftly to clear the teary haze as Mindy leans close to her. "Think you can handle being the star quarterback's girl?"

"Five years." Jules shakes her head numbly as she watches another play. "He didn't play for five years and he walked right into the starting QB spot. I..."

"He had motivation." The tone of Mindy's voice pulls Jules' focus from the field. "He had two goals coming out of Crestdale - win you back and prove to you he was worth another shot."

Jules shakes her head. "He's worth it with or without football."

"I know that and you know that, but I don't think he did."

The thought tugs at Jules' emotions as she settles in to watch this side of the man she loves. Her eyes stayed glued to West throughout the game. She feels every sack he takes as if it were her getting run over. Every scramble and forced throw catches her breath until the game is done. Four hours later she's running down the stadium steps as the clock winds down and West is coming off the field after another brilliant touchdown throw.

"Hey, Rutledge!" she shouts to his back as he stands and goofs off with a few players while the extra point is kicked.

He looks around before he turns and sees her. His face is red, his hair is a sweaty mess, but he has never looked sexier to her than at this moment. Every movement he made on the field today was filled with confidence and strength. It's something she's never seen in him before. The smile on his face and the way his eyes light up as he winks at her and holds his wrist up to point out the time all work towards confirming her suspicions. He is in his element; this is what he loves and she wants to cry with happiness at seeing him living out one of his dreams. He isn't playing ball because he thought it would get her back. He's playing because it's part of who he is.

She waits at the fence as the final seconds tick off and West disappears into the melee of players, coaches, and press. The rivals shake hands and speak to each other while another group of players kneel and say a prayer. As the band plays the fight song behind her, and the crowd cheers, she sees West giving an interview one reporter after another as he tries to move. Finally, he is free and he locks his eyes on Jules as he makes his way to the fence, fist bumping and patting the butts of players who approach him.

"You lied to me!" she accuses when he's almost to her and his brows rise. "You said you'd get to take 'some' snaps. You're the freaking starter, West Rutledge, and your brother filled me in on how you're on track to break records."

He ignores her and reaches over the fence, pulling her face to his as he bends down and presses a kiss to her lips.

"And you are gorgeous."

"West?"

"It's what I do. I play football. That's nothing."

"It's amazing!" She can see the hesitance to accept her accolades so she tones it down and switches to teasing him instead. "I'm very impressed and you should know it's extremely sexy."

"It is, huh? I might have showed off a little for a certain girl I knew would be watching."

"So what you're saying is I should come to every game so you can cream the puny opponents?"

"It would help," he agrees, kissing her again. "By the way, it's not fair for you to text me things like that when I can't see you, it kills me. If we're going with boat analogies, though, I will respond with you are my moon. You are the gravity that pulls me wherever you go."

"You do know the moon isn't part of a boat, right?"

"Stickler for details, are we? Fine," West tilts his head toward the sky, his face the picture of concentration. "You, Buffy, are the waves in the ocean-"

Jules bites her lip to keep from laughing and West gives her a sharp, yet playful, stare.

"No? My rudder? My map? The wheel? All of these things guide me."

Full-blown laughter erupts from Jules as she tugs on West's jersey, their faces only inches apart.

"Damn, this is hard. You took the good ones. Can't I just say that I would follow you forever if you let me?"

Jules sobers. "No. You're not following me. We're taking this journey side by side this time."

"Hell, that's what I should have said," West whispers. They are standing in the midst of a still crowded stadium, a fence between them, and yet they are all alone. Two people deeply in love and not afraid anymore.

Twenty-Six

<u>Jules</u>

The next day, West shows up at Jules dorm at 9:30 with an armful of roses, a duffle bag, and a smile. Jules is still in her tank top and baggy pajama bottoms when she answers the door with her hair in a mass of tangles and a frown on her face.

"I'm pretty sure when you dropped me off after midnight last night we didn't make plans for anything before noon." She yawns and steps back to let him in.

"Hi to you, too."

"Hi," she replies, leaving him to shut the door himself and crawling back into bed. She pulls her pillow over her face when the mattress sinks below her hip as West sits down.

"I wanted the whole day with my girl," West tells her sweetly as he plucks the pillow from her hands. "You're still not a morning person, huh?"

Jules groans and rolls to her back, looking up at West's smile. "Do you have coffee in that bag of yours?"

"No."

"Then, no. I am still not a morning person."

West laughs at her as she closes her eyes. "Come on, gorgeous, get up and get dressed and we'll go get you some coffee." He tugs on her arm and Jules sits forward reluctantly. She leans against his back and rests her head on his shoulder.

"How are you awake so early on a Sunday? And so…"

"Functioning?" He chuckles. "I get one day a week with you, baby. I'm making the most of it."

Those words wake Jules up as effectively as a cold bucket of water. "One day?"

"Hear me out?"

"What do you mean one day?"

"Jules?" West scoots back some to a more comfortable position and Jules can better see his face now. He doesn't look happy about what he has to say and she begins to worry he's going to backslide. He's going to run, again.

She shakes her head as she slides back against the wall and brings her knees to her chest. "West, I can't do this back and forth thing. Don't tell me you're scared of screwing up again. I swear you will not like what happens if you pull that line with me."

He laughs and Jules wants to punch him for making light of her concern.

"Buffy, no, baby. I… look, Carson and I were talking and he made me realize something the other night that I hadn't thought of." Jules considers punching Carson as West takes a deep breath.

"A year ago we rushed into a relationship after the tornado and while it was as close to perfect as it could possibly be on the outside, we both know there were a lot of things wrong with it. Not the relationship, but us. I don't want us to mess this up this time. I want to date you. To win you back the right way."

Jules relaxes a little. "You've already won me back."

"I have, but I haven't. First of all, you ran to me. I'm thoroughly pissed at myself for not being to one to run to you. I have a lot to make up, love."

"I thought we agreed we were putting that in the past."

"Yeah? Kinda like you just did? The moment I hesitated and asked you to listen to me you jumped to the conclusion that I was scared." West points out and Jules feels guilty.

"Sometimes you can't quiet the monsters in your head," she quotes and West grins, immediately recognizing the words from one of his letters.

"No fair, using my own words against me."

"You're right, though. I'm sorry. I shouldn't have jumped to conclusions. We need to let the past go if we're going to move forward."

"Our past will make us stronger, Jules. You and I, we're going to be invincible."

She smiles at his sweet words and then frowns at a new thought. "Speaking of past, my dad and I need to have a conversation." West doesn't reply so she continues. "I can't believe he didn't tell me the whole truth, West. They knew what your leaving did to me and they said nothing."

He stares thoughtfully at the wall opposite them, the painted cinder block is covered by a collage of pictures and Jules can almost see the wheels spinning in his head.

"I had a lot of time to think about this when I was at Crestdale. Try not to be too hard on them. Your dad only did what he thought was best. He was protecting you."

"By hurting you? That's not acceptable and he hurt me, too."

"Jules, I was mad at first. My own father practically had me committed to a loony bin." Jules gasps in horror at the mental picture she receives at his words and West chuckles. "I'm kidding, babe. It wasn't that bad, not really. My point is I needed help and if it wasn't for your dad I don't know if I would have gotten it. I'll agree it was a little extreme of both of our fathers, but look at us now."

He picks her hand up from her lap and kisses her palm. "Like I said, we're invincible." He winks.

Moving to her knees, she slides to West's side and wraps him in a sideways hug. Everything he said warms her heart enough that she decides to drop any thought of calling her parents right now. She doesn't want to ruin her reunion with West by fighting with her parents.

"So, tell me your brilliant plan. How are we going to get to see each other with our busy schedules?"

"Sundays and game days. I know it's only thirty minutes, but that's an hour back and forth for either of us and, with my practice schedule on top of school and whatever you have going on, that's too much. You need to enjoy school and your friends, too."

"So we only get weekends?"

"When we can, yes." Jules groans and he squeezes her arm that's wrapped around his waist. "We have a chance to start fresh, right? Let's take it. I'm going to call you and text you and woo you for the next three weeks. That's two away games and one home, and then playoffs, too. We'll make plans for game days or Sundays and we'll talk like teens the rest of the time."

"That kind of sucks."

"Yeah, it does, but it's kinda cool too, don't you think? Do you know how excited I was all day yesterday waiting to see you? I was a kid on Christmas morning and we'd only gone two days without seeing each other. A whole week is going to be-"

"Miserable?" she points out with a pout.

"Sweet misery, Buffy. I'm looking forward to the torture."

"Did you turn into a masochist while we were apart?"

"Maybe," he teases, wagging his dark brows.

She presses a kiss to his shoulder before falling onto her back again with a groan. "Okay, three weeks, it can't be that bad and then once the season is over we'll have more time, right?"

"Yep. And playoffs."

"And playoffs," she repeats with a smile, knowing that will add two, maybe even three more weeks to their dating woes.

Taking her by surprise, West jumps onto the bed and straddles her body underneath him. His hands situated on either side of her head as he stares into her eyes. "This is going to work, Juliet Marie.

Starting today."

She laughs at the use of her full name and leans up onto her elbows so she can press a quick kiss to his lips as he towers over her.

"So then what's on the agenda today?" she asks, looking at his clothing as he sits back on his legs and she works her way out from under him. He's wearing gym shorts and a football tee and Jules gets a little nervous.

"Today, we get a little bit of everything." He hops off the bed and picks up his bag on the floor producing a protein bar and bottled water. "Fuel up, babe. We're going for a workout and then I thought we would spend the day at the lake."

"I'm excited by the lake part, but a workout?"

"Yep. Austin told me he helped you with your workouts so I figured I would pick up his slack and keep you in shape."

"And this is what you call a win-Jules-back date?" she points out sarcastically.

"No, Buffy, you said I've already won you. This is a take care of my girl date."

"Touche'."

They spend the morning jogging and then competing with each other on the circuit equipment at a local park. West pushes her to be better and faster with every snarky comment he makes and Jules rises to the challenge. When they're wiped out physically they head to the lake an hour away, eat street tacos from a food truck, and lay on the shore all afternoon. They agree, for today, to talk about good things. West tells her about football, his plans to start for A&M next year, and about Mindy and Carson's New Year's Eve wedding.

"So, I'm asking you now. What are you doing New Year's Eve?"

She scrunches her face, trying to look thoughtful as she playfully responds, "Hmmm, let's see. This is the 4th of October sooo, we have roughly three months and I don't usually plan -" Her rambling is interrupted by West grabbing her waist and tickling her.

"Gah!" She laughs and falls back on the blanket they're using.

West rolls over her and continues to dig his hand into the curve of her hip, right where she is most tender while he asks again, "What are you doing for New Year's Eve, Buffy?"

She bucks at him trying to fight him off, but he is too strong for her and all too soon she is giving in.

"Okay, okay. I'm going to a wedding with you," she cries, her breath coming in gasps as his tickle assault continues. "I wouldn't want to be anywhere else."

"Are you sure?" He asks slowly, his eyes narrowing, his lips fighting against the pull to smile.

"Positive." His hands still and she takes a deep breath, looking at his face above hers. "You can have all of my days, West. As long as you want them."

West's brown eyes soften and he lowers his face inches from hers. "How about forever?"

"You can have it."

"Good answer," he whispers into her mouth as their lips touch.

"One twelve hour day a week isn't nearly enough time with you," Jules complains as she's talking to West two weeks later.

She's only been able to see him once in two weeks due to an away game this past Saturday that kept him out of town until late. Tomorrow's game is away as well, meaning they will have one more day to be miserable. As much as they both wanted to sneak in a visit or two during the week, they'd had midterms to study for. So they kept to the plan he'd offered and spent last Sunday together all day, just as the one before and just like they plan to do this weekend.

"I know, Buff. A few more weeks and then I'm all yours. All the time."

Jules can hear the exhaustion in his voice. He's been working three times as hard as he was before, trying to prove to the coaches at A&M he's ready.

"All the time, huh? You mean until spring camp and then summer camp."

"Would you want me to quit?" he asks out of the blue.

"No! How could you even think that?" she jumps at him immediately. "West, don't you dare ever quit football again! You love it."

"I do, but I -"

"Nope! Don't even say it. I would never ask that of you. Football is part of who you are and I love it."

He doesn't answer and she listens, hearing his deep even breathing. "West?" she asks. "West!" she says a little louder and he grunts.

"Hmmm? Oh, babe, I'm sorry. I need to get to sleep. This week has been killer and the bus ride was crap."

"Nooo, I'm sorry. I should have let you go a long time ago. Get some sleep, Number Twelve. I'll be checking in for updates, so you better bring your A game. I love you."

"I love you, too. Night, gorgeous."

They hang up and Jules falls to her bed thinking of Sunday morning when West will show up at her door with some sort of amazing surprise date for her. She can't wait to see him. Sunday's have become the best day of the week.

Twenty-Seven

<u>West</u>

There is nothing more appealing to West than the sight of Jules when she is laughing. He is standing in the large backyard of the Sigma fraternity house watching Jules as she plays volleyball with her friends, Jeff, and several others. He can't help but smile. Two weeks ago he'd been trying to force himself to let her go and now here they are. It's one a.m., he's wiped out from a hard played game and a long, hot bus ride home, and yet here is he at a frat party because he couldn't stand not seeing her for another seven hours.

"You're so whipped," he mumbles to himself, shaking his head and heading towards the court.

He navigates the groups of party goers with expert ease, dodging the groups he's sure will try to stop and talk to him and giving others brief waves and nods. His internal GPS is set to Jules and nothing will detour him from that course. When the game is between serves, he sneaks to the back side of the pit, holding his hand up to wave off anyone from giving him away as he rushes Jules. Grabbing her by the waist, West picks her up and swings her around as she squeals.

"Room for one more?" he asks, laughing as Jules recognizes him.

"West!"

Jules spins, jumping up and into his arms the moment he places her bare feet in the sand; her sand-covered hands grasp his neck and pull his lips to hers.

"We're in the middle of a game, Romeo. Take your girl off the court."

Recognizing Jeff's voice, West lifts his hand and flips his best friend off as he tightens his grip on Jules to move them out of the way.

"Mmm, no," Jules finally moans breaking their kiss. "We're in the middle of a match. Play with us," she invites as he sets her down for the second time.

"No couples on a team!" Katie calls from across the net.

West smiles at Jules and looks around at the others playing. It's a mix of football players, frat boys, Jess, Katie, and a few other girls he doesn't know who stare back at him curiously.

"Do you mind?" he asks nobody in particular.

"Come on, Rutledge, get over here so we can finish kicking their ass."

"Oh? So I'm going over to the winning team then? Cool," he teases, winking at Jules as he ducks under the net and puts himself opposite of her spot.

"Not for long, Spike."

He chuckles at her game face and gives her back a good gamely ribbing. "Yeah, babe. All five foot four inches of you at the net totally intimidates me."

"Game on, Twelve."

The ball is served from behind his head, flying across the net where a tall blonde sets it for Jeff who jumps and tries to use his power to spike it. Unfortunately for him, West is there to jump up and block his aim.

"Denied!" he taunts as the ball deflects to the sand and West's team wins a point.

West's team rotates and Katie is up to serve. The ball barely makes it over the net where Jess is stationed.

"Gah!" she yells as she brings her hands up to volley, missing the ball completely causing a shirtless frat boy to dive into the sand at her feet. He catches the ball before it hits the sand, sending it flying backwards and straight into Jeff who is ready and waiting for it.

"Jules!" he shouts as he hits it up lightly in her direction and West grins as he watches Jules move.

Her tan legs spring from the ground, and her long arm shoots forward, the slap of her palm making contact with the ball ringing out. The volleyball slices through the air and *SMACK!* knocks West right in the head before he even thinks to move. The move causes his team to groan and Jules' team to laugh and high-five.

Jules gasps, covering her mouth, but not before he sees a smile.

"You all right there, QB?" asks Scott, a tight end for A&M, as he picks the ball up and tosses it to Jules' side.

Jules mouths 'sorry' while he shakes the sand from his face and nods ruefully. "Yeah, just got distracted by a sexy little number, won't happen again. Sorry, guys."

The game goes on, West's team is clearly the more superior team with more ballplayers on their side. For the most part, the game is a contest between the guys to serve aces or spike the ball. The girls, on the other hand, tend to shuffle in the sand; set the ball; or, in the case of Jess, scream when it flies at them. Jules impresses him, though. Each time she's in position she sets, spikes, or volleys perfectly. Her serves are strong and she never cowers when going for a play. He's had to restrain himself twice as he's watched her throw herself to the ground to save a point. When Jeff knocks her to her knees hard as they both go for the ball he finally breaks.

"Dude, save it for the NFL!" West yells, ducking under the net and pushing Jeff aside as he tries to help Jules up.

"Chill out -" Jeff replies, throwing his hands up and taking a step back.

"Chill out? You want my ass to plow into Katie and see how you feel?"

"West!" Jules snaps.

She's helping herself up since he was too busy arguing with Jeff to actually offer her a hand. Her face is red and angry. Very, very angry. Brushing the sand from her legs, she pushes at West's chest with a grunt.

"Get on your side."

A smile breaks on his face at her feisty attitude and he moves to argue back at her, but thinks better of it when she narrows her eyes at him. Grateful the rest of the players are cutting up with each other and paying little attention to the skirmish, he moves back to his side of the net. Jeff taps Jules' hip and West watches her turn, her brows raised as Jeff speaks a few low words to her. She nods with a smile, turning back to the game.

Three more points are scored for his team with little fuss and the match is won.

"Drinks on JP!" one of the veteran players calls out as they high-five each other and make their way to the large bar set up under a newly constructed pavilion on the property.

West stops Jeff before he leaves the court. "Hey, I shouldn't have jumped on you. Sorry, man."

"She's tough, bro. It's all good."

West hangs back as Jules talks with two girls from her team and waits for them to leave before he approaches her. She hasn't looked his way since she snapped at him and, while her anger is adorable, he doesn't want to fight. He's tired, more so after playing half a volleyball match, and wants to bring her to the nearest empty bed, snuggle up, and sleep.

"Hey, tiger. Quite a performance there. Sure you don't want to go out for the team?" he teases, hoping to bring back her smile. He's rewarded with an icy glare. "Okay… clearly you're not amused."

She looks about, stepping into the grass and brushing her feet off to slip on her flip-flops. He follows her closely, causing her to bump into his chest when she turns back to him. His hands grasp at her wrists as she sighs heavily and steps back looking up at him.

"*Clearly,* you think I'm made of porcelain."

"No. *Clearly,* I worry about you too much. I'm sorry; I was a prick to Jeff. I apologized."

"And to me?" she asks pointedly.

"Baby -" he looks down at her with his hands pulling her wrists into his chest. She shakes her head as a small grin appears.

"Oh no you don't, West Rutledge. You do not get to 'baby' me. I'm a big girl. I don't need you going all caveman on me because a friend bumps into me. Your best friend, I might add."

"I know."

"I'm not made of glass and I can take care of myself, you know. I've grown a lot. I'm not the -"

She rambles and West swoops down, stopping her words with his mouth. He doesn't linger or try to kiss her deeply; he presses one hard, long kiss to her firm lips and then pulls away. She's still glaring at him, but the angry bluster is gone and he gives her a little smile before speaking again.

"Jules, it is two in the morning, I'm worn out and I do not want to stand here fighting with you, baby."

"Oh my gosh. I sound like such a shrew. I'm sorry." Jules pouts, propping her chin on his chest and looking up with her big puppy dog eyes. "You came to surprise me and I sound so ungrateful."

She rubs her cheek against his shirt and allows him to move her arms around his back before he lets go and hugs her with his own. Glancing around, she sees that the majority of the party has moved to the pavilion now. There are a few groups sitting around in chairs and a small group of guys shooting hoops, but for the most part they are alone where they stand.

"God, I missed you. I'm so glad you came."

"I was kinda banking on you letting me stay with you tonight. I'd never make it home." Uncertainty flicks across her face when he mentions staying the night and he quickly amends his statement. "I can stay with Jeff, it's fine."

"No. I don't, that is… I want you to stay with me, it's just that -" she stops and he chuckles.

"Buff, I'm talking sleep. That's it. Remember we are taking this slow. I wouldn't have the energy anyway."

She giggles, "Really?"

"Hell no, not really! Do you know how hard it was for me to not jump across that net and drag you into a dark corner? Every time you went for that ball, you were sexy as hell. I'm amazed you only nailed me once," he complains, and Jules laughs again, the sound music to his ears. "My point is, I want you, but we aren't ready for that. We're doing everything right this time."

"Let's put you to bed, Number Twelve. You look ready to fall."

West agrees whole heartedly, letting her go and rubbing his sore neck muscles as his body starts to protest from the few hard hits he took today on the field.

"I'm so excited. I get all these extra hours with you." Jules smiles as they start for the front of the house. "Oh! Let me run and tell Katie, though. Maybe she could bunk with the girls or Jeff."

"No worries, babe. I already cleared things. She's staying with Jeff tonight."

Her face scrunches up, one smooth and perfectly arched brow lifting. "You totally planned this out, huh?"

"Maybe." He shrugs. "It was an eight hour bus ride, I had a lot of time to think about you and how much I miss you during the week." He tugs her back into his arms lightly and hovers near her ear. "I spent a lot of time thinking about kissing you for hours and hours, and hearing your little gasps when I touch this spot right here," he teases, lightly touching the sensitive spot under her ear with his tongue.

She doesn't disappoint him as she sucks in her breath and lowers his hand, pressing against her lower back tightly. "So yea, gorgeous, I made some plans. I hope you don't mind my being so presumptuous."

"You can be presumptuous all you want if it means I get to be with you," she whispers hotly against his cheek.

"I'm never letting you go again, Jules," he murmurs and rubs up against her. "Damn it, we need to go."

Jules laughs at the tension in West's voice. "Yes, I think we definitely should."

Twenty-Eight

West

They're barely out of the elevator before West picks her up and carries her towards her room, her legs wrapped around his waist and her lips leaving trails of hot kisses along his jaw, neck, and collar bone.

"Keys?" he orders, his fingers digging into her backside.

"Oh no!" Jules sits back and West has to throw her against the door before she falls backwards. "I didn't bring a key. Katie had her purse."

He jiggles the handle to verify it's locked and bites his lip to keep from laughing at their predicament. His shorts are sporting a very noticeable bulge, his girlfriend's heavenly body is wrapped around him and begging for a little attention, and he's locked out of the only room with a bed he can get into unless they want to drive thirty minutes.

"Well, damn." he mutters, meeting her hot gaze and laughing.

Her face brightens and she slaps his arm. "Cassie! Next door. She should be here."

"I should probably put you down then," he teases and presses her back to the door, kissing her soundly before letting her legs slide to the ground. "Stay in front of me though, unless you want Cassie to get a look at my excitement."

Jules' face goes crimson as she glances between them; the corners of her mouth turn up into a smile as her hands adjust her skewed shirt.

"Proud of yourself, huh?"

"Maybe a little," she shrugs playfully. She moves to slide out from between him and the door and West pulls her back against his chest. One hand presses against her lower abdomen while the other wraps around her shoulder across her chest.

His face skims her neck and he takes a deep breath of her scent in. She's a mixture of sweat, flowers, beach, and the same strawberry shampoo he smelled on her in the seventh grade. "You just wait until I get you in that bed, Buffy. Payback is hell, baby."

He feels her body go limp against him as she tilts her head to the side, allowing his lips access to kiss on her neck.

"Just sleeping, huh?"

"Well, maybe a little fun." He flicks his tongue on her neck once and lets her go, smacking her butt as she hurries to Cassie and Jess' door.

Jules knocks on the door as West comes up behind her and pulls her back in front of him. As tired as he is, he can't stop touching her and he props his chin on the top of her head as Jules knocks again.

"Cassie, it's Jules," she whisper shouts, her lips close to the door.

A moment later, Cassie opens the door. West had met her briefly three weeks ago at his game, but since then he hasn't seen her. She's wearing an oversized tee shirt and yoga pants. Her dark hair is piled on the top of her head the way Jules wears hers when she's hanging out and West can see a computer sitting on the bed in the room behind her.

"Um, hey?" she says awkwardly, looking at them standing before her at two-thirty in the morning.

"Did we wake you? I didn't have a key, so sorry," Jules apologizes, stepping into the room and pulling West with her.

"No. I was just, um…" she glances at her computer. "I was

watching a movie. By myself on a Saturday night."

"Is that a Bourne movie?" West asks when he spies a paused scene he recognizes.

"Yeah. I might have a thing for kick ass movies."

"That's cool. You know, I think the first was my favorite, but the fight scenes in the second, man-"

"West, hun. You want to stay and watch the movie?" Jules asks, tugging on his hand as she crosses the room.

He flashes a smile at Cassie before heading through the bathroom and into Jules' and Katie's room. Behind him, Jules apologizes to Cassie for bothering her again and he hears the click of a door. She pokes her head into her dark room as West fiddles around for the switch on her bedside lamp.

"Hey, I'm gonna wash up real quick."

The light clicks on and West finds himself standing in Jules' room alone. He looks at the items on the table next to her bed and smiles when he sees her notebook and pencil sitting there, recalling how she kept the same one by her bed back home. She'd told him once that she was a doodler and her mind would wander at night and drawing or writing would help calm her so she could sleep. The toilet flushes in the bathroom and he hears the water turn on; he figures he only has a minute, but he wonders if it's still there.

Picking up the flower covered spiral notebook, he flips through the first few pages, smiling at her pictures and bold writing. A few pages in he finds what he's looking for and the reaction he has surprises him.

The click of the bathroom door opening startles him and he drops the notebook like a guilty thief, stepping back.

"My turn."

"What were you doing?" she asks, looking at her desk and then him as she pulls out her ponytail.

"Nothing. Just standing here, looking at your room." He shrugs and she tells him to feel free to shower off if he wants.

"I don't want sand in my bed."

West nods and cleans up quickly, stripping off his clothes and shaking his boxers and shorts in the shower before rinsing off. After he squeezes a bit of toothpaste onto his finger and runs it over his teeth, he opens the door with his shirt in his hand and finds her sitting cross-legged on the bed.

She's changed into a small tank top that clings to her curves in the most appetizing way and a checkered pair of shorts. The copper hair he loves so much is pulled to the side leaving one shoulder uncovered and begging for a kiss; suddenly West starts to think it was ridiculous for him to assume he could sleep with her and not *sleep* with her. He's about to suggest he sleep on Katie's bed for her own safety when he realizes she has her notebook sitting in front of her.

"Jules?"

"You were looking at my notebook?" she asks, looking up at him with those crystal blue eyes.

"Busted," he confesses.

He drops his shirt on the chair and gets into her bed. Moving to lie against the wall, he props his head on his elbow and looks at her. "Sorry?"

"Oh, I'm not mad at you. I just, why did you lie to me? It's only my random stuff." She flips to the back of the almost full notebook and points at the little stick drawings, happy faces, and flowers she's drawn. "I did these when I got back the night we made up."

She flips the page to one covered in hearts with arrows and his name scrolled everywhere. He sits up next to her and smiles at her pictures.

"You want to know what I was looking at?" he asks, pushing her hair off her shoulder so he can see her face. She nods and he flips to the front of the notebook; back to the page he was looking at previously.

Her head snaps to look at him. He's turned to a page with a

loose piece of paper tucked in place. The paper is covered with three words that evoke immediate pain in him. 'Who Am I?'

"Remember the night we went out for your birthday? You were getting ready and I felt so bad because I'd lost my phone and you told me to leave Carson's number in your notebook?" he asks and her eyes register the memory.

"It… you left it in here. It's in the front," she tells him.

"Yeah. When I did, this paper fell out. Look at it, Jules."

She frowns sadly. "I was being eaten by guilt over Tanya and I felt as if I'd lost myself."

"I know, baby. Look at it," he says again, handing her the sheet. Her fingers tremble as they reach for the paper and she studies it. A tear eases down her cheek and he forces himself to not hold her.

He doesn't have to watch her search the page to know when she sees what he is showing her. Her gasp gives her away and her hand covers her mouth in a small sob.

"When?" she asks, turning to him, her eyes brimming with unshed tears.

"That night," he admits, taking the paper from her and looking at it.

In one corner of the paper she had written in large print 'Who Am I?" and underneath it he'd responded:

You Are Mine
~W

He tucks the paper in the notebook and tosses it gently to the floor.

"I never saw it. I wish I had."

"Me too. I wanted you to know exactly who you were, but I was wrong."

"How so?"

"You're not mine, Buffy. I don't own you any more than you

own me, and I think that's where we went wrong the first time. We were bound to erupt eventually. We were too hot, too loaded with guilt and regret… and pain." She smiles, scooting down and pulling him with her so they were lying side by side.

"You're not that girl anymore. You are the strong, confident Jules Blacklin from before the storm. The one I fell in love with after I kissed her in the closet at a party. And I sure as hell am not that scared boy, not most of the time anyway."

Her hand brushes the naked skin of his torso as they look at each other. Her nails teasing up and down his side completely turning him on.

"I get what you're saying, but I want you to know I am yours." He tries to disagree and she presses her finger to his lips. "Shhh. I am yours, West. I've only ever been yours and I will always be yours. You're my anchor. Even in the bad times, when you were gone and I wanted to dissolve into a puddle of nothing because you'd left me alone… no, don't look so sad," she urges when her words tear at his soul. "You were my anchor. I used the thought of you to pull me up. Every hard moment in physical therapy, every sad song, and sappy romantic movie, everything that reminded me of you only gave me motivation. I was going to show you I could be okay again."

"Baby, you are more than okay and I don't know what I did to deserve you. But I'll be damned if I'm letting you go now."

"It'll be a cold day in hell before you lose me again, Spike."

Gripping his side, Jules rolls to her back and pulls him on top of her. Their mouths meet and sparks fly as they both give everything they have to one another. No more fear, no more doubts. This is right. This is meant to be. They are made for each other.

Twenty-Nine

Jules

"You're not peeking are you?" West asks for the tenth time in thirty minutes since they left the restaurant.

It's the Saturday night after West's last regular season game and all of the girls, including Cassie, and even Jeff were able to make it to watch since it was a late one and A&M had played at eleven that day. No one discusses the fact that Austin didn't come. Jules feels guilty, wondering if the news that she and West are back together has bothered him more than he is willing to admit. She's barely seen him over the past few weeks and West said he's been staying in the dorms so he hasn't had time with him either.

They went for a victory celebration dinner at a local burger joint afterwards and cut up for over an hour before everyone claimed fatigue and left to head back to A&M. Jules was staying with West at his house for the night.

After they'd hugged their friends goodbye and jumped in his truck, West had turned to her with that little half grin of his.

"Do you trust me?" he'd asked and she'd immediately become suspicious.

"Yee-es."

"I have a surprise for you, but you have to put this on." He produced a red bandanna and handed it to her.

"Around my neck? Are we into robbery now? Are times that desperate, Twelve?"

"No, smart alec. Over your eyes, like a blindfold."

"Oh. Duh." Jules grins and feels a little blonde at the moment. She ties the cloth around her face and sighs as he tells her not to peek.

It's been thirty minutes since they left the parking lot of the restaurant and she is thoroughly confused about where they are going or what they might be doing. Her birthday is in two days and she assumes the secrecy has something to do with that, but it's likely after midnight at this point and she can't imagine what he has planned.

The car pulls to a stop and she hears West turn the engine off. Through the fabric covering her eyes she can barely make out the glow of the interior lights as he opens and closes his door.

"Stay there and I'll come around," he warns and shuts the door.

She waits impatiently, listening for him, before he opens the door and lifts her down from the truck.

"Walk or carry?"

"Excuse me?" she asks, confused.

"Do you want to walk, blindfolded? Or do you want me to carry you?" West explains, his fingers weaving into hers and giving her a tight squeeze.

"How treacherous is the territory? I mean, am I likely to kill myself walking?"

West laughs and bumps into Jules side before she feels his arms go under her knees and around her back; suddenly she is being lifted into his arms and carried. Her arms go around his neck as she complains about his giving her a choice and then making the decision for her.

"Sorry, Buff, I wanted to carry you," he replies, kissing her cheek.

"Where in the world are we?" she asks as she listens to the surroundings in an attempt to hear something.

She hears the loud roar of a motorcycle engine in the distance, but no voices, no other cars. So they're somewhere more secluded. However, the air is silent, no bugs chirping, no sticks or leaves popping or cracking as West walks; this makes her rule out the woods or a field.

"Okay," he finally says after he's walked around for a good five minutes. He sets her down, her boots sinking into the soft ground and her hand goes to remove the blindfold. "No! Not yet!" he yells, grabbing her arm.

"West!"

"Patience, girl, patience." He pauses and she bites her tongue. "Okay, now."

He yanks the blindfold up from her head and she blinks her eyes as they automatically start watering from being covered. When they adjust to her surroundings, she is completely thrown for a loop and then utterly overwhelmed.

They're standing back in Freemont's football stadium in the dark, except for lanterns that are spread out before them on each ten-yard marker lighting the field in a romantic glow. Those and the parking lights outside of the small stadium are the only lights around.

"Oh my... West!" She fumbles with words, her free hand pressing against her chest while he holds her other one tightly. "Are you... no, are *we* going to get in trouble for being here?"

"No, I've got it covered."

"It's beautiful. The way the lights glow on the grass."

"I know it's not A&M's field and maybe I can make that happen next year, but -"

"A&M?" she gasps and then breaks into histerical laughter grabbing him and hugging him tightly. "My bucket list!"

"I can't believe you did this. It is so perfect." She feels like a little kid as she takes a few steps onto the field clapping her hands and leaving West behind.

The lights are set up closer towards the center of the field instead of on the sideline and it reminds her of a runway for a plane as she steps onto the turf at the twenty yard line. Turning, West is slowly following her and she stops walking. "Wait, how in the world did you set this up?"

He smiles wide, lifting his hand and pointing into the dark corner of the far end of the field. "I may have a little help from my friends," he confesses and Jules laughs when she spots the movement of people.

Katie, Mindy, Jess, and Cassie emerge from the darkness along with Jeff and Carson, both of them tossing footballs in the air as they walk onto the field.

"What do you say, cheerleader? How about a little four on four?"

Jules looks at the huge cheesy grin plastered on West's face and can't help but run into his arms and kiss him.

"Game on, Twelve."

They decide to play boys against girls, and even with a one player advantage it really is no match. At five-six, Jess is the tallest of the girls and, despite all their years of watching football, none of them can stop the guys when West throws rockets across the field to Carson and Jeff.

"Dude! I've missed this." Jeff shouts at West as he hauls another ball in for a touchdown. The guys' high-five each other, hooting and hollering, as Jules and Katie fall to the ground, exhausted at trying to cover Jeff.

"New rule!" Mindy calls out, pushing into Carson as he taunts her. "No more throwing."

"What? No throwing!" Jeff and Carson argue and Jess and Cassie join Mindy in the argument.

"Come on, this is way unfair."

Jules is lying on the ground looking up at the clear night sky when West's hand comes into view. Reaching up, she lets him pull her to her feet and into a tight hug.

"You done, princess?" he teases as he kisses the tip of her nose and she shakes her head ruefully as he lets her go.

"Ok, new plan. Touch football. No passes, no hard tackles, but you can do a shovel pass." West calls out as they regroup in the center of the field.

"Shovel pass?" Cassie, the only football rookie on the field, asks. The guys snicker and Katie knocks Jeff in the gut.

"It's like an underhand toss," West explains as he steps back and demonstrates, passing to the ball to Jules. They throw out a few more rules and break.

The girls huddle and Jess decides to take charge. "Okay, ladies. We've got this now. Mindy cover Carson, Katie, you get Jeff. Jules and I will center and snap it to Cassie." She looks at Cassie whose eyes bulge. "You then pass it to whichever one of us isn't covered and we'll go from there."

"We'll go from there? That's your game plan?" asks Katie.

"We've moved the ball five yards in ten plays. Yes, if we can actually get it to an open player then 'we'll go from there.'"

"Come on girls, the night's not getting any younger." Jeff taunts.

They line up, Mindy and Katie across from Carson and Jeff, West directly center across from Jules and Jess, and Cassie lined up behind them. Jess snaps the ball to Cassie and they all start moving. West runs for Jules, immediately covering her as if they are playing basketball, so she can't break away.

"Ahhh, you butt," she says as she tries to outwit him and get around his large body.

Her eyes dart to her left where, somehow, Katie and Jeff have ended up tangled together on the ground and to her right where she sees Cassie throw a little underhand pass to Jess - who is wide open. When she passes the line of scrimmage, Carson shouts out as Mindy trips him and throws herself into his body knocking him off course. The stadium echoes with the sound of laughter as Jess runs and the guys try to detangle themselves from the girls to go after her.

West's trick to keep Jules occupied backfires on him as he tries to turn away and she blocks his path. It's either steamroll her or give up and Jules banks on him being a gentlemen.

She underestimates him.

Laughing at her as she counters his steps, he turns and runs backwards before cutting back up the field and Jules can't catch up. He is fast and soon he's tackling Jess softly to the ground.

"Not fair!" Jules complains, running up behind him. "Your Coach would kill you if he saw you backpedaling like that."

"Only if I had the ball," he points out as he helps Jess up. "Plus, it's only back if you don't make the play and, as you saw, I made the play. Sorry, baby." He winks and ruffles her hair as he lines up with the guys again.

Using a few dirty tricks, tripping, holding, and sexual innuendos included, the girls are able to take few more snaps and move the ball to the twenty yard line. They're now eying a touchdown and, as they huddle, they strategize for one last big play.

"Quarterback sneak?" Jules suggests and Katie nods.

"Football For Dummies, please." Cassie reminds them and they explain.

Getting into formation with Cassie snapping to Jules and the other three covering the guys, Jules shouts playfully, mocking West's audible, "Hut, fifteen, Pizza, twenty-four, chocolate, twelve!"

Cassie snaps the ball and Jules runs to the left and makes a break for the goal line as the girls do everything in their power to stop the guys. Carson breaks free of Mindy and tries to catch her, but it's too late and she crosses the line as his hand skims the fabric of her shirt causing the girls to scream for joy.

"Yes!" Jules hollers, spiking the ball and dancing as the guys watch and clap reluctantly.

"We actually scored?" Cassie asks as they dance in circles, hugging like little girls.

"We did," Jules confirms hugging her football-hopeless friend. Her eyes connect with West's over Cassie's shoulder and she smiles at him as he looks on.

Then she is reminded of her bucket list and her ramblings from once upon a time and she steps away, leans back, and wobbles.

"Ow, ow," West cat calls as she lifts her arms and shakes her hips with all she's got.

Katie joins in, followed by the others, and soon they're all singing 'wobble baby, wobble baby, wobble baby, wobble', dancing and laughing.

"Water break!" Katie announces and the touchdown celebration ends.

"Another item's off the list, huh?" West asks as he joins Jules and pulls her into his side.

She stops, letting their friends and family go ahead of them, and wraps her arms around him. "Thank you for this." He shakes his head and she forges on. "No, don't shake me off. I know game days are exhausting for you and I know you'd probably rather have me all to yourself, but this…" She looks around again and sentimental tears flood her eyes. "This is amazing and I love you for it."

"First, there is nothing I'd rather do than put a smile on your face, Buff, tired or not. Second, I'm gonna have you alone all night and into the day tomorrow, so you might say I'm pretty pleased I get to have my cake and eat it, too. And last, but not least, we aren't done here."

"We're not?"

"You scored yourself a touchdown, cheerleader, now do you think you can kick an extra point?" he challenges her, pointing at the uprights.

"Ummm, I took off my boots, remember?" she reminds him, lifting her barefoot in the air.

"Well, go put them back on and I'll show you how it's done."

Jules complies, stopping to grab a water bottle as she fetches her boots, and returns to West's side near the five-yard hashtag.

"Five?" she asks with a frown, dropping to the turf to slide on her socks and boots. Extra points are typically kicked from the ten-yard line.

"I figured I'd make it a little easier. It's not as easy as it looks, babe." He laughs at her as he waves Jeff over. "Hey, Jeff, come hold for me."

Jules cracks open her water bottle and watches as Jeff spots the ball and West attempts a goal. He takes his time meticulously stepping back six steps and then three to the side before he moves forward and kicks the ball. It sails in a pretty little spiral up and over the goal post; West raises his arms in the typical referee signal.

"Ace." Jeff shouts, jogging to get the ball.

"Damn, you're such a show off, little brother."

West and Jules both turn to find Austin coming across the field, his hands in his pockets. West grins and meets his brother half way and they hug, slapping each other on the backs. She sees Austin say something to West before they part and Austin walks to Jules side. West hangs back for a moment, allowing them time to speak.

"Hey," says Austin.

"Hey, yourself. I'm glad you're here." She looks him over before adding honestly, "I've missed you."

She's not sure how that will go over with West, but she can't deny she's missed Austin's friendship. He stares back at her in silence only breaking when Jeff makes his way back.

"Hey, man," he nods to Austin and looks at West. "Dude, the ball sailed. Maybe you should walk on as special teams?"

"Are you crazy? They are going to be begging him to play QB," Jules argues, giving Jeff a dirty look.

"That's my cheerleader," West laughs, rejoining the group

"Rutledge boys at A&M, it's tradition." Carson chimes in as he joins the group and punches Austin in the arm. "Sup, brah."

Jules rolls her eyes as Austin punches back and the guys all start rough housing and talking smack.

"I thought I was getting a lesson here?" she finally asks, throwing herself in the middle of their pile.

The girls walk up and Katie grabs the back of Jeff's shirt and pulls him back. "Hey, I want one, too."

"Well, West is the only one who can kick so he can play tutor."

"Really?" asks Mindy as she reaches their group with Cassie in tow. "Baby, you can't make a field goal?" She looks at Carson and he groans.

"Baby, field goals are typically kicked from thirty yards or further. So, no. I can't. I don't even think West can make that distance. Extra-point kicks are easier -"

"And no, he can't make those kicks, either." Austin interrupts, looking at Mindy with a laugh.

"Neither can you, you shit." Carson throws back at him, but Austin doesn't notice.

His laughter dies the moment he looks Mindy's way and he's frozen, his face clearly surprised.

"Hey," he says and all eyes follow his. He is staring at Cassie, who is chewing on the side of her lip

"Hi. What are you doing here?" she asks.

"What am I doing here? I'm West's brother. What are you doing here?"

"Wait! Have you two not met? Seriously?" Jess asks, looking between Austin and Cassie.

"I never introduced you two." Jules offers, stepping to Austin's side. She looks at Cassie, "You were never around. Cassie, this is Austin. Austin this is Cassie, Jess' roommate."

"Cassie," he repeats and his lips form into a smile.

"Yeah," she says shortly with a smile of her own and Jules can feel the tension in the air. Evidently, the others can too because Katie grabs Jeff and pushes Jess away.

"Come on, West, show us how to kick. Mindy? Carson?" she calls and everyone walks away slowly.

"Did you come to play ball?" Cassie asks Austin.

"Yeah, I did. I had some other things going on earlier, but I hated to miss West's big surprise for Jules so I took a chance." He looks at Jules. "Sorry, I couldn't be here earlier."

She shakes her head. "You two have obviously met before, you seem surprised to see each other."

"*Cassie*," Austin says, putting emphasis on her name, "and I have met, at the library. Although I didn't know her name and so I had no idea she was your roommate. Small world."

"That it is," Jules agrees.

"Yep. Excuse me, I'm gonna go learn to kick that ball." Cassie says, giving Jules an apologetic smile. She leaves without glancing at Austin again and the moment she is out of hearing range Jules jumps on him.

"What did you do to her?" she hisses softly so her voice doesn't carry.

"Nothing! I swear. I helped her at the library one day and then -"

She gasps as the word *library* hits her. "She's the girl, the one you mentioned? How did you not know her name, it's been weeks? And she never mentioned you to me!"

"We haven't exchanged names. I got the feeling she hates jocks so I never told her who I was and she refused to tell me. She thinks I'm cocky."

"No kidding, you?"

"Ha, ha," he deadpans.

"You're right, by the way, she doesn't like jocks. Actually she's not a big fan of guys in general."

Austin's face tightens, "Why?"

"I don't really know."

"Jules, get yourself over here so I can show you how it's done," West calls.

"You and I are going to talk about Cassie later," Jules points out, grabbing his arm and pulling him along with her.

"Hey, Jules, I need you to know one thing," Austin says and he stops walking and looks at her seriously. "I'm not upset about us. I am thrilled for both you and West, okay? You're meant to be together and I'm good with that."

"You're one of my best friends, Austin," Jules whispers, throwing her arms around him. "I was scared things would change. You stopped coming around and barely answered my messages."

"No, candy girl. I love you and I love West. Nothing is going to change. I just needed a few weeks."

"I get that," Jules agrees, letting him go and giving him a look. "So, I bet I can get more goals than you."

"Ha! You're on," he agrees and they rejoin their friends.

Despite the cool demeanor of Cassie towards Austin for the remainder of the night, Jules has the time of her life. Surprisingly, she makes one field goal and Austin makes none. She can happily knock another item off her bucket list and she has bragging rights over a Rutledge boy; life is sweet.

As they drive away from the stadium with her hand in West's, she's struck by how much her life has changed again. This time for the better.

"I'm so happy," she mutters when they're almost to the house.

West kisses her knuckles and shoots a smile her way.

"I didn't think I'd be this happy again after the storm."

"I'm happy, too. I never thought I'd find a love like this."

"Isn't that a song?" she teases and West laughs.

"If it is, I wasn't quoting it. Seriously. After my mom died, I didn't want to attach myself to anyone. You changed that for me."

"I really need you to stop saying such amazing things to me, Rutledge. You're going to spoil me."

The truck pulls into the driveway of the house West shares with his brothers and he turns to her, his face dead serious. "Let me spoil you then, because I will never get tired of telling you how much I love you," he says, leaning over the middle console and touching her hair.

"And I will never get tired of hearing you tell me how much you love me," she replies, pressing a light kiss to his lips. "Nor will I ever get tired of *showing* you how much I love you," she says suggestively and West's eyes darken with passion at her words.

Coming around the truck, he carries her into the house, nodding at Mindy and Carson who are standing in the kitchen talking while Jules laughs and covers her face in embarrassment. West takes her straight to his room where he drops her on his bed.

"Show me," he orders, his voice hoarse with desire as he leans over her.

"My pleasure, Number Twelve. My pleasure."

Thirty

<u>West</u>

"Rise and shine, princess." West rubs his nose along Jules' neck and kisses along the smooth curve.

Jules gives a half moan, half sigh as she stretches and her fingers move into the hair at the base of his neck holding him close as she moves her body closer to his.

"Sleeeeep," she grumbles, burying her face into his shoulder. "Wait, why aren't you in bed?" she asks sleepily as she realizes he is on top of the sheets.

"We've got things to do, love. We're celebrating your birthday today."

"Can't we lay here all day and celebrate?"

His mind contemplates the pleasure he would take in that. "Don't you want breakfast? I thought we'd get pancakes and then I have a surprise for you."

Her longs fingers play with his hair as her lips start to kiss on his bare shoulder. He's lying alongside of her and she finds his hand on her hip and pulls it up, guiding it under the thin sheet covering her body and placing it on her warm naked curves.

"I can skip breakfast, if you can," she whispers and she pushes his hand lower.

"Well hell, I guess we can do brunch," West moans, pulling the sheet down to her waist.

"Or linner," Jules purrs.

"Dunch."

"Yes, we'll do dunch." She laughs before his lips crash into hers.

Once they are showered and dressed a few hours later, they grab lunch at a deli and West surprises her with his idea for the day.

"You can totally say no to this, okay?"

Popping an olive from the salad bar in her mouth she smiles, "Okay."

"Dani wants to meet you."

"Dani? Oh, Dani!" Jules sits up and West holds back a smile as he watches her look down at her clothes and fiddle with her hair.

"You're gorgeous," he reminds her, reaching across the table and grabbing her hand mid-primp.

"But, I'm not dressed to meet her and, oh wow." She breathes in and takes a long sip of her iced tea. "The thought makes me incredibly nervous."

"Babe, we don't have to. It's your day. I just, Dani called the other day to wish me good luck for the game and to ask about you, of course. She mentioned they were having visitor hours this weekend and it got me thinking."

"I'd love to meet her."

"Are you sure?" he asks, searching her face for any hesitation. When she agrees, they finish their lunches quickly and hit the road.

Crestdale Victory Center is located outside of Houston, a little less than two hours away from A&M. The drive flies by as they sing along to the radio and talk about random things.

"I can't believe you were this close to Tyler the whole time and I didn't know."

The comment comes out of nowhere and West debates on discussing it or dropping it. Before he can make a choice, Jules drops another bomb.

"Hey, my parents want me to come home next weekend. They were pretty ticked I didn't come this weekend for my birthday and I didn't want to have it out with them by phone, so I blew them off. But, I should go, if for no other reason than to see Jase."

She sounds as if she is asking for his thoughts and he has to bite back how he feels about her seeing her mom and dad and telling them they are together. He trusts Jules but he worries her parents, or her dad specifically, might try to bully her into not seeing him.

He decides to avoid a discussion about her parents and sticks to a safer one, for now. "How is Jase, by the way? Still terrified of storms?"

"He's better. He isn't a fan of bad weather still, but he's not as scared as he was. He still loves Star Wars and he loves football. Of course, my dad has a lot to do with that."

He avoids talking about her parents, again.

"I wish I could go home with you, but I'm stuck until after playoffs. I mean, we could make the trip on a Sunday, but that's a lot of driving and I doubt coach would be happy."

"And playoffs run the next few weeks, right? When will the championship game be?"

West grins. "If we make it to the championship game it would be December fifth."

"What about Thanksgiving, you won't be able to come home to Tyler?"

"Babe, we haven't done Thanksgiving in Tyler since the year my mom passed."

"Oh, that's right. You came home early last year." He notices her shudder and he squeezes her knee, leaving his hand to rest on her thigh. He doesn't allow himself to think about the year before. They still have several weeks before they hit the anniversary of that night and there's no reason to allow himself to dwell on it right now.

"Yeah, I can't wait till football is done to go home," she says. "I'll go home this weekend and confront my dad."

The truck pulls into Crestdale and she stops talking as West gives his name at the entrance gate. Jules looks out the window as they drive around a winding road and park. He takes a moment to address her before he looks at the place he lived for seven months.

"Jules? Whatever happens with your parents, I'm here for you. You know that, right?"

"Of course." She unbuckles her seatbelt and sits forward, twisting in her seat. "Nothing they say will change how I feel about you, West. Once my dad is aware you weren't at fault for anything that happened, he will understand. I promise," she says sweetly, leaning across to kiss him.

"Also, you realize Dani has issues, right? I mean, we haven't talked about her much and she'll probably act completely normal, but watch what you say. She's more fragile than she acts."

She nods and they exit the truck and walk towards Crestdale's main doors.

Walking into the main building is surreal. When he was admitted almost a year ago, it was with a reluctant and disbelieving attitude. He agreed because Jules' father was adamant he would not let him see her until he got counseling. He agreed because that same night after her dad left, his own father sat him down and told him how his mom wouldn't want him to keep punishing himself. He did it for Jules and his mom; he thought he was fine. It wasn't until he met Dani that he realized he wasn't as fine as he thought.

He smiles at the front desk workers and nurses, recognizing them all, and they come around to hug him and say how happy they are to see him looking so good.

"You know Dr. Steel will be angry you came on a Sunday," the head nurse over weekend shifts admonishes him.

"I know. Maybe we could keep the visit to ourselves?" He winks and asks about Dani.

"My lips are sealed, gorgeous," she teases back. "As for Dani, she's where she's always at. Or she was last time I made rounds."

Thanking the ladies at the desk, he holds Jules' hand and heads to the courtyard where he knows he'll find his friend sitting in the shade of the large oak trees. The hallways of Crestdale are all painted a light creamy yellow color. The brick walks devoid of artwork, with the exception of a landscape picture or two. He sends a fast glance Jules way to see her reaction to where he spent his time and catches a glimpse of her chewing her bottom lip.

"You okay?" he asks when they round the corner and approach a set of glass doors leading out into the common area.

She nods silently.

They open the doors and enter back into the late afternoon sun; the October air today finally has a small touch of fall in it.

"There she is." He points towards the largest tree.

From where they stand, they can barely make out the person lying under the tree, but West knows. It's the spot they used to sit under daily, and her sweat pant covered legs are propped up with her knees in the air. Jules squints across the paved commons.

"It's her favorite spot," he explains. "Come on."

"Old habits die hard?" he asks when they make it to Dani's side. Her eyes are closed and she doesn't move, except for her mouth. Her lips crack a small smile and West smiles in return, happy to see her again.

"So nice of you to finally visit me," she says sarcastically, turning her head their way and opening her eyes.

Dani sucks in a deep breath and sits up, pushing her black hair back as she takes in Jules by his side.

"I brought someone to meet you," he points out.

Dani rises as West steps forward and lets go of Jules' hand. He hugs her hard as she whispers, "I missed you."

After a few moments, West pulls back and looks her over. Her tall frame looks skinnier than before and he wonders if she's been sliding back into a depression since he left. It's easy to fall back into old habits.

"I missed you, too," he tells her as he looks back at Jules, who smiles.

"You didn't lie," Dani grumbles playfully. "She is beautiful."

Jules' cheeks go pink and she moves closer to hug Dani, gushing, "I'm so happy to meet you."

Dani's big eyes grow even larger as Jules holds her and West laughs. Like him, Dani finds it difficult to accept affection from others. It was one of the things they bonded over in the short month they'd hung out together at Crestdale.

When Jules finally lets Dani go, they sit in the grass together.

"I have to admit, when West kept giving me updates and you two weren't together, I thought my sending the letters didn't work and I truly thought you must be the coldest girl on the face of the earth to be able to resist those words."

"Resist those... Dani, did you read my letters?" asks West, shocked.

"Oh, just one or two. I didn't want to send them if they weren't good."

"You weren't supposed to send them at all," he reminds her, and Jules giggles as Dani makes a face at him.

"If I hadn't, I have a feeling you'd still be moping around," counters Dani.

Jules bumps into West shoulder with a smile. "I'm totally fine with her reading them and I'm absolutely grateful she mailed them." She turns serious and looks at Dani sitting across from them. "Seriously, thank you for mailing them. I needed the push."

"Sometimes we all need a push. You're welcome."

They spend the next two hours sitting under the oak and talking. Dani asks about school and talks about her newfound love of football, thanks to West.

"I wish they televised your games, but I've been watching your brother."

"You could come to a game, you know," West points out and Dani frowns, offering an unenthusiastic 'maybe.'

When it's time to go and they're standing at the main lobby again, Jules excuses herself to use the restroom, giving Dani and West a moment to speak alone.

"Dani?" he asks seriously, and she shakes her head.

"Don't, West."

"Don't what? I didn't even say anything."

"No. It's what you're not saying. I recognize that voice. I'm fine."

"Are you?"

She nods and looks out the glass door to the parking lot. She swipes at her cheek and then faces West. "I'll be okay. This summer has been harder than I thought. You left and I got a little depressed."

"I'm sorry, D."

"Don't be stupid. You don't have to be sorry. I'm so happy for you and for Jules. She seems pretty amazing."

"She is," he agrees.

"I want that someday."

He decides to pull her into a hug. "You'll get it, you need to take care of you first," he says, repeating advice she once gave him.

She snorts, pushing him away and rolling her eyes. "Using my words against me, huh?" She laughs before telling him seriously, "I'm trying. I had a slip back, but I'm recovering."

"Can I help in anyway?" he asks, taking her slender hand in his.

"Just be happy. Make your dreams come true and live." Her face changes into a smile and he looks behind him to see Jules returning.

"Hey, Jules, you keep this guy in check, okay?"

"No worries, I plan on doing that for a long, long time."

They hug and Jules thanks Dani, again, for mailing her West's letters and promises they will come back soon to visit. Once they're back in the truck and on the way home, Jules finally asks all the questions he's sure she's been dying to ask.

"You told her to come to a football game. Can she come and go as she wants?"

"At this point, yes. She was only sixteen the first time her grandparents sent her to Crestdale. She's been in and out for two years now. Once she turned eighteen, over the winter, she was technically able to leave. She doesn't have an order to be there. It's voluntary."

"Why does she stay then?"

Dani's story is Dani's story and West doesn't feel right telling it for her, even to Jules. Instead, he explains it the best he can. "Remember all the guilt you felt after Tanya's death? Dani's family died and she feels the same. She hasn't gotten over it yet. She wants to, though. She's smart, baby," he tells her when he sees the sadness overcome Jules. "She stays at CVC because she wants to get better."

"When we first walked in there, I started to feel sick to my stomach because it felt cold and lonely and I hated knowing you had to be there," she explains, and he nods, recalling her quiet looks before she met Dani. "Dani changed that. I could see how much she cares about you and I'm glad you were able to be there for her and her for you."

So many things happened over the last fifteen months; each bad moment leading to something good. The realization puts a smile on his face. The tornado brought them together. The car wreck got him help and introduced him to Dani. *There is a purpose to the madness,* he allows. He'd stop believing in the purpose for a while but now he is reminded of Jules' words at the vigil two months ago. Studying her sitting next to him in his truck, he feels a peace he's never felt before and he repeats her words to her.

"Sometimes happy endings take time."

"I have one last thing for you," West tells Jules a few hours later when he's bringing her back to her dorm after dinner. He'd given her a leather bound journal at the restaurant for her to keep at her bedside, but he wasn't done.

They park and West gets out, pulling his seat forward and producing a white box with a pink bow on top. He's smiling at Jules as she walks around the front of the truck.

"Another present? You shouldn't have," she says as she claps her hands greedily. "Give me!"

"Ha! Hang on. Come with me."

They walk past her building and West searches for a place to take her. It's a little after nine and the campus is still buzzing with students hanging around, couples walking together, people drinking coffee and groups chatting on benches. It takes them ten minutes before they finally find a bench where he sits her down and hands her the box. She pulls the top off with giddy excitement.

"What in the world could this be?" she wonders aloud as she moves the tissue paper. When her eyes see the gift, she laughs and pulls the blue and white Freemont number twelve jersey out of the box.

"I figured my girl should wear my number. It's a woman's cut, especially for you."

She holds the jersey up and turns it around to look at the back where his name is written.

"Awww, you signed it!" her voice breaks and West lowers her arm to see her eyes wet with tears.

He'd written 'I love you, always' in his number and signed his first name for her. He'd signed the jersey as something of a joke – the big shot QB signing something for a fan – but afterward he realized he didn't want people to think she was just "another fan". So he wrote 'I love you' to show everyone she is more than some chick that he'd autographed a shirt for. He'd started to think it was stupid to be so territorial, but her tears tell him he did the right thing.

"I'm so proud of you, you know that right?" She asks.

He shakes his head, not needing her praise tonight, but it doesn't deter her.

"I mean it, West. I want you know how amazing I think you are. You came back to this sport and you've rocked the hell out of it. Your mom would be so proud of you."

He touches the jersey in her hands and smiles at her comment. "Did I tell you about the plan?"

"The plan?"

"Dr. Steel had this plan. It was her idea to get me to try to walk-on here. Before I would even open up to her about my feelings, about you or my mom, the only thing we talked about for the longest time was football. The only reason I agreed at first was because I thought it would get my dad off my back and -" He stops, not wanting to put pressure on her with the truth.

"And because you thought it would help win me back," she finishes for him softly. He looks at her, startled that she already knows.

"Mindy told me I was your motivation," she admits.

"Yeah, you were at first. Then when I thought you were with Austin, I kinda snapped out of that. I threw myself into training even harder to prove to myself that I could do it. That first game it hit me like a ton of bricks, babe. There are two things in this world I don't want to live without - you and football. I know how much it sucks for me to be so busy all the time and us not getting to see each other-"

"No." She reaches out and presses her fingers to his cheek as she shakes her head. "I don't care how hard it is, you are living your dream and I wouldn't want it any other way."

Theres a tense quiet in the air between them and West smiles to break the unexpected seriousness this moment has taken. "You know, those colors might be a bit dangerous for an A&M girl to have."

She laughs, holding the shirt up in front of her. "This is so perfect. I will be honored to wear these colors, even here on campus."

"Don't go overboard now, babe. I promise to give you an A&M jersey once I make the team." West coughs and nods his head toward the box. "There's one more thing in there."

Jules tucks the jersey in her lap and sets the box on the bench, looking in and pulling out a simple brown box and she looks at him.

"Katie knew where you kept it and snuck it to me the other night." West takes it from her fingers. "You're not mad, are you? I was hoping you'd consider wearing it again," he explains as he takes the lid off and pulls out the rose gold anchor ring he gave her for her eighteenth birthday last year. "I thought about buying you something new, but this one has so much meaning."

She sits there, staring at the ring, and West begins to think he's made a terrible mistake when she finally speaks.

"Again, I think it's perfect. I loved that ring. You know I didn't take it off until June." West looks at her, his pulse racing. "I took it off right before I left for school. That's why I got the tattoo, actually. I needed something to remind me of you, of us."

He holds the ring up, his brows lift as he meets her blue eyes, "May I?" She nods and he slides the ring back onto her ring finger where it belongs.

Thirty-One

Jules

Jules throws her bag down on the table in the large library next to Cassie on Wednesday afternoon, startling her and earning dirty looks from those around them.

"You can't ignore me forever," she says, sitting down and propping her chin in her hands...

"Ignoring you? Why would you think that?" Cassie asks innocently.

"You have a thing for Austin, don't you?"

"What!" she gasps, and again dirty looks are thrown their way with a chorus of shushing. Cassie mumbles an apology to a girl glaring at them nearby before turning back to Jules. "I didn't even know his name until Saturday night. No, I do not have a thing for him."

"Then why did you give him the cold shoulder? He totally likes you, it's so obvious and he even told -"

"Jules!" she whisper-shouts, interrupting Jules. Pushing her chair back, she prepares to stand. "Don't. I'm not interested, okay? He's wasting his time with me. I need to get something, I'll see you later, okay?"

Cassie hurries away without waiting for Jules to say anything and Jules is thoroughly confused. She twirls her ring, and then smiles when she realizes she's doing it.

She meets Jess and Katie for lunch in the commons, having a hard time holding in her thoughts when Jess mentions that Cassie has been acting strange the past few days.

"Do you mind if I stay here this weekend?" she asks Jules. "If there's something going on with her, I'd hate to leave her here alone."

"No. I agree. I wish I could put the visit off, but Jase begged me; he wants to go trick or treating with me one last time. He says he'll be too big next year." She grimaces and Katie laughs.

"Did you not remind him how we were still going when we were in high school? Free candy, man."

"Yeah, he's funny about things."

"Well, I'd go home with you, but I've got the DZ party."

"Nah, it's fine. I'm leaving Friday after class and I'll probably get up super early Sunday to get back and spend time with West. God, I will be so glad when football is over," Jules says with a sigh.

"I don't know why you don't stay at the house with him. It's not as if you're saving it for the wedding," Katie points out with a teasing wink.

Jules shrugs. The thought has crossed her mind to stay with him, but he's never asked. They'd agreed to go slow and then shot that to hell when he'd shown up at the frat party two weeks ago. Apparently, it wasn't in them to go slow. The feeling of need she remembered from high school was back in full effect. Every moment they are apart is another winding twist of the second hand on a clock; the tension getting wound tighter and tighter until she's ready to explode if she doesn't see him. West describes their being apart as sweet torture and he is right. The misery and anticipation is some of the best foreplay ever, but she's ready to have him all the time.

Jules is still thinking about the misery of only seeing West one day a week when she pulls up to her house a little before five p.m. Friday afternoon. Obviously watching from the front windows, the front door is yanked open as she's pulling her weekend bag out of her backseat, and she finds Jase rushing out to greet her.

"Jules!"

"Hey, bud," she calls back, facing him as he throws his arms around her waist. "Have you gotten taller?" she asks honestly, messing with his hair. He reaches her chest and she's amazed at how much she misses while she is away at school.

"You haven't been home in three months. Of course I've grown. Lost a tooth, too." He smiles, showing her the new gap in his mouth.

"Dude, quit growing up."

"I wish that worked," her mother calls from the front steps, wiping her hands on a dishtowel. "I tried it with you for years."

Jase takes the small laundry bag she's carrying from Jules' hands and starts up the walk with Jules behind him. She stops at the bottom of the steps and looks up at her mom. This is the woman who laid with her night after night after the car wreck and let her cry on her chest over West. The woman who held her hand when she went to her first counseling appointment and cheered her on when she took her first steps in therapy after her fracture and breaks healed. Yet, looking at her now, the only thing she can see is the woman who knew the truth about West being sent away and never told her. The betrayal runs deep for Jules. She's not sure how she will get past it, but she gives her a smile and speaks as if everything is fine.

"Hey, mama."

They step into the house and Jules sniffs the familiar scent of her mom's famous pot roast in the air. Her stomach growls on reflex and she excuses herself to put her stuff in her room. She pulls out her phone while upstairs and shoots a quick text to West, letting him know she made it to Tyler fine. He replies quickly with a heart.

Jules joins her mom and Jase in the kitchen where they fill her in on all the local gossip while they wait for her father to get home from work.

"Did mom tell you I'm the fastest in my class?" Jase asks out of the blue. Obviously, the gossip over the town floozy isn't enough to keep him entertained. She shakes her head and he excitedly explains.

"We have to run laps, right. Remember doing that? So, the other day Ms. Furman named who had the most laps in the class and said I did. Well, Nick got mad. He said it didn't matter because he was still faster than me."

Jules frowns, knowing this Nick kid to be a brat who always bosses Jase and the other boys around, but Jase just smiles at her.

"So, Ms. Furman heard him and decided to let us all race and I won. Twice!" he finishes and laughs evilly. Her mother shakes her head ruefully while Jules joins the laughter and gives Jase a high-five.

"Well, that's not a sound I hear every day," Jules father booms as he opens the garage door off the kitchen. "I could hear you all laughing from the garage." He smiles, putting the computer bag he carries on the floor inside the door as he meets Jules' eyes.

"College girl doesn't give her dad a hug anymore?" he teases when Jules doesn't get up as she usually would.

Reluctantly, she slides off the bar stool and meets her dad halfway, letting him hug her. Her father ruffles Jase's hair and kisses her mom hello. A short while later, they all sit at the table for dinner, as if it's a normal night.

"So, tell me about school. How are your classes?" her dad asks once they've passed the food and are eating.

"They're fine."

"Good, can you elaborate?"

"Not really," she replies smartly as she focuses on Jase. "Hey, Jase, when we're done, why don't we go outside and toss the ball around? I've been brushing up on my playing skills."

"You've been playing football at college? I thought all you got to do was study."

"Nah, I've got lots of friends who play football, you know that," she says meaningfully, shooting a quick glance her dad's way. "In fact, I have a signed jersey in my bag for you."

Jase's screech makes her ears ring as he jumps up from his seat. "Can I get it? Please?"

Jules smiles happily, telling him it's in her bag. She can tell her parents are not happy without looking at them. Her mom's fork is arrested halfway between her plate and her mouth; her dad's is on his plate, having clattered against the porcelain the moment Jules referenced all of her football friends and she glares at him.

"Could that not have waited until after dinner, honey?" her mom finally asks when Jules keeps eating silently, looking at Jase's empty seat.

"What? The jersey? It just occurred to me and I couldn't help it. You know how I can't keep secrets," she murmurs, stuffing a bite of roast in her mouth. "Mmmm, this is really good, mom. As always."

"This is awesome!" Jase yells as he comes back to the kitchen with the jersey pulled over his clothes. "And you got Austin's number. That's so cool Jules, thank you."

Jase pulls the jersey away from his body and flashes it in front of her dad as she goes on about the signatures. Her dad's face goes a little pale as he looks at proof that, if nothing else, Jules now keeps in contact with one Rutledge.

"You know Stuart sent me a signed hat, but this is way cooler than that." He sits back down to eat and her mother tells him to take the shirt off so it doesn't get dirty, but Jules barely hears that. All she hears is how Stuart sent a signed hat.

Not bothering to ask to be excused, she pushes away from the table and walks out to the back porch. The click of the door opening and closing doesn't surprise her at all and she whirls around on her dad, wanting to get the first words in.

"Why would Stuart send Jase a hat? I mean, he liked Jase alright when we were together, but he barely talked to him. He wouldn't do it out of the kindness of his heart, dad."

"Juliet…"

"Why!"

"There is no need to shout at me, young lady. Since it bothers you so much, I'll tell you. I told you last year I used to talk with his dad about games. I called Stuart to wish him good luck when the season started. He's a hell of a player, Jules, and he still asks about you, you know."

She almost chokes on her ire at that comment. "I'm sorry, he still asks? So you talk to him a lot?"

He must realize he's made a mistake in bringing it up and he softens his tone. "A few times, not a lot. He's a good young man, with a lot of promise."

"Oh my God," She moans, running her hands through her hair angrily. "As opposed to West?"

"What the -"

"I mean, that's what you're saying here, right, daddy?" she laughs and walks past her father and into the kitchen where Jase and her mom are sitting still.

Her mom looks at her angry face and tells Jase to go upstairs. Jules stands there and nods to Jase as he leaves the kitchen.

"Why don't you tell me what West Rutledge has to do with me talking to Stuart?" her father asks calmly once they hear Jase's door close upstairs.

Jules laughs in disbelief at her father's obtuseness. "Did you think I wouldn't find out?"

She stands angrily behind her chair, her fingers gripping the back until her knuckles are white, and she watches her father.

"Wouldn't find out what, honey?"

"Really, mother?" she spits the words out in complete disgust, and her mom winces.

"She doesn't know," her dad says softly, his hands going into his pockets.

"I don't know what? What are you two talking about?"

Jules feels relief rush through her knowing her mother didn't lie to her all this time.

"Priceless, daddy. I'm amazed that you've kept in touch with my ex-boyfriend for over a year. The one I clearly didn't love and was over, but you sent the man I loved and *needed* away. What a touching display of love you have for your only daughter."

"Juliet Marie Blacklin, do not speak to your father that way. Your father loves you."

"I'm not sure I want that kind of love, momma," she says dismissively, spinning on her foot to leave.

"Don't you walk away!" her father shouts. "You don't understand the ins and outs of it all. What did his brother tell you?"

"His brother?"

"Obviously you talk to Austin, since you gave Jase his jersey. It makes sense you would know him, but -"

"But nothing, daddy. I didn't get my information from Austin. I got it from West."

Her mother presses her hand to her chest as her face exhibits shock at hearing West's name, but it's her father's demeanor that is truly interesting. His eyes go wide and his mouth opens and closes as he works to say something.

"Don't tell me you really thought we'd never talk? Did you think I could love someone that much and then let him go without a word? Without closure?" Her eyes tear up as she looks at her father's face and her mother steps to her side, putting a hand on her arm.

"*He* went to West's father," she tells her mother saying 'he' like it's a dirty word. She rounds on her father as her mother's face falls. "You went to him, without my knowledge, and you convinced him to send West away. You convinced him West needed help. You made West think he was to blame for everything. EVERYTHING!" She screams, stepping back from her mom and standing in front of her father. "I am the one who ran away that night. I lied to West, told him you guys were fine. I begged him to tell me where he was. He wasn't to blame that night."

"Jules, you had changed so much. You were moody and you came home smelling of alcohol more than once. You never behaved that way with Stuart."

"My best friend was killed by a damn tornado! I lost my school. I almost died! I had nightmares every single night. You think West is to blame for all that, too? West is the only reason I got through those months. The only one. And then you ripped him away from me."

Her father's face drains of color with every point Jules makes.

"Is this true Jim?" her mother asks, her voice full of hurt and accusation. "How could you do that to your daughter?"

"I thought I was protecting her."

"You know what? I could actually, someday, possibly accept that as truth. Except for one thing, dad. You lied to me. You lied to me for months. You could have fixed it all and told me the truth, but instead you swept it under the rug and hoped you'd never have to address it again." She shakes her head and looks at her mother. "I'm going to my room for the night."

Her parents spend the night fighting while Jules spends the night playing with Jase.

After spending the early part of the day at Jase's baseball game and then at lunch, they get ready and Jules takes Jase trick-or-treating Saturday night. When they return to the house, Jules tells him she is taking what she calls 'a customary five-percent babysitting fee' out of his candy. Jase protests how he didn't need her to babysit, telling her she should pay him instead for allowing her to trail along. In the end, she gets her cut as they sit on the floor and sort through the large pile.

The time spent with Jase helps alleviate the anger she has

worked up throughout the day. Her phone rang off the hook all afternoon with updates from Mindy on West's first play-off game, each call making Jules angry that she'd skipped such a huge moment for him to come home and fight with her parents. Her dad tried to approach her twice and she'd rebuffed his advances. Her mother attempted to have a conversation, as well, but there was nothing she could say to help the situation.

It's nearly eleven Saturday night when she walks into the living room and sits on the chair in the corner without a word. Her mom is reading a book and her dad is watching sports highlights. Upon her taking a seat, he mutes the television and waits.

"West and I are back together." They sit there with blank faces and she continues on. "I know you have to know he's playing ball again, and I imagine you know he won his playoff game today. I came here, instead of watching a huge moment in his life. I won't do that again. I want to make that clear. I love him, and you either support us or you don't. That's up to you, but I want you to know he comes first in my life now."

Her dad sits forward on the edge of his chair. "Honey, you are nineteen years old."

"We were nineteen when we met," her mother says quietly, and Jules gives her a small grateful smile as she sets her book down and sits up.

"Sure, but we didn't have the baggage -"

Jules stands up, putting her foot down on the conversation. "I'm not arguing this with you, daddy. What you did to me and to West is unforgivable. I'm struck with the thought that had it been Stuart, you'd have hugged him and consoled him that night, instead of giving him the cold shoulder and then blaming him for everything. I wanted you to know where I stand. I'm leaving around six in the morning." She walks to her mother and gives her a kiss on the cheek before stepping back and looking at them both. "I'm dying to get back to my boyfriend and congratulate him on his success."

The next morning, she is surprised when her mother walks into the kitchen as she's filling a coffee mug to go.

"You didn't have to get up to say good-bye."

"Of course I did, darling." She hugs Jules tightly. "Please tell West I am sorry for what your father did. Tell him I am proud of him."

"Thank you, momma, I will. He loves me so much. You know that, right?"

"Oh, baby, I know he does. I knew it last year; I saw it on his face every time he looked at you. Your daddy will come around. He's being stubborn. Drive carefully. I love you, baby girl. Even though you're not a baby anymore."

"I will, and I'll always be your little girl." She smiles at her mom, hugging her once more. "I love you, too."

Jules wants to ask her mom why she didn't step in last year when West left, why she didn't talk to him or his father and make sure they knew he wasn't to blame. She wants to ask her, but she doesn't. The truth doesn't matter so much anymore. Her parents know where she stands and West is waiting back at school for her to come home. Everything is as it should be now.

Three hours later, Jules strips off her jeans grabs one of his tee shirts and climbs into West's bed with a deep sigh of peace.

"Mmmm, hey, baby," he groans, bringing her into his side as she wiggles under the covers.

"Shhh, sorry. Go back to sleep."

"What time is it?" he asks sleepily, kissing the top of her head. His hand skims across her hip, causing her skin to break out in goose bumps.

"It's only nine. I missed you." Jules kisses his neck. "Now sleep."

Thirty-Two

<u>Jules</u>

The days start to fly by as the air finally turns cooler. To Jules' surprise, her mother calls her and asks where West's next play-off game is, saying that she and Jase want to show up to cheer him on. Jules doesn't ask about her father, and tries to pretend it doesn't hurt that he won't be there, but it does. West's team wins the South West Division Championship, all but, securing him a spot on A&M's roster next season.

Even with the regular season now complete, West and Jules stick to their weekend only dating rule as West continues to have daily football practices. Freemont has one last game to play, either a bowl game or the National Championship, they just have to wait two weeks for final rankings of all the other teams.

"Do you have a sec?" Cassie asks the day before Thanksgiving while Jules is studying alone in her room.

"Of course."

"I wanted to tell you, I'm sorry about the library." She sits on the edge of Jules' bed and smiles hopefully at Jules.

Up until now, both Austin and Cassie have avoided talking to Jules about their strange confrontation that night on the ball field. Austin told her Cassie isn't studying at the library anymore, but he didn't elaborate what had happened between them previously. She looks at Cassie sitting before her now and decides to let her two friends confide in her when they are ready.

"It's fine. I'm sorry I pushed you," she says, sending her a smile.

Cassie looks down at the hem of her shirt and tugs at a loose string. "He's not a bad guy, is he?" she half-states and half-asks the question.

The desire to prod her suite mate for information plagues her. "Not at all. I mean, he's not a saint by any means, but he's a great guy. He's super smart, too. I was shocked when I figured that out."

Cassie smiles at that. "Imagine that, a jock with brains."

"Right?"

The girls share a light laugh before Cassie gets up to pack.

"Jess mentioned you are going to Tyler with her for Thanksgiving. She's going to give you a tour of our old stomping grounds." Jules teases, trying to keep the mood light whenever she talks about Cassie's mother, Gwen.

"Yeah, apparently Gwen decided to take a little cruise with her boyfriend instead of having me come home." She waves her hand dismissively, letting Jules know she is fine with the end results.

The situation with Cassie and her mother makes Jules reconsider her own weekend plans. After some heavy thinking, she calls home to tell her mom she's planning to celebrate the holiday with West and his family instead of coming home. West begs her to reconsider, arguing the need to forgive her father, but she stands firm.

On Thanksgiving day she is surprised when she is helping Mindy set the table at the house and her mother and brother walk into the house, followed by her dad.

She eyes West, who looks guilty, as Mindy whisks her mother and brother into the kitchen and Jules hears Carson asking Jase to play corn hole in the back yard.

"What are you doing here?" Jules asks her dad as she goes back to setting the silverware.

"I came to apologize. To both of you, Jules," he says sincerely.

Jules laughs angrily, displeased at the surprise entrance of her family. "Oh really? Good luck," she replies sarcastically, setting a spoon down with a little extra force.

West rounds the table and stills her hands, sending her an encouraging glance, "Baby, just listen to him, for me. Please?"

Jules takes a deep breath and turns, crossing her arms over her middle as she faces her father for the first time in weeks.

"Honey, I know now I didn't handle things the right way. You have to understand where I'm coming from, as your father. Forget all of the issues you were having by that point and my worry about your behavior, and consider that night. You ran out after you were told no, you went to a party where you and West both drank, and then you got into a car. I know what happened after that wasn't West's fault. But, back then, I couldn't think clearly. I walked into that ER in the middle of the night to find West covered in your blood and being told they were doing everything they could to save you." His voice cracks slightly and the blood rushes to Jules' face as her eyes water.

"It was the second time in only a few months where I thought I'd lost you and I was angry. I couldn't be angry at God, so I got angry at West. I know it was wrong, but when I saw you... I flipped, sweetheart."

"But why then didn't you ever tell me the truth. You acted like you had no idea where he was or why," she points out, and West's hand goes around her back.

"I was trying to protect you from getting hurt. I thought you'd get over it. As time went by and you slipped deeper and deeper into a depression, I realized I might have done the wrong thing, but I couldn't change it at that point."

Jules swipes at her cheeks as her father stands there waiting for her to say something.

"He called me earlier this week, Jules. We talked for a while and I forgave him." West turns her cheek to look into her eyes. "What really matters is that we are together now."

"No thanks to him."

"You're wrong. He may have handled it wrong, but in the end what he and my dad did... it helped me. If I hadn't worked through my grief about my mom, and then about you and the guilt I felt, I'd still be that scared guy waiting to screw up again." He looks at her, his thumb caressing her cheek. "Forgive him. He loves you."

She nods, looking at her father. "I'm still angry with you. What you did to us hurt, but you've been my biggest supporter my entire life and I know you love me."

Rushing forward, she allows her father to haul her into his chest for a tight hug.

"You have to accept that we are together, daddy. I'm going to marry him some day." The second she says it, she curses herself mentally.

Her father pulls her back and looks a bit shell shocked at her, "Marriage?"

"Well, I mean -"

"Yes, sir." West steps in as she stumbles to find an excuse for her words. "I plan on marrying your daughter someday, but don't worry. I'll ask for permission first. If she lets me," he teases.

Thirty-Three

West

New Year's Eve.

It was always West's mothers favorite holiday and, as West dances under the stars with Jules, he can't help but think of how much she'd love this night. Tonight was a night for lovers as they watched Carson and Mindy tie the knot in a small, romantic ceremony on a beach in St. Lucia. It was intimate and perfect and something his mother would have planned. When they'd decided on New Year's for their wedding date, they knew it would be best to go small, so they chose a destination wedding with only Mindy's parents, her best friend growing up, Jules, Austin, West, and their Dad. They decided to have a huge reception party in mid-January for all of their friends and the extended family.

Jules, standing there across from him in her strapless cream dress and her red hair tied up, exposing her long neck to his gaze, had made him crazy all night. He couldn't stop thinking about the moment when he would pledge his life with hers someday.

Last year for New Years, he sat in his room at Crestdale and looked at the ceiling in misery that he would never get her back. This year, he's the MVP of the National Junior College Football Championship game, he's waiting for the official word that he will be starting for A&M in the fall, and if that's not enough, he's dancing in the Caribbean with the love of his life and contemplating taking her gown off as soon as the new year rings in.

"What are you thinking?" she asks.

They've been swaying to the music of the waves for the last thirty minutes, the sound of revelry from the resort in the distance. He looks down at her and smiles at the way she is watching him.

"I was thinking how much I'd love to undress you right now," he admits boldly.

She smiles and drops her hand to his pant pocket, removing his phone and checking the time.

"Only five minutes, and then you can have your way with me."

"Promise?"

"Absolutely. I'd be offended if you didn't," she smiles and laughs, kissing him deeply as they resume their dancing.

"What are *you* thinking about?" West asks a moment later.

She smiles up at him, the moonlight shining in her blue eyes. The warm water laps at their feet as they stand in the sand.

"I was thinking about how far we've come."

He kisses the tip of her nose, "How so?"

"I cheered for your team when you played Pop Warner in fifth grade. You probably don't remember-"

West chuckles softly. "Are you kidding me? Of course I remember. Where do you think that crush I had on you came from?"

She stops swaying and shakes her head with a rueful smile. "Our paths were always on course with each other's, West Rutledge. From fifth grade to kisses in a closet, to finding each other in the wreckage and creating this beautiful love out of the ruins of our lives after the tornado. We were meant to be, weren't we?"

"Baby, we've been through more storms than two people our age should have to go through, but you know what? We're still here, together."

A few minutes later, the music cuts off and they hear the party guests start to count down from twenty-five.

"Hey, cheerleader?"

"Yes?"

"I'm going to love you for the rest of your life. You're okay with that, right?"

"Promise?"

"Absolutely."

"You know, you're not really such a bad boy, Rutledge."

He leans down and presses a kiss to the ticklish skin below her ear and whispers, "I would be happy to show you just how bad I can be, Buffy."

"I have no doubt you would enjoy that." She smiles and pushes him back. "However, I've decided you are now my Angel."

"Seriously? I'm Angel now, huh? The one you want to be with, even though you shouldn't be?" he challenges, raising his brows. Jules shakes her head.

"No. You're the guy I want and always belonged with, but things happened and life got in the way. Buffy and Angel — everyone knew they were meant to be together from the first time he walked into her life."

"That's some damn fine logic," he whispers into her ear as the revelers behind them celebrate and shouts of 'happy new year' fill the air and fireworks light up the sky.

"You know what?" he whispers, pulling her gaze from the colorful display over the ocean and leaning down to kiss her. "I want you to know that when all is said and done, no matter where we are or what we have, we will be okay even if our love is all that remains, because I don't need anything as long as I have you. I know it's not going to be easy with football and school, and I know we're young-" He stops pointing out their obstacles when Jules frowns at him.

"My point is this is a new year and it's the first year of the rest of our lives. Happy new year, love."

"Happy new year. Now kiss me and take me to bed."

"Yes ma'am," West laughs and scoops Jules into his arms,

kissing her deeply as a rainbow of colorful fireworks light up the sky.

My dearest reader,

From the moment I began writing From The Wreckage, my intention was to write a book as real as life itself. I didn't wrap every storyline up with a pretty bow, and I didn't touch much on some plot points after the initial mention because you don't always get all the answers in life.

I will let you in on a secret though. My goal is to write more about these characters in the future. Right now I have two other stories I MUST finish, but I am hoping to come out with a series of standalone stories based on the From The Wreckage characters in 2015. The series will be called 'Wrecked" and the best part is you will get to follow-up on Jules and West. So if you were hoping for that 'happily ever after' ending you might try checking these books out.

I hope this prospect excites you. I'd love to hear from you and know who you'd like to get their own book.

Thank you for sharing this series with me. I sincerely hope you loved reading it as much as I loved writing it. I put my heart into Jules and West and will always love them.

As always, I'd love for you to take a moment and write a quick review on the site where you purchased the book or on other online book sites. It's super easy and it helps me out a bunch since I'm an Indie author, and we need all the help we can get. I appreciate any time you take to leave a review and always try my best to read all of them. Also, share! Word of mouth is our best marketing tool, so please tell your friends to check out the From The Wreckage series, I would appreciate it beyond belief.

I love hearing from readers, please feel free to chat me up on

Twitter or my Facebook page. Check out my Pinterest page too for cool pics, quotes and other things that show you more of my creative side and inspirations when writing my stories.

Most of all, keep reading! I hope that you will try out my other titles, but also those of other Indie authors. There are a ton of amazing stories out there waiting to be discovered by you!

acknowledgments

To all of the people who buy, read and review my books, thank you. Plain and simple. I am especially touched by those who take the time to send me notes on Facebook. I can't tell you how I feel when I see a new note telling me what you think of a character or a new review talking about the storyline. A million thanks to each of you.

My street team - Chele's Belles - these ladies help give me advice when I'm stuck, they BETA for me, they check out the teasers I create and help pimp me out. For that I am forever grateful.

Cheri Gracey, Samantha Eaton-Roberts, Kayla Hargaden, Danielle Young, Tanya Johnson, Megan Bagley, Jessica Smith, Chelcie Holguin, Mandy Anderson, Marla Wenger, Destiny Love, Megan Hornyak, Nancy Byers, Courtney Willging, Laura Helseth and Tess Watson.

To the bloggers and book pimpers: you ROCK! I can't say it enough. Each person who has liked, shared, re-tweeted me. I am grateful.

To the hundreds of authors I am blessed to interact with, you inspire me to be better every day. Thank you for your guidance, laughter, wisdom and your sharing and pimping. They let me know I'm not alone in this imaginary world I create.

My #Fierce5 sisters, Christy Foster, Mindy Hayes, Starla Huchton and Sarah Ashley Jones - words are not necessary.

You girls complete me.
To Jonathan, Grayson, Gabe and Belle- thank you for allowing

me the freedom to work so hard to achieve my goals. You sacrifice so much so that I can work. You are my true inspirations!

A Special thanks to the professionals who help me look good:
Rick Miles and Kris Pittman with Red Coat Public Relations
Samantha Eaton-Roberts, Editor
Starla Huchton with Designed by Starla, Cover Designer

About The Author

Michele is the author of six books, ranging from Coming of Age Fantasy to Contemporary Romance to New Adult Romantic Suspense.

Having grown up in both the cold, quiet town of Topsham, Maine and the steamy, southern hospitality of Mobile, Alabama, Michele is something of an enigma. She is an avid Yankees fan, loves New England, being outdoors and misses snow. However she thinks southern boys are hotter, Alabama football is the only REAL football out there and sweet tea is the best thing this side of heaven and her children's laughter!

Her family, an amazing husband and three awesome kids, have planted their roots in the middle of Michele's two childhood homes in Charlotte, North Carolina.

Email: authormichelegmiller@gmail.com
Facebook: https://www.facebook.com/AuthorMicheleGMiller
Twitter: https://twitter.com/chelemybelles
Pinterest: http://pinterest.com/chelemybelles/
Website: http://michelegmillerbooks.com
Goodreads:
http://www.goodreads.com/author/show/6975382.Michele_G_Mill
er

If you loved this series, you might check out:

Killing Me Softly by Devyn Dawson

And

Me After You by Mindy Hayes

These two CLEAN New adult romances are fabulous tearjerkers.

Made in the USA
Columbia, SC
16 December 2019

85069980R00139